What Others Are Saying...

Laura V. Hilton has penned a touching story of love and its impact on a hurting heart. A compelling story line and unforgettable characters make *Patchwork Dreams* a must-read!

—Penny Zeller
Author, *McKenzie* and *Kaydie*
(books one and two in the Montana Skies series)

Laura V. Hilton's book captured my interest from the start. It opens with raw emotions and doesn't let up.

—Mary A. Hake
President, Oregon Christian Writers

Laura Hilton captures the complicated relationships that spin out of the expectations of family and church. This poignant story is sometimes touching, sometimes humorous, sometimes bittersweet. Readers will find themselves rooting for Becky's broken heart to heal and to turn to Jacob. Hilton keeps us guessing until the last page.

—Suzanne Woods Fisher
Award-winning author, *The Search*

Laura Hilton combines her expert knowledge of the Amish with exceptional storytelling to create a fast-paced, poignant romance. You will fall in love with her bigger-than-life hero in this first book of her series The Amish of Seymour.

—Mary Ellis
Award-winning, best-selling author,
Sarah's Christmas Miracle and *A Widow's Hope*

With an amazing twist that makes it fresh, *Patchwork Dreams* is a wonderful new Amish story that you will want to read from front to back without putting it down.

—Cindy Loven
Book reviewer, cindylovenreviews.blogspot.com

Laura V. Hilton conveys a true depiction of God's transforming love in *Patchwork Dreams*. It's a wonderfully written love story between a broken woman with a marred past and the man determined to restore her heart.

—**Ruth Reid**
Author, *The Promise of an Angel*

A gentle, sweet romance with enough twists and turns to keep you guessing. Laura's beautifully written novel will satisfy any romance lover!

—**Miralee Ferrell**
Author, *Love Finds You in Tombstone, Arizona*,
and *Finding Jeena*

Laura Hilton weaves a delightful tale of love, hope, and forgiveness as she carries you into the world of the Amish of Seymour. I thoroughly enjoyed the road to romance in *Patchwork Dreams*, and I look forward to reading the rest of the series!

—**Susette Williams**
Author, *Something About Sam* and *New Garden's Conversion*

If you love Amish romances, you'll find Laura Hilton's writing style engaging and tough to put down.

—**Tammy Barley**
Author, The Sierra Chronicles
(*Love's Rescue, Hope's Promise*, and *Faith's Reward*)

Patchwork Dreams is an uplifting tale of hope for tomorrow and the power of second chances.

—**Ginny Aiken**
Author, the Silver Hills Trilogy
and the Women of Hope series

Patchwork Dreams is a joy to read.

—**Diana Lesire Brandmeyer**
Author, *Wyoming Weddings* and *Hearts on the Road*

Patchwork

a Novel

Dreams

LAURA V. HILTON

- *The Amish of Seymour* -

a Novel

Patchwork Dreams

LAURA V. HILTON

WHITAKER
HOUSE

PATCHWORK DREAMS
The Amish of Seymour ~ Book One

Laura V. Hilton

ISBN: 978-1-60374-255-9
Printed in the United States of America
© 2011 by Laura V. Hilton

Whitaker House
1030 Hunt Valley Circle
New Kensington, PA 15068
www.whitakerhouse.com

Library of Congress Cataloging-in-Publication Data

Hilton, Laura V., 1963–
    Patchwork dreams / by Laura V. Hilton.
        p.   cm. — (The Amish of Seymour series ; bk. 1)
    ISBN 978-1-60374-255-9 (trade pbk. : alk. paper)
    1. Single mothers—Fiction. 2. Amish—Fiction 3. Seymour
(Mo.)—Fiction. I. Title.
    PS3608.I4665P38 2011
    811'.6—dc22
                                            2011000700

1 2 3 4 5 6 7 8 9 10   **w**   17 16 15 14 13 12 11

Acknowledgments

I'd like to offer my heartfelt thanks to the following:

The Swartz family, for allowing me a look at the inside of an Amish home and the outside layout of their farm. And for giving me a taste of their homemade jams and jellies.

Susanne Woods Fisher, for contacting her sources to settle a few questions to which I couldn't find the answers.

The residents of Seymour, for answering my questions and pointing me in the right directions.

The Ozark Folk Center in Mountain View, Arkansas—specifically, Scott Reidy—for giving me a crash course in blacksmithing.

The amazing team at Whitaker House—Christine, Courtney, and Cathy. You are wonderful.

My agent, for believing in me all these years.

To my critique group—you know who you are. You are amazing and knew how to ask the right questions when more detail was needed. Also, thanks for the encouragement.

To my husband, Steve, for being a tireless proofreader and cheering section, and my sons, Michael and Loundy, for taking over the kitchen duties when I was deep in the story.

And in memory of my parents, Allan and Janice, and my uncle Loundy, and my grandmother, Mertie, who talked about their Pennsylvania Amish heritage.

Dedicated to:

Steve, *my best friend,*

Loundy, *my favorite song,*

Michael, *my adventurous one,*

Kristin, *my precious daughter,*

Jenna, *my sunshine,*

Kaeli, *my shower of blessing,*

and to God, who has blessed me with these.

In loving memory of Allan and Janice Price, my parents, and my Uncle Loundy, who have blessed me with some knowledge of our Pennsylvania Dutch ancestors.

Also to Tamela, my agent, for not letting me give up and for giving sage advice.

Glossary of Amish Terms and Phrases

ach	oh
"Ain't so?"	a phrase commonly used at the end of a sentence to invite agreement
Ausbund	Amish hymnal used in worship services. Includes lyrics only.
boppli	baby or babies
bu	boy
buwe	boys
daed	dad
danki	thank you
dawdi-haus	a home built for grandparents to live in once they retire
Englischer	a non-Amish person
frau	wife
grossdaedi	grandfather
grossmammi	grandmother
gut	good
gut nacht	good night
haus	house
hinnersich	backward
"Ich liebe dich"	"I love you"
jah	yes
kapp	prayer covering or cap
kinner	children
kum	come
maidal	an unmarried woman
mamm	mom
nein	no
onkel	uncle
Ordnung	the rules by which an Amish community lives
rumschpringe	"running around time," a period of adolescence after which Amish teens choose either to be baptized in the Amish church or to leave the community
ser gut	very good
verboden	forbidden
"Was ist letz?"	"What's the matter?"
welkum	welcome

Chapter 1

J acob Miller hunkered on the middle seat of a white van. He wasn't a prisoner, but he might as well have been.

Could he say, "I quit"?

Could he say, "Stop this ride, I want to get off"?

No, to both questions.

Despair roiled in his gut as the van passed a McDonald's on the right, then pulled off the southbound lane of Highway 60, turned left at the light, and continued down a road covered with snow. The ice-laden trees, while beautiful to behold, did nothing to settle his inner turmoil. The heat from the van's air vents only dispelled the outer chill. This was possibly the worst thing that had ever happened to him—having to leave his girl as he was tossed out like an old copy of the Amish newspaper, *The Budget*.

Jacob leaned forward, his black felt hat clutched in his hands, as the vehicle lurched over a bump. Or something. Seymour, Missouri, wasn't too far from Springfield, which the driver called the "Queen City of the Ozarks." But the trip dragged by as if in slow motion. Maybe because he'd been dreading it for so long.

Fearing it.

Having nightmares about it.

Mamm's fourth cousin twice removed lived somewhere in this rural Missouri town. What would his family be like? Would Cousin Daniel be a harsh disciplinarian like Daed? Or would he be more easy-going, like Mamm? Jacob blinked hard, remembering Mamm's tears when he'd boarded the transport driver's van for a ride to the bus station.

He wished he could use his contraband cell phone to call home to talk to Mamm. But his parents didn't own a phone; there was only the community one in a shack a couple of miles down the road.

Jacob grimaced as the van rumbled past several small businesses and then turned down a narrow dirt road.

"Not too far now. A bit anxious, are you?" The driver glanced at Jacob in the rearview mirror, then reached forward and adjusted the heat. "Getting a mite warm in here."

Jacob made a noncommittal grunt and looked away. The driver had made a couple of attempts at conversation since picking him up at the bus station, but with nausea clogging his throat, he didn't want to risk opening his mouth to speak.

How could Daed do this to him? It seemed wrong in so many ways.

Instead of building his farm in Pennsylvania, Jacob would be working the rocky red clay of southern Missouri. If he were home, he could be drinking a mugful of hot apple cider made from the family's orchard and then going out to prune the fruit trees, working alongside his brothers—something he'd always imagined himself doing for life.

Jacob pushed that thought away. Better not to think of what might have been.

Instead of marrying sweet Susie during wedding season, he'd be spending a year helping out a distant cousin he'd never met. Susie's warm, brown eyes flashed in his mind. Her quick laugh. Her willingness to try new things, never content to settle for the old. Ach, he already missed her. He reached for his cell phone to send her a text message but couldn't get a signal. No coverage.

Well, if Daed thought this would destroy their love for each other, he had another thing coming. Jacob couldn't imagine living without Susie for a week, let alone a year.

Bare trees dotted the edges of someone's property, and in the distance, the rolling hills made a rather hazy background picture. Pretty, though not at all like home.

Would he be able to get past the homesickness—and this streak of bitterness toward Daed—to embrace this as an adventure? A chance to learn about another part of the country, to expand his boundaries, and, more important, to minister to this needy relative and his family?

Too bad his pep talk wasn't convincing. He didn't like his bad attitude, but it seemed impossible to get rid of it.

All too soon, the van arrived in the gravel driveway of a large, two-story farmhouse. The trees surrounding the house would provide plenty of shade during the hot summer months, though now they were decorated with dripping icicles. Jacob imagined the wide front porch would be a good place for the womenfolk to shell peas or shuck corn during the harvest. A porch swing hung at one end, possibly a silent testament to a courtship from days gone by.

A whitewashed barn stood sentry several yards away. With a casual glance around, Jacob noted cows, horses, chickens, goats, and pigs, plus the usual array of dogs and cats.

The driver pulled to a stop in front of the house. Almost immediately, the front door opened, and a woman appeared, her honey-blonde hair pulled back into a bun and tucked under a prayer kapp.

She peered out at the van, then disappeared behind the door before reappearing with a wrap tossed over her slim shoulders.

Jacob opened the sliding door and clambered out of the vehicle as the driver went around to the back to get his luggage.

"Hello, Tony." The woman stopped on the porch. She spoke to the driver, but her blue eyes were fixed on Jacob.

"Miz Becky." The driver bumped his hat in what Jacob took as a greeting. "Brought your cousin by."

Becky nodded. "Jah. That I see. Welkum, Jacob."

She didn't smile, and her eyes remained somber. Distant. As cold as the wind that howled around the corner of the house.

Jacob hoped the rest of the family wasn't as distant. Maybe she wanted him here as much he wanted to be here.

Not so much.

Jacob straightened his shoulders. Like it or not, he was here. He pulled in a deep breath, trying to get the nausea under control. "Hello, Becky." He hoped that the smile he aimed in her direction would convey excitement about this new venture. Might as well turn on the charm and start making the best of a bad situation.

⌘

Becky Troyer didn't want to look at this Jacob. She didn't want him here. Not now. Not ever. Besides, she thought the bishop had said that they were sending several boys—not just one—down from Pennsylvania to settle in this area, bringing new blood to the small district. And not the middle of February. In the spring, sometime. Or maybe early summer.

Maybe the rest were coming later. Or maybe not. All Becky knew was that Mamm had gotten letters from her family in Pennsylvania saying that they were sending Jacob out. Now. In February. Made her wonder what this man had done to make his family send him away so soon. And did they really want him here, potentially defiling the community?

Ach, her attitude. Becky had thought she'd gotten it all worked through, but seeing this stranger brought it all back.

Still, she couldn't keep her eyes off this man. He was tall, even standing next to Tony, and she'd thought Tony was big. Jacob stood at least half a head higher. And he was very handsome, with sandy blond hair and eyes that were so blue, he might have fallen straight from heaven and soaked up the color from the skies as he passed through on his way to earth. He was clean shaven, too, a sign he wasn't married. Broad shoulders. A dimple in the left cheek.

Her stomach flipped.

There was a spark of something in his eyes, a glint that reminded Becky of the mischievous boy who used to sit across from her at the one-room schoolhouse when she was young enough to go, right before he reached forward and stabbed Lindy Beuler's braid to the wood desk with his pocketknife.

Jah, this one was trouble. Too cute for his own good, and dangerous underneath.

Becky straightened, realizing she was being rude, staring like she was. The driver had unloaded the van of luggage, along with a blue bicycle, and now he and Jacob stood there next to the vehicle, both of them staring up at her. Behind her, her younger sisters jockeyed for position, trying to move her out of the doorway so they could see.

Becky forced herself to move and felt the hem of her skirt brushing against her bare ankles. "Ach, sorry. Please, welkum, welkum. Won't you kum in? Daed is in the barn, and Mamm has gone to a quilting, but she should be home soon." She gripped the shoulder of whichever sister was pressed up against her and looked down. "Abbie, run to the barn and tell Daed that Jacob has kum."

Abbie twirled a lock of hair around her finger, stared at Jacob for a second longer, then took off at a run toward the barn.

Jacob reached down and picked up some of his bags with one hand while removing his felt hat with the other. "Nice to meet you, Becky." His accent was different from those around here. As he climbed the steps, Becky moved further from the door, allowing him access to the house. He'd be sleeping in the dawdi-haus next door, in the spare room upstairs across from Grossmammi and Grossdaedi's room, but Grossmammi had gone to the quilting bee with Mamm, and Grossdaedi had taken the buggy to the store an hour ago. She didn't feel comfortable sending him over there for the first time when no one was home.

It was getting hard to breathe with Jacob standing so close to her. She backed up another step and noticed that her fourteen-year-old sister, Katie, held the front door open. "Go on in. I'll make you some tea.

Or coffee. Whichever you'd like." She looked back at Tony, who had followed Jacob with another bag. "Can you stay for lunch?" she asked him.

"Oh, no, no. Have to get back to the missus. Thanks for the offer. We'll be seeing you, Miz Becky." He placed the rest of Jacob's luggage inside the door.

Following Abbie, Daed approached from the barn, so Tony turned away to speak to him. Becky followed Abbie, Katie, and Jacob inside to the warm kitchen. The scent of bread baking filled the air. Pans of cookies waited to go into the oven as soon as the bread was done. Daed's sweet tooth always expected a couple of cookies when he came in from the fields, and their supply had run low.

Katie had already seated Jacob at the long table and had filled the kettle with water, putting it on the stove to heat. Becky grabbed some potholders, peeked inside the oven, and checked the bread. It was nicely browned, so she opened the door and removed the five pans, one at a time.

"Care for a crust, Jacob?" Katie lifted a knife.

"Jah, sounds good."

Becky glanced around in time to see his nod. But his eyes weren't on Katie. Instead, they were locked on her.

Her heart pounded. Could he feel the strong attraction that made her almost forget to breathe? She told herself to concentrate on the cookies so that she wouldn't drop them or burn herself on the hot oven rack. But she couldn't look away. Instead, she wished she could pull up a chair, plunge into his friendship, and delay the inevitable.

The door banged open. Cold wind swirled in with her father.

"So, Jacob. You have arrived. You had a gut trip, jah?"

"Jah." Jacob's jaw lifted, his gaze still holding Becky's. Then, he glanced away. She looked at the open oven door and silently slid the tray of cookies inside the oven. She knew Daed had seen the whole exchange. And she knew what he thought.

She didn't turn to check. After all, he'd be wrong. No man would want her. Not when he learned the truth.

Chapter 2

C ousin Daniel pulled off his leather work gloves, laying them on a counter. He washed his hands, then sat down at the table. Instantly, a young teenage girl put a slice of buttered bread in front of him. "Cookies are in the oven, Daed."

Jacob took advantage of his distant cousin's preoccupation to glance toward the woman busy at the stove. Becky seemed the exact opposite of his sweet Susie in every way. Pale blue eyes instead of dancing brown. Light blonde hair instead of strawberry blonde. Quiet instead of talkative—although that might be a good thing. And apparently unhappy rather than cheerful.

It seemed odd that she didn't act happier about his arrival. After all, Jacob's backbreaking labor would be helping them out. Or maybe his arrival put her beau out of work.

Didn't matter much, though. He was here, and here he'd stay—for a while. He straightened his spine. He would be home in time for wedding season in November, if he had anything to do with it.

And in the meantime, he'd work on seeing a real smile on Becky's face. She'd be pretty if she smiled. Well, prettier. She had a delicate beauty that appealed to him. He squared his shoulders. He liked a challenge, and he sensed that erasing that gray cloud of doom that hovered over Becky would take a significant amount of effort.

Her daed, his cousin Daniel, reached for another slice of buttered bread, drawing Jacob's attention. He was sure that each person had been introduced by name, but he couldn't remember any of them. For some reason, the only name that stuck was Becky's.

One of the girls, she looked to be about seven years of age, placed a cup of coffee in front of Jacob, along with a pitcher of cream and a bowl of sugar cubes. He dropped two cubes into his mug and was starting to pour the cream when the older man cleared his throat"So, Jacob. You are looking forward to settling in this area, jah?"

Jacob's hand wobbled. A drop of cream landed on the table. He set the pitcher down with a thud. "Excuse me?"

"No special woman back home, is there? Is that why you agreed to kum out here to marry?"

"Marry?" Jacob was certain his eyes were wider than a newborn calf's. "I'm sorry, I don't understand. I'm here to help you out with the farm work." He reared back in the chair, his jaw tightening. "At least, that's what Daed told me."

Daniel frowned and glanced away, and then his gaze returned to Jacob. "So, you have someone at home, jah?"

"Jah. Plan to marry during wedding season."

"You are here to help out." Daniel's eyes narrowed.

"Jah." Something wasn't right. Jacob's stomach cramped.

Daniel leaned forward. "Our bishop put out a request for young men to be sent to our area to marry and settle down. Your name is on that list. Your daed told us that you were coming out early to get a start looking for property. To get first pick of the women."

That made Jacob sound selfish. Prideful. Both sins.

Jacob's stomach churned. He wanted to rake his hand through his hair or, even better, get up and expel his anger through some sort of physical labor. But sensing that all the eyes in the room centered on him, and not knowing where or how to escape, he bowed his head to hide his emotions. Daed had sent him down here to marry him off? And he'd lied about it? What else had he lied about?

Jacob rubbed his sweaty hands across the rough material of his pant legs.

Would Daed be telling lies to Susie, too?

⌘

All the color had faded from Jacob's face. Becky's hands tightened around a potholder. She'd never figured that this distant cousin would pick her to be his bride, although she had harbored some faint hopes of being chosen by one of the incoming men. Whisper-thin hopes. Mostly, she'd decided she'd keep her distance from him. From all of them. After all, the local men didn't want her for a frau. Why should she expect anyone else to?

She shouldn't.

Couldn't.

Wouldn't.

Still, she certainly hadn't expected Jacob to be taken already.

And she hadn't expected that his daed would lie to Jacob about why he was being sent here. What was so wrong with the woman he planned to marry that his family would go to such lengths to separate them? Could it be that she wasn't Amish? Was a family feud to blame?

The silence stretched awkwardly as Jacob stared down at his hands, a muscle working in his jaw. And Daed, after sending Becky a confused glance, gazed into his cup of coffee, as if expecting answers to this dilemma to float to the surface.

She was fairly positive they wouldn't.

How many full cups of coffee had he studied when she'd entered her rumschpringe? Hundreds, for sure.

Daed's hand landed on the table with a loud slap, and Becky jumped. Jacob glanced up, but the muscle still worked in his jaw.

"Well then, Jacob. We'll make the best of this situation. You are here. You will help me. And if you happen to have your eye caught by one of our local girls, you'll stay. But if not, then I'll make sure you catch a bus back to Pennsylvania whenever you want to go."

"Danki, sir. Appreciate that." Jacob poured some cream into his coffee. His gaze locked on Becky. "The cookies smell gut."

Becky blinked. *The cookies!* She spun around and opened the oven. Heat billowed out of the open door. She gripped the pan with the potholder and lifted it out before sliding the next pan in. Thankfully, the chocolate-chocolate-chip cookies weren't burned.

"As soon as you finish that coffee, Jacob, I'll take you on a tour of the farm and show you where you'll be sleeping," Daed said. "You want a cookie first, though, ain't so?" Daed's gaze swung from Jacob to her. "Becky, as soon as the cookies cool, Jacob and I would both like one or two."

"Of course." Becky turned back around and picked up a spatula. "Just a minute, Daed." She lifted a cookie off the tray and laid it on a cooling rack. But as she slid the spatula under the next cookie, a wail filled the room, and the cradle in the corner began to rock.

Daed stood, going quickly over to the cradle and lifting the three-month-old baby. He cradled her in his arms and walked back over to the table, cooing softly. "And this, Jacob, is Emma."

"Nice to meet you, Emma."

"Jah, she's a sweetheart," Daed said. "No boys in this family. Yet. But I thank the gut Lord for the girls."

Jacob smiled. "And that would be why you need help with the farm, jah?"

Daed shrugged. Smiled. "It would appear that way, jah. But then, things are not always as they appear."

Chapter 3

The next morning, Jacob woke up to strange surroundings, from the scent of rosewater that filled the room to the look and feel of the colorful quilt as he tugged the bed back together after his restless night's sleep. A strange house. A strange town. A strange state. And the sickening knowledge that Daed had lied to him. Funny how that changed everything now.

Daniel had showed Jacob around the farm the afternoon before. He'd seen the site of the small blacksmith business they had on the side. It allowed Daniel to keep the buggies in good repair, plus he made some decorative crafts to sell to tourists. Then, Jacob had gotten to see the garden shop the womenfolk ran on the premises. It had been quiet lately, but it would soon be bustling when they started the seedlings in the greenhouse to get ready to sell to the locals for their spring planting.

Jacob's stomach rumbled, a reminder that he'd barely picked at his lunch and supper. He'd even turned down the apple pie, and that was one of his favorite treats. He figured he could give a good meal the attention it deserved now, but he knew the usual order of things: certain chores first, then breakfast. He pulled on his loose-fitting pants, a blue shirt, and suspenders, slapped his black felt hat on his head, yanked on his coat, and headed downstairs. The rest of the dawdi-haus was quiet, with everyone already up and gone.

Jacob pushed his way into the barn through the hanging doors.

"Nice you could join us, Jacob," came the good-natured comment from a dark corner. A lantern hanging from a hook lit a small area of space. Jacob rubbed his hands together to try to warm them, but it didn't help much. The windchill had to be in the single digits. The barn seemed only a little warmer. He pulled in a breath, inhaling the strong, musty odor and the scent of animals. He saw the older man, the grossdaedi, climbing down a ladder from a loft where a gray cat waited at the top. Then, turning, he spied Daniel in with the cows.

"How can I help?" Hay crunched under his feet as Jacob walked over to where Daniel sat on a low stool next to a milk cow.

"Guess you could take over here. Or, you could get started feeding the animals."

For a second, Jacob stood in indecision. He wasn't used to options. Daed communicated with orders. It seemed rather feminine of Cousin Daniel to talk like that. But he supposed that in a houseful of women, some of their ways rubbed off on him.

He slapped his hands together, then rubbed them briskly. "I'll finish the milking." He glanced around as Daniel stood. "Sorry I was late."

"Ach. I just got started. You're fine. I was teasing. Besides, it wouldn't have hurt for you to sleep in a bit your first morning here. I know you had a long trip."

"Jah." Not to mention the huge shock at discovering the truth, which had hampered his ability to fall asleep.

Well, there also had been a bit of fascination with the blonde beauty who was probably even now baking up a storm in the kitchen. She certainly would make a good frau. Maybe for one of his friends who'd signed up for that swap Cousin Daniel had mentioned yesterday.

Jacob sat on the three-legged wooden stool Daniel had vacated.

"I made the trip once when your great-great-grandfather died. Barely knew him; he was a distant onkel of mine. But my frau thought it'd be nice to see the extended family. That was...." Daniel hesitated, then hoisted a bag of feed. "That was before you were born, I'm thinking."

"Jah." Jacob didn't know what else to say. He quirked his mouth and looked down at the milk flowing into the pail, then cut a glance at the gray tabby cat hovering nearby. With a small grin, he shot a stream of the liquid in the cat's direction. When he looked up, Daniel had left.

Leaving Jacob alone with his thoughts, the cows, and the cat.

And the Lord.

Jacob patted the cow's side. "How do you like singing, Bessie?" He didn't know the animal's name, but it seemed at least one cow on every farm was named Bessie—sometimes all of them, depending on the farmer's imagination or lack thereof.

With a glance up at the dark rafters, Jacob pictured Susie strumming her guitar. He guessed that was when Daed and Susie had crossed plows. Daed had been furious when he'd discovered that Susie played the forbidden instrument. And even angrier when he'd learned that Susie had talked Jacob into going with her to a few Mennonite meetings.

Daed hadn't calmed down much, even when Jacob had promised to join the church. And especially since Susie hadn't yet confessed to her sin. He'd gone off on a rant about how Jacob would be shunned if he married a worldly woman and left the faith as a result. Jacob had tried to tell Daed that wouldn't happen, but Daed hadn't listened.

Jacob would try to write Susie later today and encourage her to confess and get rid of the guitar. Maybe then, Daed would be more receptive to their relationship. After all, if she loved him, she'd want to join the church with him. Might as well start now with the way they intended to go. With a slight lift of his left shoulder, he looked back at the Holstein and started singing.

ᨅ

Becky tossed another handful of seed into the plastic dish the chickens ate from, then closed the bag. Brushing her hand against her apron, she paused for a moment as the sound of a man singing drifted in from the other side of the barn. That Jacob had a beautiful bass voice. He'd make a nice addition to the Sunday night singings the youth had—not that she'd hear him there. She'd kept her distance from those events since her sin had made her an outcast. No point in setting herself up for further hurt.

With a sigh, she put the feed bag away, blew out the flame in the lantern, and headed up the six narrow stairs to the main floor of the barn. Time to get back to the house and help with breakfast. Her mother had mentioned German pizza last night. Becky's mouth watered thinking of the breakfast casserole.

With some hot coffee and some buttered toast, it would be a wonderful breakfast.

But then *he* would be joining them for breakfast. For all meals, since her grandparents ate with the family, too. Last night, Jacob had only pushed food around on his plate. Becky felt sorry for him. It was hard enough to be in a new community, a new home, and harder still to learn that he was there under false pretenses. Even so, Becky had been hurt that he'd eaten only a couple of bites of her oven-fried chicken and hadn't touched any of the other dishes she'd fixed in honor of his arrival. He hadn't even tried a slice of pie. She couldn't imagine anyone turning away a slice of her prize-winning apple pie. But he had.

Pulling her coat more tightly around her, she pushed through the barn doors and made her way toward the kitchen.

Once inside, she found Mamm busily peeling potatoes and slicing them for lunch. They'd be placed in a kettle of water and pushed to the back of the stove until it was time to cook them for the noon meal.

Becky washed her hands, checked the casserole, and then set out jars of apple butter, fruit preserves, and jams. "Are you going out today, Mamm?"

"Jah. We need to finish Sadie's quilt soon. The bishop has given permission for her to marry John Beuler. Since they are both struggling after losing their spouses and have young children, they agreed it would be best for them not to wait until fall to marry."

"Ach, gut. I know Sadie was concerned about that." Becky slid a knife through a loaf of bread.

"You're going to kum today, ain't so? We could use your help on the quilt."

"Nein." It was hard enough helping with normal quilts. But a quilt that was specially designed for a marriage bed? She couldn't.

"Emma stirred a bit ago. I sent Abbie to change her diaper and get her dressed."

"I'll go feed her, then." Becky turned toward the door as Katie came inside, carrying a couple of glass canning jars of corn they'd put up last summer. Since they kept them in the root cellar outside, the chilly air must have been what made Katie shiver.

"Morning, Katie," Becky greeted her.

"Morning. I'll take over in here."

"Jah. I'll be right back." She wanted to have Emma fed and be back in the kitchen before Daed, Grossdaedi, and Jacob came in. But why, she didn't know. Even if she and Jacob somehow managed to forge a relationship, he'd surely shun her just the same as everyone else when he learned about her sins.

It seemed the kneeling confession she'd made before the church hadn't helped at all.

Had she really expected it to?

⋘⋙

Jacob couldn't keep from glancing around the kitchen when he walked in. Five girls of assorted sizes, plus the grossmammi and Daniel's wife were all busy in the kitchen with some sort of cooking duty. The youngest girl set a fork and knife down on the table and then stopped to stare at him. Becky wasn't in the room. He shrugged, bothered that he'd even looked for her. Daniel pushed past Jacob and headed for the sink, where he began to wash up. The grossdaedi hung up his coat on the coat tree.

As if summoned by his thoughts, Becky came in through the connecting door from the living room, carrying the boppli close against her chest and whispering.

His heart clenched.

She'd make a great mother. A fantastic frau. For someone else, of course.

The fact that she wasn't married yet made Jacob wonder if the men around here were blind. Or maybe she was picky and wanted to hold out for that shipment of men Cousin Daniel had mentioned. After all, new blood would mean less risk of the DNA-related health problems some Amish families faced with their children.

Or, maybe that gloomy attitude she sported scared the men off. Most men wanted a cheerful frau. Jacob included.

He smiled. Jah, that would be his mission. Cheer up Becky so she could get married.

Jacob rubbed his hands together to warm them, then crossed the room toward Becky, trying to ignore the way his heart rate increased as he neared her. "Here, let me take your sister. What was her name again?" He slid his hands under the baby's arms and tugged. After a second, Becky loosened her hold on the boppli and stepped away.

"Her name is Emma." Becky looked down, then up again, a defiant expression ablaze in her blue eyes. Her chin lifted. "And she's my daughter."

Chapter 4

B ecky had released her daughter and watched Jacob hold her close to his shoulder as if it were second nature to him. He'd looked down at her and given a soft coo, which had ended abruptly when Becky had made her bold declaration. Now, he stared at her, his gorgeous blue eyes widening with surprise.

He stepped back, his gaze turning to assessment.

Becky squared her shoulders and brushed past him, not wanting to see his inevitable look of condemnation. But maybe he'd think she'd been married. She wasn't too young. Some Amish girls wed at seventeen. A few even had their first child by then.

Of course, there was no husband around.

Nor would there ever be.

Becky ignored the man invading her world and bustled over to the stove, picking up a couple of crocheted potholders en route. The German pizza her mother had put together filled the air with the aromas of sausage, eggs, cheese, and potatoes. Breakfast casseroles were a rare treat at their house, reserved for special occasions. Apparently, Becky's mother considered this Jacob worthy of the honor. Becky pulled open the oven door and carefully lifted the dish from the rack. She deposited it on another potholder in the middle of the table, then turned to find a knife.

"Breakfast is served," Mamm said in an overly bright voice as Becky finished slicing the casserole into pieces. "Jacob, you can sit in the same chair you used last night." She motioned to a wooden chair she'd moved to a spot between Daed and Grossdaedi.

In most Amish families, the men sat on one side of the table, the women on the other. With only two men in the family and a large table to fill, they didn't always observe the normal seating arrangements, though Mamm did place Jacob on the same side as Daed and Grossdaedi. Apparently, she was trying to make a nod toward convention.

Katie grabbed a stack of plates and placed them on the table, along with assorted serving utensils, and Becky set the salt and pepper shakers within reach. Then, almost everyone quietly took a seat. Jacob wordlessly handed Emma to Mamm and sat down. Mamm laid the boppli in the cradle in the corner, then joined the others at the table. Becky dipped her head for the silent prayer, thankful that she didn't have to look at Jacob for another few minutes. Maybe that would give her time to collect her thoughts.

⌘

After they'd finished breakfast, Jacob followed Daniel out to the blacksmith shop. His thoughts still reeled, confused by Becky's blunt declaration. He was familiar with the notion that some Amish districts allowed bundling, a bed courting method, but pregnancies out of wedlock were rare. His Ordnung spoke against bundling. She wasn't widowed because she didn't dress in mourning clothes. So, what had happened to Becky's beau? Had he left the district? Married another girl? Jumped the fence?

Ach, any of those incidents definitely would have caused Becky to feel abandoned and might account for her unhappy countenance. She must have loved this boy, whoever he was. Perhaps he'd return someday. Most Amish eventually finished their rumschpringe and joined the church. After all, Jacob planned to join as soon as he returned home to his Susie. In time for wedding season.

He kicked at an ice-covered rock in his path, then winced when it refused to budge. Somehow, the idea of that young man returning to Becky didn't make him as happy as it should have. She deserved better than some guy who'd run off and left her in disgrace, whatever his reasons.

Two open-air buggies waited in the blacksmith shop. "Courting buggies?" Jacob swallowed, regretting his choice of words immediately. There was no excuse for them. He'd been thinking of the man who'd courted Becky.

"Nein. Only type that are allowed." Daniel handed Jacob a pair of safety glasses and some leather work gloves. "Do you know anything about blacksmithing?"

"Nein." Jacob donned the glasses and followed his cousin to the blazing flame. The intense heat almost overpowered him. He glanced from his cousin's hands, blackened by work, to his own unstained hands. With a grimace, he shook off his coat, hung it on a peg, rolled up his sleeves, and slipped on the gloves. "Show me what to do."

"Ach, first thing to do would be to start the fire. Kum over here to the forge, and I'll show you what to do. Bring that bucket of coal, if you don't mind. And the coke."

Jacob raised his eyebrows and looked around for a can of soda. He didn't see any. "Coke?"

"Ach, sorry." Daniel came over and lifted a plastic lid off of one of the buckets. "Coke." He picked up a piece of burned charcoal and pointed to some white pieces mixed in with the black, saying something about keeping it moist and needing it to keep the fire at a certain temperature. Information Jacob didn't understand and couldn't see himself needing to know. After all, apple orchards were in his future. Not a blacksmith shop.

Instead of listening to Daniel as closely as he should have, he thought instead of Susie, and his daed, and Mamm. His older brothers were all married with children, and they all worked on the farm with Daed. Jacob frowned. Mamm had always said that when Jacob married, she and Daed would move into the vacant dawdi-haus and let Jacob and his frau have the main house. After all, the family should be together. The way God intended it to be.

Jacob kicked at a clump of black coal on the black gravel floor. This shop was a stinky mess. It smelled like smoke, but the odor was different from the annoying odor of cigarettes. This was heavier and thicker; it seemed to permeate everything.

He couldn't wait to get home and farm the nice, clean earth.

But then, there was fire. Jacob watched the flames, fascinated, as he cranked the handle on the forge that Daniel told him to turn in a slow, steady manner while he dumped a bucket of coal around the fire that he'd begun with wood and crumpled paper. The coal made a dome around two sides of the fire.

"There, listen to that. Hear the roar of the fire? That's what we're looking for."

⁕

Becky hoisted the laundry basket and the pail full of clothespins before hurrying outside to the clothesline. She shivered in the cold wind, wishing they could dry the clothes inside like some of their Englisch neighbors. After placing her load on the ground, she reached for a pretty little pink dress belonging to her four-year-old sister, Mary. Becky missed wearing the beautiful, bright colors permitted for little girls. She glanced down at her dark maroon dress, more suited for hard, potentially dirty work.

At least she could enjoy the colorfulness of the quilts the women made. The tumbling block pattern on Becky's bed featured various shades of blue, her favorite color. A double wedding ring quilt in lavender and purple covered her parents' bed. She wondered what Jacob thought of the quilt she had spread across his bed. It was a log cabin pattern, and she'd helped to make it. It was supposed to have gone into her hope chest.

No point in letting her thoughts go there. She forced her attention back to her task.

Men's voices carried on the breeze, but she couldn't understand the words. She glanced toward the shop where Daed and Jacob worked. A couple of cars and buggies were parked outside the small, open building. Maybe they were customers needing some blacksmith work. Or maybe they'd come to shoot the breeze. She knew Daed had a lot of fun out in his shop, and sometimes it seemed like the local hangout.

She picked up another dress—a bluish-gray one of her mother's—and shook it out. What did Jacob think of their community? How did it compare to his own in Pennsylvania? More snow up north, maybe. But wouldn't one district be pretty much the same as the next? She shrugged and deliberately pushed Jacob out of her mind, turning her attention to other chores that required her attention.

Mamm needed a fruit cobbler to take to quilting on Monday, so Becky figured she'd make two. Her sisters and Daed wouldn't be happy if she didn't provide one for them to enjoy. She'd need to make the cobblers today, Saturday, as Sunday was a day set aside for the Lord and for family. The kitchen floor really needed to be scrubbed. Probably after she'd made the cobblers. Mary and Abbie would likely want to help with the baking, and the floor, table, and chairs would be sticky when they finished.

Becky hung up the last dress and then hurried toward the house, eager to start the rest of the day's work.

Maybe, if she finished quickly, she could go visit her friend Annie and tell her about Jacob from Pennsylvania.

Chapter 5

Jacob stared at the fire he'd finally managed to build according to Daniel's specifications. Daniel's lecture about the all-important blacksmith fire that he'd fed Jacob seemed to dissolve as fast as the sparks in front of him. He didn't believe for a moment he'd remember a word of it tomorrow. But then, maybe the old idiom was true that a burned hand teaches best. He glared down at his sore, reddened fingers. Not that they'd been burned yet. Daniel had warned him that there is no such thing as a first-degree burn in a blacksmith shop. It would be either second or third degree. Neither appealed to him. He would have to remember to wear his work gloves.

Daniel showed him how to heat the metal, holding it in the fire. "You want an orange-red color, because that is the temperature that is best to work with. Any hotter will melt the metal." He nodded with satisfaction at the color on the tip of the metal piece he held, then picked up a farrier's hammer. "See how this is flat on one side? I like using this type the best, because I can get it more even." He laid the metal piece on an anvil, pounded a few times with a clanging sound, then reheated the metal. He handed the hammer to Jacob. "You give it a try."

Jacob swung the hammer a few times, stopping when Daniel told him to reheat the metal. Finally, Daniel stopped and examined it.

"Ser gut. Now, dip it into this solution. This will harden it up. It is a mixture of blue Dawn dish soap, salt, and water. I'll show you how to make it in a few days."

Jacob dipped it in the solution, watching as the hot metal sizzled.

"Gut. Now, dip it in that barrel of rainwater." Daniel pointed to another black bucket in the corner of the room.

Jacob's family didn't do any blacksmith work. They took broken buggies down to old Mose, who'd been in the business for years. Everyone in their district went to Mose. But here, the popular blacksmith seemed to be Cousin Daniel.

While Daniel might have been up to the challenge of both teaching the job and doing the work, Jacob wasn't up to learning it and doing it. His head hurt. The thick smoke clung to the insides of his throat and lungs, making him feel strangled.

Wasn't this black coal stuff the thing that caused disease in miners and killed them? Maybe Daniel should be providing him with a breathing mask and oxygen tanks. Jacob coughed.

Daniel heated something and grabbed the hammer, swinging it down, talking all the while. The words seemed to go over Jacob's head. In one ear and out the other. Or, nein, maybe they got stuck in his brain and swirled around in a bunch of confusing nonsense.

The seemingly constant clanging as they pounded a piece of orange-red metal on the anvil got on his last nerve, and Jacob dashed toward the open shed door and fresh air. Pure, cold, invigorating air. He gulped it in, praying that the headache would depart. He rolled his neck and tried to rub the tension out of his temples.

Would he ever grasp this?

At that moment, he thought not.

Out of the corner of his eye, he caught the movement of clothes flapping on the line in the wind. He turned in that direction, hoping to catch the attention of whoever was hanging them. Maybe she'd be kind enough to fetch him a glass of cold water to quench his parched throat. But no one moved near the clothesline. Apparently, whoever had done the laundry had already gone inside.

Daniel poked his head out of the doorway of the shed. "Jacob?"

Jacob cleared his throat. "I need a glass of water. I'll be right back."

"Water. Jah. If you're getting frustrated, you need a break. I don't want you getting hurt." Daniel grinned. "Don't worry. You'll get it."

Jacob thought the "You'll get it" was in reference to his new job as a blacksmith apprentice, but he wasn't sure. And he didn't ask. Instead, he nodded and headed toward the house. He could have gotten a sip from the outside pump, but he bypassed it in favor of a full glass from the kitchen. He was further enticed by the thought of the sweet scent of baked goods that lingered there. At home, the kitchen always smelled like cinnamon. Mamm specialized in apple cinnamon treats, as they always had apples in abundance. After all, they couldn't sell the bruised, wormy, bird-pecked, or misshapen ones. So, they were used in baking.

His stomach rumbled at the thought of apple fritters as he went up the porch steps.

It still seemed strange to open the door of someone else's house and walk in, but since he was living here for the time being, he decided he'd better get used to it. After closing the door behind him and taking a few steps inside, he stopped to sniff and smelled a strong, lemon-scented cleaner mixed with something sweet. His stomach rumbled. Then a small sound akin to a whimper caught his attention, and he looked down to see Becky, kneeling in the entry-way, a rag in her hands and a bucket of soapy water by her side.

Jacob swallowed, hoping he hadn't tracked dirt inside. Had he stepped where she'd already scrubbed, or was she getting ready to wash that area? He didn't know. Either way, it wasn't good.

He stepped back, deciding to tease about it. "It's okay, Bex. You don't need to bow to me."

Her eyes widened, but he didn't get the smile he'd hoped for. Her lips didn't even twitch. "Bex?" Her voice came out in a squeak. "Bow?"

Jacob grinned. "You are too cute. I just want a glass of water. I'll be out of your way in a moment."

❧

Becky watched Jacob as he stepped around her and went to the gas-powered refrigerator for a pitch-er of cold water, then to the cupboard for a glass. Nobody had ever called her "Bex" before. She wasn't sure how she felt about it. She wanted to dislike it. But she did like something about the implied famili-arity, the sound of her name tumbling off his lips in that carefree way.

And telling her she was "too cute"? What did that mean? Did he find her attractive? Or did he mean it as someone might describe one of those stray tomcats that are so ugly they're cute? Was he referring to the newborn puppy sort of cute? She wanted to ask. But her courage fled even as she considered voicing her question.

Why bother asking? He'd hesitate to tell her if it was negative.

He turned to face her as he downed the liquid in one long gulp, then set the glass in the sink. With a wink, he stepped around her again. "Smells gut in here. You'll be a gut frau someday." The door closed solidly behind him.

That wink had sent her nerves sizzling with hopefulness.

She gave herself a mental shaking as tears burned her eyes. She'd never be a good wife. Maybe a mother's helper. Everyone knew she was destined to be an old maid. She hoped he hadn't intended to be unkind. Maybe he didn't realize how hurtful his words were.

Becky blinked the moisture away. She needed to focus on her task, not her situation.

She finished scrubbing the floor, then took the cobblers out of the oven. They were done to perfection, lightly browned, and smelled delicious. She set them on the counter, glanced at her sleeping boppli in the cradle in the corner, and went looking for Mamm.

Becky found her browsing through a seed catalog.

She looked up at Becky and smiled. "This came in the mail a while back. Since I didn't have a chance to look at it then, I decided to take a short break. Kum join me?"

It always seemed odd to Becky that the catalogs came in the mail the first few weeks of January, too soon to think about gardening. But they'd be starting seedlings in the greenhouse in the next several weeks so that the Englisch could be supplied with tomatoes, peppers, and other vegetables and fruit ready to plant. Not only Englisch. The Amish took advantage of them, too.

"What do you think of this, Becky?"

Becky sat next to Mamm and glanced at the picture of an heirloom tomato and read a shortened version of the description. "A type of yellow fruit, known for its sweetness."

"Sounds gut to me. But yellow tomatoes don't sell as well as red."

Mamm lifted a shoulder. "We'll keep it for ourselves."

"Jah." That would work. "Do you need me for anything else, or can I go visit Annie for a spell?"

"Maybe after lunch. Can you help Katie with the mending?"

Her shoulders sagged. Annie would have to wait. She took a deep breath and nodded. "Jah. That'll be fine."

❧

The morning crawled by as if in slow motion. Daniel patiently tried to talk Jacob through problems, but most of the time Jacob felt hinnersich. Still, this was his first day as a blacksmith apprentice—a career he never wanted. Maybe he'd have more appreciation for Mose when he returned home.

But there was something mesmerizing about pounding the hot metal into shapes and watching the forms appear that Daniel wanted.

The clanging of the dinner bell coming from the house signaled a welcome break. Jacob looked forward to whatever Becky had been baking when he'd been in the kitchen earlier.

When he came in, the table was already laden with bread-and-butter pickles, chowchow, jams, fresh baked bread, and pickled eggs. One of the girls—her name escaped him, but she looked about twelve—was just finishing setting the table.

Jacob followed Daniel to the washbasin, watching out of the corner of his eye for Becky. She wasn't anywhere in the room. Probably taking care of her boppli.

Funny how her situation upset his stomach. He needed to pray for her—and the man who had wronged her.

Jacob sat down at the table, his hands on his lap, watching the women bustle to load more food onto the table—Salisbury steak, mashed potatoes, and corn. They'd no sooner placed the last serving dish on the table when Becky hurried in, skirts swirling—though he tried not to notice—and slid into her chair, bowing her head for the silent prayer.

Jacob followed suit. At least with his head bowed he didn't have to pretend he didn't notice her.

If only she'd smile.

He heaved a sigh and closed his eyes, forcing his focus away from the woman sitting across from him and onto the Holy One who deserved his undying devotion. Jacob offered up thanks for the bounty in front of him, adding a plea for help for Becky.

And for a measure of wisdom for him. There must be some way to tease a smile out of her.

Did the youth have singings here? He imagined they would. Maybe he could talk Becky into taking him to introduce him around. He could help her find a potential husband. Surely, she went. She was still in her rumschpringe. Right?

Chapter 6

After the silent prayer, Daed took a helping of the meat and mushrooms, then passed the white serving dish to the left. Jacob accepted it, but as he reached for the fork, he glanced up, meeting Becky's eyes. He grinned and winked. Her face warmed, and she hastily looked away, passing a dish to her sister.

"So, Bex, are they having a singing tomorrow night?" He didn't clarify who "they" were, maybe figuring she would know. And he'd called her Bex in front of her family. What did they think about that?

Becky knew whom he meant by "they." But if he wanted to know who would be hosting it, she didn't know that. She hadn't been to youth functions since before....

She wouldn't go there. Not mentally, and certainly not physically.

Just at that moment, Ruthie passed the bicolor sweet corn. Did Becky read pity in her sister's eyes? Becky glared at her. What would an eleven-year-old know about life?

She stabbed the serving spoon into the bowl of corn. Thankfully, it seemed everyone else at the table was ignoring the conversation that Jacob had initiated. Except maybe Daed. He wore that knowing expression. The one he'd put on when he'd come into the kitchen the day Jacob had arrived. The one that said he knew a secret.

Becky passed the corn on to Abbie and accepted the mashed potatoes, all without answering Jacob. As if the question would go away if she ignored it long enough.

She caught a look from her mother as she passed the potatoes on to Abbie—the one that Mamm wore to say silently that rudeness would not be tolerated.

Becky knew that her mother was right. But really, this stranger was going down roads she didn't want to travel. And he was taking her with him.

That didn't change things. And Mamm's expression promised Becky an earful along with a tongue-lashing if she didn't answer, and quickly. Becky acquiesced, with only the briefest of glances at Jacob. "I haven't been to a singing for a long time. I'm sure they'll be having them. I can find out tomorrow." Since tomorrow would be a non-church Sunday, they would visit family around the area. Even if no one asked Becky to join the singing, she knew they would ask Jacob.

He was, as the Englisch girls say, hot.

Becky's face heated just thinking that word.

But she wasn't blind. Just—unwanted.

Poison.

⌘

Last night's letter to sweet Susie lay crumpled in Jacob's back pocket. He needed to run it to the mailbox right quick. After all, she needed to know his address. And he wanted to beg her to give up her music so they could be together. Not that the music would stop Jacob. But it would make a difference whether Daed accepted her. Whether they would wed with his blessing, or with Jacob ending up being shunned. Besides, there was the rather large issue of the Ordnung not allowing instruments. And he didn't want to leave the Amish church. Though he would, for Susie.

A wave of homesickness hit. He yearned for the scent of apple blossoms, though it would be early for that, as he worked with his brothers and Daed in the apple orchard. Yearned to enjoy the same orchard later that night as he strolled with Susie. He needed to get home, sooner rather than later.

At the end of the meal, Jacob and Daniel each had a second cup of coffee and another serving of blueberry cobbler. While they ate, Jacob watched Becky move alongside her sisters as they made quick work of the dishes. Comparing her with Susie. He studied the brightness of her blonde hair under her white kapp and the sway of her reddish-colored skirt as she moved around. The trimness of her ankles when her skirt shifted enough for them to come into view. The curve of her neck.

The two women were so different.

After she finished, she grabbed a coat from the closet and pulled it on, then lifted her boppli out of the cradle, wrapped her in a thick pink blanket, and placed her into a sling. "I'm going over to Annie's now."

Already started on her baking, her mother raised a hand in acknowledgment.

"Ready to get to work, Jacob?" Daniel pushed his chair back with a smirk. Unsaid but implied was, "Since you won't have anything to watch in here."

Jacob shot Daniel a look that his daed would have considered disrespectful, and his face warmed as he stood. "Jah. Let me run this out to the mailbox first." He pulled the letter from his pocket. But whether he needed to remind Daniel or himself that he had a girlfriend, he couldn't have said.

Jacob bolted out the door after Becky, leaving Daniel and his frau to come to whatever conclusion they would.

"Bex! Wait up."

He slipped a little on the ice as he scampered after her, catching up halfway down the driveway. She had turned with eyebrows raised, shifted the sling holding the boppli, and watched him approach.

"I need to mail a letter."

One eyebrow quirked higher. "The mailbox is right there." She pointed toward the black box not even a hundred feet away.

"Jah. Danki." Even without looking, Jacob knew where it sat.

She turned to go, but he grabbed her elbow, stopping her. He didn't let go, even when unexpected sparks shot up his arm.

Becky jerked her head up to stare at Jacob, her eyes wide. She pulled back enough to dislodge his hand. "What?" Her voice sounded strangled.

"Why'd you quit going to the singings?" Ach, talk about blunt. Jacob hadn't meant to ask so plainly. But there it was. Laid out in the open.

She stared at him, his shock mirrored on her expression. She just stood there, not answering. But he could read the "none of your business" that she wanted to say in her eyes. Instead, after what seemed half of forever, she looked down, then up again with a suddenly coy look in her eyes. "Why? Did you want to take me home?"

With that, she scurried off, leaving Jacob staring after her.

Wondering.

Why did he feel sparks with this woman? The possibilities excited him, but they were tempered

with guilt. He intended to find her a date with someone else. Not him. Never him.

The crunch of tires on gravel drew his attention
from the fleeing woman to the mail truck edging to
the box. All of a sudden, he remembered the letter in
his hand and the girl waiting for it back home. Jacob waved the envelope, catching the mailman's attention, and hurried the few yards separating them.
He replaced the crumpled envelope in his pocket and
pulled out another one addressed to Mamm, instead.
Then, leaving the family's mail in the box, he turned
and sprinted—almost skating on patches of ice—back
to the blacksmith shop.

Not that he was in any hurry to get back to that
hot, dirty job. He didn't exactly want to face Cousin
Daniel, either. But the more distance between him
and Becky, the better.

Whatever had possessed him to touch her?

Chapter 7

Becky hurried the mile to Annie's house, holding the sling carrying Emma tight against her side. Her face burned from embarrassment as she scurried down the road, beneath the trees that looked as if they'd been painted by God's own hand. Ice still encased some of the branches from the winter storm they'd had two days before Jacob's arrival. But the ice was starting to melt, and the roads were mostly clear.

Whatever had possessed her to tease Jacob about wanting to bring her home from the singing? He wouldn't be interested in dating her, even if he didn't have someone waiting for him back in Pennsylvania. At least by hurrying off, she had saved herself the embarrassment of being rejected outright.

If only....

No point in pursuing that thought. She couldn't change the past, even if she wanted to. And she cherished Emma. She often wished that she'd done things in the right order, however: marriage first, and to a good, solid Amish man. Not running around with Kent in his fancy red car and being taken in by his smooth-talking ways.

Ach! She set her jaw. She would not think about this.

Emma squirmed and cried out, and Becky adjusted her hold. She must have squeezed her too tightly. Positive proof that she didn't need to be thinking these things. Instead, she'd tell Annie about Jacob the minute she got there. Annie would surely be interested in the good-looking addition to their community, and maybe Jacob would take her home from the singing. She wasn't seeing anyone; hadn't since Luke had gone and jumped the fence to the Englisch world.

Word was that Luke had cut his hair and wore Englisch clothes now. And Becky had heard he'd even bought a black pickup truck.

Emma cried out again, and Becky pulled the material of the sling back far enough to press a finger to her soft cheek. Emma giggled. "You are worth it," Becky said.

But still....

Images of Jacob floated through her mind. If only she'd waited.

Arriving at Annie's house, she stomped her feet on the stoop, knocking most of the dirt and ice off her boots, then opened the kitchen door and slipped inside. Annie and her mother were baking heart-shaped cutout cookies, probably to sell in the bakery.

"Becky, welkum!" Annie set her cookie cutter down on the table and hurried over. Taking Emma, she unwrapped her and pressed kisses on her little cheeks. "How is the wee boppli?"

Annie's mamm took Emma next. "I've been hoping you'd stop by. I haven't seen Emma in over a week. My, how she's grown!" Cuddling the boppli close, she headed over to a carved rocking chair, one her husband had made in his furniture shop.

"Can I help with the cookies?" Becky took off her coat and hung it on a wall hook.

"We're almost finished. This will be the last batch. When the cookies are cooled, we'll give you some to take home to your family. Care for some coffee?"

"Danki."

"So, what is going on at your haus?" Annie poured the coffee and set a cup in front of Becky and one beside her Mamm. "We saw Tony dropping someone off at your haus a couple of days ago. Do you have family visiting?"

Becky leaned forward, hooking her fingers through the handle of the cup. "Jah. Not family, exactly. He's a very distant cousin of Daed's. We thought he came out to be part of the swap. Jacob said he was sent out to help Daed, and he has a girl back home. But, Annie, maybe he'll stay. You've got to meet him. He'd be perfect to take your mind off Luke. He's so gut-looking."

Shoving Jacob in Annie's direction hurt more than Becky had expected it to. She wanted to snatch the words back and hold them close.

Annie shrugged. "I don't want to take some other girl's man. That'd be wrong."

"Jah, but you could help him change his mind." Why did she keep talking? "You've got to see him, Annie. He is so cute."

"Maybe you want him for yourself, jah?" Annie's mamm said with a quirk of an eyebrow.

Becky's eyes widened. "Me? Nein. I'll never marry. Besides, I'm used goods. He wouldn't have me."

"What? You'll never marry?" Annie slid the last tray of cookies into the oven. "I wouldn't be so sure. I overheard Bishop Sol talking to your daed about marrying you up with Amos Kropf. His third wife recently died, and he's got all those kinner who need a mamm. I heard Amos has his eye on you, since you've got Emma and no husband."

Becky's skin crawled, and her stomach heaved with the force of sudden, rising nausea. By God's grace, she kept the contents down.

Not Amos Kropf. Please, God. Nein.

If only someone else would have her. Someone like Jacob.

❧

The afternoon seemed to go by a little easier. The orders from the morning's customers had all been taken care of, and now the only person waiting was a man who appeared to be approximately the same age as Daniel. Since this man wanted to talk privately, Daniel had sent Jacob out to get him a drink and a couple of cookies. The errand wouldn't take long but would give the men the privacy they wanted.

When Jacob walked into the kitchen, he saw Daniel's frau working on some sort of baking. He'd made sure to wipe his feet first this time, not wanting to track anything on Becky's clean floor. "Excuse me, ma'am. Daniel wants something to drink and a couple of cookies."

Daniel's frau turned around and smiled. "Call me Leah." She nodded toward the counter. "Help yourself to the cookies." Elbow-deep in flour, she kneaded a lump of dough.

Jacob nodded, washed his hands, and grabbed two cookies from the apple-shaped cookie jar. He placed them on a napkin, then took a cup out of the cupboard and filled it with water.

He had almost reached the door when Leah spoke again. "Are you liking it here so far?"

Jacob stopped, turned, and shrugged. He hadn't really had a chance to decide how he felt—about the location. "So far, so gut." What else could he say? Becky fascinated him too much for his own good, and he missed his family and his girl. That was the whole reason Becky fascinated him. Had to be. Plus, he had absolutely no desire to become a blacksmith.

And there, his attitude had reared its ugly head again.

Following God's will meant that he would make the best of being here.

Daniel certainly didn't seem to need Jacob's help, but he still put him to work. Jacob didn't have any idea why God would have sent him here. Unless it was to prompt him and Susie to break up. God must be on Daed's side.

Jacob held back a sigh.

He still wanted to cheer Becky up so she could find a husband, but so far, that project had been like ramming his shoulder into the side of a barn. Not one bit of give on her part, and a whole lot of aches and pains on his. Not to mention frustration.

"Well, let us know what else we can do to help you feel at home." Leah plopped the ball of dough into a bowl and covered it with a towel.

"Jah." Jacob nodded. Armed with cookies and water, he headed out the door. Back to the blacksmith shop.

Jacob arrived to find the shop empty. Looking around, he saw Daniel and his visitor walking side by side toward one of the fields, still talking.

He found a clear spot on the worktable and set down the napkin, cookies, and water, then set to work checking the fire. Next, he put away the hammers and tongs that had been left out. He didn't know enough about the job to risk starting a new project. If Daniel had his way, however, Jacob would probably know enough about blacksmith work to rival Mose when he returned home. Maybe enough for Daed to build a forge where Jacob could do the family's repair work.

Or maybe enough to support Susie with his own business.

Even if it wasn't one of his choosing.

Daniel strode back into the shop, his expression drawn, his shoulders slumped. The other man climbed into the buggy outside, and at a word he spoke, the brown horse pulled it down the gravel drive. Daniel didn't watch the man go. Instead, he went and checked the fire, then headed over to get one of the tools Jacob had just put away.

Without a word.

He picked it up and put it down again, staring at it as if he'd never seen it before.

Jacob flexed his jaw, wishing he knew Daniel well enough to ask him what bothered him. However, they had met just days ago, and he felt sure Daniel wouldn't want to confide in him.

But he didn't want to just stand there doing nothing, either.

"Can I help?"

Daniel jumped. "Nein. Go...go see what Grossdaedi is doing."

Jacob hitched his shoulder. "Jah. Danki."

Leaving his coat and hat on the hook, he headed out. He'd check the barn first, having no idea how the patriarch of the family spent his days. It certainly wasn't in the blacksmith shop with Daniel.

He found Grossdaedi in the barn, mucking out the horse stalls. Jacob grabbed a shovel and moved in beside the elderly man.

⌘

Becky trudged home with Emma bundled in her sling, a basket of cookies hanging on her arm, and her thoughts weighing her down. Amos Kropf had already buried three wives. Becky certainly didn't want to be number four. She had no desire to marry a man his age. He must be in his early forties, at least.

Daed surely wouldn't agree to this match, would he? Not even if the bishop recommended it? Was this the only way she could hope to get married? To a man she barely knew? A man she suspected had abused his last wife?

"Lord, I don't want to marry Amos Kropf. I'd rather remain a maidal all my life. But if it's Your will, help me to accept it."

The smoky smell from the blacksmith shop greeted her as she entered the edge of their property, though she didn't see any cars or buggies outside it now. And she couldn't hear any voices.

Going up to the house, she opened the door. Daed sat at the kitchen table, staring into a cup of coffee. Jacob was nowhere in sight.

He looked up with a sigh. "Ach, Becky."

She set the basket of cookies in front of him. "Annie sent these." They had covered the cookies with pink icing while she'd visited. She unwrapped Emma and headed for the other room. "Are you alright?"

Daed nodded. "I will be."

"I need to go change her diaper. I'll be right back."

"Jah."

"Where's Mamm?" Becky paused and turned back. If only she dared ask what bothered him now. Surely, Jacob couldn't be so inept that it had sent Daed up to the house to brood over a cup of coffee. Besides, if he was truly that bad, then Daed wouldn't have left him alone in the shop.

"Upstairs working on the mending."

"And Jacob?" She felt her face flush with heat just saying his name.

A ghost of a smile flickered across Daed's lips. "Helping Grossdaedi. I needed a break."

"Ach. Hinnersich, jah?"

"Nein. He's smart. Wonderful-gut help."

Ach, if only she could sit down at the table with Daed, have a cup of coffee and some cobbler, and listen to him recite Jacob's virtues.

But Emma needed attention.

Feeding this foolish fascination with their guest would only cause her more heartache. After all, he'd be leaving in the not-so-distant future, maybe sooner rather than later, and then where would she be?

Best to think about him as little as possible.

With a sigh, Becky draped the pink blanket over the back of the cradle and hurried upstairs to tend to Emma.

And to put all thoughts of one Jacob Miller out of her head.

Chapter 8

With the stables mucked, Grossdaedi declared he needed a nap, and since Daniel had disappeared from the blacksmith shop, Jacob hurried up to the house. He walked into the empty kitchen. Bread cooled on the counter, a plate of iced heart-shaped cookies sat on the table, and a full cup of coffee had been abandoned near a half-eaten cookie. The cradle in the corner was empty, except for a pink blanket carelessly tossed over the edge, the only evidence that Becky had returned.

Silence filled the house. Jacob went into the room next to the kitchen, where some chairs were arranged and the big family Bible rested on an end table. Macintosh apple-scented candles were the only decoration in the room, aside from a cabinet full of quilts that stood in one corner. Its doors were open, and colorful material spilled out from the overstuffed shelves. A couple of books and *The Budget*, the Amish newspaper, lay on another end table under a gas lamp.

A seed catalog was open on one of the chairs, with notepaper and a pen beside it. Some notations were visible on the paper.

A creaking sound came from the stairs, and Jacob turned to see the youngest girl coming toward him, clutching a faceless doll. "Katie?" He made a guess at the name. "Where's your daed?"

"Daed wanted to talk to Mamm, and I'm Mary. M-A-R-Y. I'm four. My birthday is in two days." She held up five fingers.

"Danki, Mary. Um, where is...." Jacob hesitated, not sure whom to ask for next.

"Abbie won't play with me." The child gave a small huff. "She's making a quilt for her doll."

"I'm sorry. Perhaps she'll play with you later. What about your other sisters?"

"Ruthie is reading, Katie went to visit a friend, and Becky is feeding Emma."

Jacob nodded. "Danki." His family always took a brief quiet time during the afternoon, too, and again in the evening when the work was done, so they could relax before bed. Daed always claimed he could work better if he took several breaks throughout the day. "I guess I'll, uh...."

"Have a cookie? That's what Mamm told me to do. She said that Becky brought them home from Annie's."

"A cookie sounds ser gut." With a cup of coffee, especially.

Mary nodded, her braids bouncing against her shoulders. "My dolly is going to have one, too. Her name is Rachel, the same as my friend. And my friend named her dolly Mary, like me."

Jacob smiled. "That's nice." He glanced up the stairs again, willing someone else to come, but no one made an appearance. "Let's go get that cookie, then. Would you like a glass of milk with it?"

"Jah, and one for my dolly, too."

Jacob blinked, not quite sure how to handle that one. But maybe by the time he was ready to pour the milk, someone else would have come downstairs. He followed Mary into the kitchen and headed for the refrigerator. He took out the milk, then turned and saw Mary place two little cups on the table. Little toy dishes, really, like his sister had played with when she was little. "Does your dolly want her milk in this?" he asked.

Mary nodded. "Jah. And me, too." She plopped herself down in a chair. "Why'd you kum here?"

Jacob shrugged, not sure what to tell a four-year-old. How much had she heard, anyway? He seemed to remember her being in the kitchen during the initial conversation, but she might not remember any of it. And even if she remembered, she probably had not understood.

"My daed said I had to kum." He filled the two little cups with milk and then returned the milk jug to the refrigerator.

"Are you sad?" Mary asked.

Jacob smiled. "I miss my home. But your home is nice." He moved over to the stove and poured some coffee into a mug. When he heard a swish of a skirt, he turned to see Becky step into the room without Emma. His heart rate increased.

"We're having cookies, Becky." Mary bounced on the chair. "And Jacob poured me and my dolly some milk."

"Jah. I see that." Becky nodded, and her gaze briefly landed on Jacob. "Make yourself at home."

Was that a bit of sarcasm he sensed in her voice? He quirked an eyebrow. "Want to join us, Bex? I'll pour you some coffee." He didn't know whether to hope she would accept or decline. Honestly, this woman seemed to tie his brain up in knots. It'd be good to get back to Susie and their comfortable romance, where the only knots were caused by Daed's refusal to accept Jacob's decision.

A look of discomfort flitted across her face, and she glanced toward the door she'd just come through, as if she was trying to think of a reason to leave. Maybe a chore she had to do. Or maybe she listened for Emma.

He poured another mug of coffee and set it down on the other side of the table, deciding he'd rather she stayed. "There you go." He dared to wink when she looked back at him.

She blushed, hot red flooding her checks. Twisting her skirt with her hands, she lowered herself into the chair. "Danki."

"No problem. Care for a cookie?" He pushed the plate toward her.

"Nein."

"I want one. And so does my dolly." Mary reached out and snagged two. Jacob grinned at her.

"So, you must miss your sweetie, jah?" Becky asked in a tight voice. "Tell me about her." Her face turned an even brighter shade of red, and she dropped her gaze to the table.

His sweetie? It took him a moment to realize she meant Susie.

❧

Becky didn't want to hear a word about Jacob's girl, not a single word. But if she had to be in the same room with him, with no family but Mary between them, then it seemed better to bring up the person he loved, helping herself to remember that someone else had a prior claim on him.

Out of the corner of her eye, she saw Jacob reach out and take a cookie. He remained silent for a time that seemed to stretch by endlessly but might have been only a minute. Finally, he sucked in a deep breath. "Look at me, Bex."

She looked up, and he grinned. "I don't like talking to the top of a head. I want to see your beautiful face when I talk to you."

Ach! A smooth talker, for sure. He'd probably upset all the girls back home when he'd picked one to settle down with. The type of guy who would leave a chain of broken hearts here in Missouri when he boarded the bus to return to Pennsylvania.

Hers would not be one of them.

She had to get away from him. But, incredibly, she couldn't think of a single reason to call her away.

What chores had she done already? She tried to reverse the list to see what she'd have to undo. The laundry could be checked, since it was hanging out on the line. It would probably be frozen solid by now, cold as it was. Or maybe, she could...um....

She glanced around frantically.

"Am I so terrible to look at, Bex?"

"What?" She jerked her attention back to him.

"That's better." His grin deepened, causing a dimple to appear on his left cheek. Ach, he was so cute.

"Your girlfriend?" She prompted him when he seemed to be content sitting there gazing into her eyes.

"My girlfriend? Ach, Susie Chupp." He reached for another cookie. "She's pretty, with strawberry blonde hair and brown eyes. Lives down the road a bit."

He took a bite of the sweet.

"Her daed will be planting lots of celery this year, jah?" She thought of the long rows of the traditional wedding food that would never be planted for her. That was like a knife to the heart.

Jacob squirmed a little, discomfort crossing his face. He frowned. "Jah, that was the plan."

Becky doubted she'd get any more information from him. Amish were, by nature, closemouthed, and sharing details about courting was verboden, even though most people could figure them out. She searched for something else to say. Before she could come up with anything, though, a puddle of milk flowed toward her.

Becky jumped to her feet and hurried around the table to grab a rag.

Mary frowned at her doll. "You need to be more careful. Now I need to change your clothes." She stood and darted from the room.

Becky ran the rag over the spill, quickly wiping it up. Jacob reached out and put his hand over hers, stilling it. Shock waves raced to her heart. Her gaze jumped up to meet his.

"You'll go with me to the singing tomorrow night, jah? For moral support?"

Like he'd need moral support.

"Introduce me around?"

That would be the polite thing to do. Daed and Mamm would want her to. But still, she'd been serious when she'd said she'd never go to another one. She started to say "Nein," but the grip of his hand tightened.

"Please? You'd have fun."

She'd have fun. Right. What had happened at the last singing had not been her idea of a good time.

Becky swallowed hard. "Nein." It came out harsher than she'd intended it to. Yet, not feeling inclined to apologize, she jerked her hand from under his and turned, dashing from the room after her sister.

⎯᪥⎯

Ach, she was stubborn.

Jacob frowned, staring at the doorway she'd disappeared through.

She would go with him. If not tomorrow, then the next time. Or the time after that. He had to get her out around people, although if her own family wasn't enough to make her smile, then he didn't know how being around her peers would. But that just seemed to be the next natural step—forcing Becky out of her comfort zone so she could meet other men. Surely, Leah would babysit her granddaughter while Becky went out and had fun.

He figured he should check on that before assuming anything, though. Somehow, he had to get everything worked out so that she'd have a hard time saying no.

For her own good.

And maybe his. This sequence of rejections was beginning to wear on him.

He forced himself to calm down as he reminded himself of reasons why she'd refused so quickly.

She didn't know him. Didn't trust him. And he'd expected her to warm up to him quickly? Plus, he had a girl back home.

Ach, he was befuddled. Besides, Becky needed time.

Time, he had plenty of.

Maybe he should back off some and let her get to know him. To learn to trust him and realize he would not hurt her. And maybe then she'd agree to go.

Jacob drained his coffee and moved to put both his mug and Becky's in the sink. He picked up Mary's two tiny play cups and set them there, as well, then wiped the table.

If it would help Becky thaw out a bit, he'd willingly do women's work.

He laid the damp rag on the edge of the sink, then straightened, turning back around as Daniel and Leah came into the room, talking quietly.

Hearing the sound of an engine, Jacob glanced out the window. A black car came to a stop in front of the shop.

Daniel grimaced. "Ach, Jacob. Ready to get to work?"

Chapter 9

U sually, Becky enjoyed Sundays. The quiet after-
noons were filled on alternating weeks with long
church services where they sang from the Ausbund,
their hymnal, and visiting relatives. This Sunday
would be a time for visiting folk, and she hoped Jacob would find someone to be friends with, even a
girl, so he'd leave her alone. She didn't want him to
hang around Seymour, though. Nein, the faster he
returned to Pennsylvania and his Susie, the better.

At least, the better for her state of mind.

Her heart might tell a different tale.

She shook her head. She'd never been so befuddled before Jacob had arrived, and she didn't like it
one bit.

Jacob had even intruded on the nightly devotions, when Grossdaedi read from the big Bible right
before they retired. If only her grandparents didn't
spend so much time with the family. Maybe if they
had their own private devotions, she could go to bed
without her final thoughts being on Jacob instead of
on God. Jacob disrupted and invaded her sleep. God
generally didn't.

Last night, she'd tried to pray before falling
asleep, but even then, her prayers had been mostly
for Jacob.

Or maybe for herself.

And her dreams...ach! How could one man affect her so? Even Kent, with his smooth, cajoling ways, hadn't captivated her thoughts like this Jacob.

It just wasn't right.

But today would be good. She would get away from him and spend time gossiping with the women. It was a sin, for sure, but one that didn't seem to stop anybody. She would enjoy it as long as they didn't talk about her.

But that was almost always how it went.

She usually tried to stay in the shadows so that she could escape notice. And eavesdrop.

And Jacob, well, he could hang out with the buwe, or maybe with her onkel and the older men.

Anywhere he wanted to, as long as it was far away from her.

Jah, it would be a good day.

She carefully twisted her hair and pinned it up, then secured her white prayer kapp over it. Grabbing her apron, she tied it over her dress and hurried downstairs. Emma still slept. Becky would listen for her to wake up while she helped get breakfast on the table.

Thankfully, the men were still in the barn when she made her way into the kitchen. While she sliced the bread, Katie laid out the butter, jams, and jellies, and Mamm scrambled eggs and fried bacon. Ruthie set the table, laying out the plates and the eating utensils and placing the salt and pepper shakers in the center, while Grossmammi supervised from a nearby chair. Breakfast was ready when Daed, Grossdaedi, and Jacob came in and washed up.

"Gut morning, Bex." Jacob's deep voice held a teasing note.

Why did he have to target her? Becky's stomach clenched. "Morning." She avoided Jacob's gaze, turning instead to see if anything else needed to be placed on the table. There was nothing left to do. Head lowered, she silently slid into her place.

At least she hadn't been outright rude.

She swallowed hard and tried to focus her attention on the silent prayer. *God, why did You send Jacob here to torment me?*

⋯⋙⋘⋯

Jacob climbed out of the buggy at the home of Daniel's brother, Onkel David, as Ruthie called him.

Children were already running around, the little ones playing what appeared to be a game of tag. Several young girls sat in the dirt near the big barn doors, playing with kittens. And a group of teenagers and young adults were engaged in a game of volleyball.

Katie went to join in the game, while Becky disappeared into the house with her mamm.

Becky needed to be outside, playing.

Jacob eyed the house for a moment, frowning. But then he turned to join the game. Maybe she'd come out later.

He'd be surprised if she did.

Jacob merged into the game on the right side of the net. He nodded to the young man next to him, then fixed his eyes on the ball. The temperature had risen to almost fifty, at his best guess. The ice had melted, so the ground was soft and muddy, but he didn't care. Clothes could be washed.

Though Becky would probably be the one washing them. He hated to create more work for her, and he hesitated for a second. But as the ball came toward him, he reined in his thoughts and prepared to play.

Sometime later, the ringing dinner bell interrupted the game. Jacob followed the others to the pump to wash up before going to the table loaded with fresh-baked bread, cold cuts, and other sandwich makings. With his plate loaded, he found a place to sit on the porch with some of the other young men his age.

A man who had introduced himself as Ben turned toward Jacob. "You're staying with Onkel Daniel, ain't so?"

"Jah." Jacob took a bite of his sandwich.

"How long are you here for?" Ben asked.

Jacob shrugged. "Until—Daniel and I haven't agreed on a date." Daniel had said when he was ready to go. And, at some moments, asking for a ticket home seemed very appealing. But then, there was Becky.

"Are you one of those who came down here looking for a frau?" Ben snickered and nudged the boy next to him.

Jacob furrowed his brow and took another bite, not saying one way or the other.

"Just stay away from Daniel's Becky." Ben gave a sage nod.

The words caught Jacob by surprise. He frowned and looked up, noticing all the other men on the porch nodding in agreement. So much for any of these guys being talked into courting Becky. Wouldn't happen. Her future husband would have to be one of the men in the exchange. "Was ist letz?" He knew that he shouldn't encourage gossip, but perhaps this would be a chance for him to offer a positive comment on Becky's behalf. Other than her unhappiness, and the boppli, he saw nothing but good in her. And the boppli wasn't bad. Just a little off-putting. How many men wanted to be an instant daed?

Though, to gain Becky....

Ben shook his head. "I shouldn't talk. She did confess, and her sins were forgiven. But...."

Jacob studied a crack in the porch floor, then cast a sidelong glance at Ben. "Her beau jumped the fence, ain't so?" Leaving her in disgrace. He struggled not to grind his teeth.

"Nein." Ben leaned closer but didn't lower his voice. "Englisch. And Kent says that the kid isn't his, that she's loose."

"But the Englisch have some sort of test they do to verify parentage," Jacob protested. But it was weak. Of course, Becky wouldn't have agreed to that. It wasn't the Amish way, even if the alternative meant ruining her reputation.

Sadly, there was usually some truth in rumors.

Jacob turned his attention to his sandwich, confusion clouding his thoughts, his emotions warring.

If only he could pull Becky away and find out the truth so that he could know how to defend her better. How to reach her.

If only she'd trust him enough to tell him.

If only he understood the need he felt to fix everything for her.

It didn't make sense. She meant nothing to him. Right?

ᴄ᙭ᴐ

Becky managed to stay out of the way of the ladies all morning, hiding in the corner of the big room with all the married women and young children and listening in on the conversations. She didn't really fit in anywhere. Not being married, she had nothing in common with those who were, and the girls her age... well, she had zero things in common with them. So, she felt like what Kent had called her once—a wall-flower. She hadn't been sure what that meant, and he hadn't explained it to her, but the description hurt. That same pain ate at her now. If only she could fit in somewhere.

Kent had encouraged her to drink some sort of liquid that had burned her throat all the way down and settled like molten lead in her stomach. He'd said it would loosen her up. Maybe it had, but all she knew for sure was that the one time she'd tried it, she'd run the buggy into a ditch on the way home and broken it, and the next day, she'd awakened with an awful headache and felt terribly sick.

Daed hadn't been happy, though he hadn't said much about it. The disappointment she'd read in his eyes had just about torn her heart out.

She'd never touched the stuff after that. The aftereffects were too horrible. And she couldn't remember what she did when she drank. It wasn't worth it.

She eased out of her corner, locating Emma asleep in her grossmammi's arms, and wandered into the kitchen, where she poured herself a cup of coffee. Then, she pulled her shawl more closely around her and stepped out the back door onto the wraparound porch. She loved the way Onkel David had built it. She used to beg Daed to copy it and make their porch a wraparound. He'd said that the big front porch was enough. At least he'd hung a porch swing, her favorite place to read.

Grasping the coffee in one hand, she started walking toward the front of the house, but male voices stopped her.

"Just stay away from Daniel's Becky," she heard her cousin Ben say.

When Jacob asked why, Ben repeated those awful words that Kent had said.

Tears flooded her eyes, and her throat burned.

She could only imagine what Jacob thought.

She gripped her coffee cup handle so tightly that her knuckles turned white. With the other hand, she dug her fingernails into her palm.

At the first singing she'd gone to after finding out she was pregnant, and after Kent had dumped her and started spreading those awful rumors, one of the Brunstetter buwe had tried to talk her up into the hayloft. She swallowed hard, remembering the scary look in his eyes, the whispers and pointing fingers and stares of the others there.

She'd refused to go. Instead, she'd slunk off into the darkness and gone home.

She'd never been back.

Becky turned to go back inside, hoping no one had heard the creak of the loose floorboard she'd forgotten to avoid. She wouldn't go to another singing. Ever. Not even Jacob's brilliant blue eyes and smooth talk would sway her. But he'd probably never ask her again after hearing those lies from her cousin.

She grabbed the doorknob and twisted it, blinking back the tears. If only she could take Emma and go home to the solitude of her room.

Something brushed her arm. She bit back a scream and jerked her shoulder, the coffee in her mug sloshing out, spilling lukewarm liquid over her hand.

"Bex." Jacob spoke in her ear. He removed the cup from her shaking fingers and set it on the rail. "Kum, walk with me."

Chapter 10

When Becky looked at him, the tears in her eyes almost undid him. Jacob never had been able to handle women's tears. At least she seemed to have them under control. They sparkled on the ends of her eyelashes but didn't run down her cheeks.

He leaned toward her and swallowed when he caught a whiff of her scent. "Please."

Her eyes narrowed, and she studied him, as if unsure of his motives.

"We'll stay in plain sight." She might open up once they were alone, but he knew suggesting such a thing would frighten her.

"Nein. They'll think we're courting."

Jacob tilted his head. "I don't care what they think. I have a girl. And your family should care enough for you to not jump to the wrong conclusions."

From what Ben had said, though, that wasn't the case. Jacob wanted to throttle Ben, especially after he'd heard the creaking of the boards behind them, then seen Becky moving away. But, even more, he wanted to know the truth about what was going on.

"Nein," she repeated, and this time, she shook her head to punctuate it. "I need to be alone. Just... go."

Jacob frowned and tilted his head. "Bex. Walk with me a little ways."

She hesitated.

"Kum." He reached his hand toward her.

She drew back, but after a moment, she nodded and headed toward the steps. Jacob moved to her side in silence.

She walked in the direction of the barn but bypassed it for the fields beyond. Jacob stayed beside her, a body width separating them as they matched step for step. With everything in him, he wanted to ask questions, to clarify things in his mind. But Daed had once told him that silence forces people to talk to fill the dead air. He waited patiently to put that theory to the test.

Becky's breath was ragged, like she'd been crying or was angry or something. Jacob looked out over the fields, to the trees in the distance, and to the neighboring farms around them and waited for her emotions to calm down.

But after fifteen minutes, she still didn't seem inclined to speak. Perhaps she had more patience than he did. Waiting had never been his strong point.

Jacob drew a deep breath and stepped a bit closer, not so much to crowd her space as to make speaking softly easier. He ventured a glance at her. Tears ran unchecked down her face, dripping off her chin.

Jacob exhaled and looked away, glancing back toward the house. He couldn't see it, not with the barn separating them. He reached his arm out to wrap his fingers around Becky's, tugging her to a stop. If only he could comfort her with a hug. He spoke with all the sympathy he could muster. "Bex—"

"It's not true."

He kept still, waiting.

She stomped her foot, a futile effort in the muddy ground, if she wanted the sound effect. "It's not true! Not a bit of it!"

That pretty much said it all. Especially when he considered her volume.

He opened his mouth to apologize but then closed it again when he couldn't think of what he had to be sorry for. Maybe for not understanding the situation completely. Jah, he definitely stood in the dark.

She jerked her hand from his and wiped her brow, which glistened with beads of moisture. "And you shouldn't listen to gossip." She spat out the words, then whirled and headed across the field. Going away from him, away from her onkel's house.

Leaving him feeling like he'd run headlong into the side of the barn. Again.

She'd said she wanted to be alone. He should have listened.

He whipped off his hat and ran his hand roughly through his hair. "Women," he muttered.

⤞⤝

Becky needed to get away. Her heart hurt, her eyes ached, and she had a sore throat. All from crying so much. Something she still couldn't get under control.

At least Jacob hadn't followed her home.

Why couldn't he leave her alone?

Emotions whirled about in her head. Jacob shouldn't have listened to gossip—but then, how could he help it? Sometimes, it seemed she was a popular topic. Her choices, decisions, sins, all held up to the young people as an example of what not to do. The young men were warned to stay away from her. It just wasn't right. And now, Jacob would be getting a warped opinion of her. He'd already been told to keep his distance.

Yet he seemed to care about her in a way that no one else ever had.

Becky hated the feelings of vulnerability that filled her. Why did she have to be the one who ran scared?

Her hands trembled as she hitched up her buggy horse. Still, she had to go someplace to calm down. Someplace far away from Jacob and the flood of emotions he'd released. She couldn't take it anymore. If he was going to invade her territory, she needed to get away.

If only she could think of someplace to go.

And she certainly wouldn't run away without Emma.

But right now, Emma was safely with her gross-mammi, which was good, because Becky could hear chocolate calling her—a big, yummy Hershey's candy bar, and maybe a cappuccino from McDonald's. Both were rare treats and served as her method of dealing with extreme stress.

Daed and Mamm knew her well enough to guess where she'd go. They wouldn't worry.

Not so long as she was home by the time Emma got hungry. She should have about two hours.

She hoped the escape would calm her down—build up her defenses—before she returned home and had to face Jacob over dinner and devotions.

And if she wasn't calm by then, well, she would think of something else. Like maybe coming down with a migraine.

She climbed into the buggy, hands still shaking, and made a clicking sound. When the horse started moving, she turned the buggy out of the gravel drive. After a car passed, she headed down the road toward town.

❦

Jacob didn't see any sign of Becky when the family returned home that afternoon. He figured she was hiding out upstairs in her room, away from everyone. It hurt to think that he might have been the cause of her distress. He only wanted to help.

She didn't seem to appreciate his efforts.

Jacob tried to read *The Budget* as he sat in the living room with Daniel and Leah, but Daniel must have caught on to his restlessness, or maybe his frequent glances toward the stairs, because he cleared his throat. "Her buggy horse is gone."

Leah let out a noncommittal hum when Daniel spoke, not even looking up from her book. Jacob didn't know how many horses they kept. He glanced at Daniel over the top edge of the paper.

"Probably went to McDonald's." Daniel caught his eye and winked.

Jacob scratched his ear. Was Daniel telling him to go after Becky?

She'd told him she wanted to be alone. McDonald's seemed a funny place to seek solitude.

And why would she want to go there, anyway? Unless she planned to meet someone. Maybe she had a date, though that would be odd in the middle of the afternoon. Dating was usually done under the cover of darkness. In Pennsylvania, at least. Missouri might have different rules.

Jacob shrugged and returned to *The Budget*. He started a new article and read two paragraphs.

"A cappuccino sounds mighty fine, jah?" Daniel spoke again.

A cappuccino? Jacob wrinkled his brow. He didn't think he'd ever had one and wasn't even sure what it would be. But since Leah ignored that comment, too, he figured it had to have been directed at him.

For some reason, Daniel wanted him to follow Becky to McDonald's.

Jacob set his jaw and stood. He didn't look forward to another run-in with that hard wall. How much would it take before the blockade around her began to crumble?

Jacob refolded the newspaper and placed it back on the end table. As he did, he caught Daniel's self-satisfied smirk.

His distant cousin played matchmaker, for sure and for certain. Probably was in on Daed's decision to separate him and Susie for good. Or maybe he thought Jacob liked Becky some.

He did. More than some.

Or maybe he just liked the challenge.

Chapter 11

B ecky sat in a corner booth with her steaming cappuccino in front of her, waiting for it to cool enough to drink. She'd already inhaled one Hershey's candy bar that she'd bought at a convenience store she'd passed, but a second one waited beside the coffee cup, just in case she needed it.

At least she'd finally stopped crying.

Actually, she'd quit before she'd reached town. She hadn't wanted to be seen with red eyes and a runny nose, although with flu season in full swing, perhaps people would assume she was sick and keep their distance. Might be a good idea after all.

She took a tentative sip of her coffee, watching the cars on the highway zoom along. What would it be like to have the freedom to go anywhere? Maybe even to Springfield? She'd been there once, when her older sister, Naomi Joy, had gone into labor prematurely and had to be rushed to the hospital. Little Regina had been kept at the hospital for months, and Naomi Joy had practically lived there with her.

Becky had considered asking Naomi Joy to raise Emma, too, but Daed had put his foot down and said Emma would be Becky's responsibility.

She was glad he had.

A shadow passed over her, and someone paused beside her booth. She silently willed the person to move on. Maybe if she ignored him, he would.

"Mind if I join you?"

He wouldn't be moving on. Becky closed her eyes. "Jacob." Couldn't he just leave her alone? Fear that he'd followed her to see if she really was "loose" warred with hope that he might really be interested in her as a person.

Of course, he might have come to dispense with some unwanted and unwelcome advice.

He slid into the booth across from her, his knees brushing against hers. "Daniel said you'd be here."

"Jah. I needed...." *To get away from you.* "I needed some quiet time." She opened her eyes and dared a glance at him. If he looked even the tiniest bit cocky, she'd get up and walk out.

He gave a lopsided smile. "And I had to go interrupt it."

Thankfully, he didn't make any comment about her claiming to need quiet and then going to a bustling fast-food restaurant.

He reached out and picked up her candy bar. "Plain milk chocolate? Have you ever tried it with almonds?" He set it down again, his gaze resting on her.

"So, did you pursue your Susie this relentlessly?"

Jacob's eyes widened. For the longest time, he didn't answer. Instead, his gaze moved past her to the window. His lips thinned as he stared outside. Finally, he looked back at her. "Nein. She chased me."

Becky rolled her eyes. Of course, she did. And when the single girls in this community caught wind of Jacob, they'd be chasing him, too.

"Did you want a coffee?" She gestured to the tall Styrofoam cup in front of her.

He eyed the cup with a wary look. "Is that the, uh, cappuccino Daniel mentioned?"

"Jah. It's an espresso—really strong coffee—with flavoring and sugar, I think."

He wrinkled his nose. "Maybe not so much."

Becky laughed. "They have normal coffee here, too."

Jacob's eyes jerked back to hers, and a slow grin spread over his face. "Bex, I'd drink a thousand of your cappuccinos just to hear you laugh again."

Her face heated. She lowered her eyes, flattered and intrigued. Ach, he was a bold one.

༒

Encouragement. He'd managed to find a small crack in her barricade. And she had a beautiful laugh. Jacob slid his hand over the table until his fingertips touched hers. "I'll be right back. I'm going to order myself a cappuccino. I'm willing to give it a try."

"I probably should be going." Becky glanced up. "Emma...."

"Emma is fine. Leah's taking gut care of her." Funny how he didn't want their time together to end.

"But...." She started to stand.

"Please." Jacob stood and placed a hand on her shoulder, gently urging her back into her seat. "Wait." After another long glance at her bowed head, he turned and strode up to the counter and stood in line.

"Well, look who's here. You miss me, babe?"

Jacob had just reached the front of the line when he heard the loud voice somewhere behind him. He glanced back and hesitated when he saw a couple of Englisch guys stop beside Becky.

Her face paled as she stared up at the two men. He saw her lips move, and although he couldn't hear her, he knew what she said: "Nein." She closed her hands around her drink and made a slight move. One of the guys, the dark-haired one, sat down on the edge of her booth, forcing her back in. The redheaded one sat on the other side. Jacob's side.

"May I take your order, sir?"

Jacob frowned at the clerk and shook his head, then stepped out of line and walked back to the booth in front of Becky's. He hesitated there, not sure whether he should interrupt now or wait to see if she needed help. Glancing out the window, he noticed the lone buggy tied to the red hitching pole.

Out of the corner of his eye, he watched the man as he slipped his arm around Becky and pulled her closer to him. "Wanna go out and have some fun, babe? There's a party tonight. I can find a date for Luke, and we can—"

"Nein. Kent, please. Go." Becky's voice wobbled.

Kent. Emma's daed. Jacob gave up pretending to look outside and openly studied the man beside Becky. What had she ever seen in this man?

He took a deep breath and reminded himself that the Amish were pacifists. Then, he strode over to the table. "She's with me."

The man Becky had called Kent looked up. Jacob's fingers itched to form a fist and rearrange his face.

Lord, forgive me. Help this to end quietly.

"Found yourself a new plaything, babe?" Kent rose to his feet. "And who might you be?"

"I might be Jacob Miller." *Plaything?* How dare he treat Becky like this!

"Chakob? What kind of name is Chakob?" The Englischer laughed as he pronounced the name the

Amish way. He stepped forward, getting in Jacob's face.

The redheaded guy, Luke, stood up, looking uncomfortable. "Let's go, Kent."

With one strong hand, Kent shoved Jacob away, then continued past him. "Yeah. She's not worth it."

She was so worth it, but still.... Jacob let them go. *Thank You, Lord.*

Becky's hand gripped her fancy coffee so tightly that Jacob feared she'd crush the cup. He hesitated at the end of the booth, looking down at her, then glanced out at the parking lot to see the two men climb into a red car.

"You about ready to go, Bex?"

The two men slammed the doors shut, and the engine roared to life.

"Jah." Her voice shook.

The car backed out and drove off.

"Let me throw my bicycle in the back of the buggy, and I'll take you home."

Jacob watched them pull out onto the highway.

"I can take care of myself."

"What?" His attention leaped back to Becky. Her eyes were the same icy color as they'd been the day he'd arrived.

⊰⊱

Becky supposed Jacob thought he was some big and mighty hero, coming to her rescue. But she didn't have any fear of Luke, Annie's old beau, and, well, she'd figured she'd be safe so long as he was there.

Even though Kent could be unpredictable. Especially if he'd been drinking.

When Jacob had come striding up and declared for the world to hear that she was with him, for a second, she'd felt valued and protected.

She'd reveled in that feeling for a whole minute before the truth had set in: she wasn't. And Jacob couldn't be her hero. He belonged to Susie.

Becky decided she didn't much like his Susie.

Probably because she'd gotten to Jacob first.

Becky pried her hand from its death grip on her cappuccino and stood. "I said, I can take care of myself."

"Jah." Jacob's expression didn't match his words. "Of course, you can."

She didn't know whether to take his comment at face value or to accuse him of sarcasm. But there wasn't a bit of mockery in his tone. Instead, it was soft and soothing.

"But, while I'm here, Bex, you don't need to. I'll take care of you as if you were my little sister." His gaze held hers.

Ach, jah. That made her feel so much better. His sister—just the person she wanted to be.

"Kum. Let's get my bicycle loaded, and then we can go."

Becky wanted to remind him that she wasn't his sister and never would be, but a glance around the restaurant reminded her that they weren't alone. And they had attracted attention. With a self-conscious nod, she picked up her cappuccino and candy bar and headed for the door.

Outside, Jacob unlocked his bicycle from the bicycle rack and wheeled it over to her buggy. He lifted the two-wheeled contraption effortlessly into the back, then turned to her, offering his hand and assistance.

She didn't want to accept either.

Instead, she gave him her cup and candy bar, then climbed up into the buggy.

Once settled, she turned back to reach for her things. Jacob handed them to her, then climbed up beside her and took the reins. He set the horse at a fast trot, and they headed away from of town, back toward the family farm.

"Did anyone invite you to the singing?" Becky glanced at him.

"Jah. Ben said that there'd be a gathering in their back field. I'll head over later. You sure you don't want to go?"

"Jah. Positive." She took a sip of her coffee. Should she warn Jacob that Ben's "gatherings" weren't where the good Amish young adults hung out, or should she leave it alone and let him find out on his own?

She should tell him. In a minute. She took another sip.

"That's gut, jah?" He nodded toward her drink.

"You never got one for yourself. Want a taste?" She held it out to him, expecting him to refuse.

With a smile that almost took her breath away, he took the cup from her. "Jah. Danki." He raised the cup to his lips and took a sip, his eyes widening as he swallowed. "This is ser gut." He held it out to her.

She held up her hand. "You can have the rest, if you want."

"Nein." Jacob winked at her. "I'll share it with you."

Her face warmed.

He took another long swallow, then handed the cup back to her. She took it, not sure how to handle the situation. Drinking after Jacob seemed rather intimate, yet he'd sipped after her without hesitation.

She'd had only a couple of sips. And it was her favorite drink. She forced her misgivings aside and took another drink.

"Would you, um, care for half of my candy bar?" she asked, peeling back the wrapper.

He shrugged. "Jah, if you don't mind sharing. But you probably need it more than I do. Chocolate always makes my mamm feel better, though she likes almonds in hers."

Ach, why had Susie gotten to him first? Becky broke the candy bar down the middle and handed one half to him. She searched for something to talk about. His home.

"Tell me about your home, Jacob. I bet you really miss it."

He glanced in her direction. "Jah, sometimes. But there are things here that aren't at home." He winked at her. Heat rose in her cheeks.

With a grin, he touched her hand. "Home. Well, Mamm and Daed have nine kinner. I'm number nine. My older brothers and sisters are married, and I have five nephews so far." Instead of immediately pulling his hand away, he let it rest there on hers for a few moments longer than she thought was proper. "No nieces. Yet."

No wonder he could view her as a younger sister. He probably wanted one.

"We have an apple orchard. My brothers all work there with Daed, and someday, I will, too."

So, he had long-term plans at home. Becky twisted her skirt in bunches with her hands.

Thirty minutes later, the cappuccino and candy bar both gone, Jacob pulled the buggy into their gravel drive and headed straight for the barn, passing the house. In front of the barn, he pulled the reins, stopping the horse. "Bex, I enjoyed our time this afternoon."

She agreed with him. Mostly. She could have handled not seeing Kent.

"Jah." She turned and climbed out of the buggy. Then, in a rare moment of boldness, she stopped and looked over her shoulder at him. "Jacob, I'm not your sister."

He looked down at her from his perch on the buggy seat. "Nein. But I never said you were. I said I'd take care of you as if you were."

She lowered her eyes. Men. Sometimes, it seemed they talked in nonsensical riddles.

Or maybe it was just that females found it important to define relationships with distinct boundaries.

Chapter 12

Earlier than he wanted to be up and active, Jacob stumbled his way to the barn. He'd had a late night out. And the gathering that Ben had told him about hadn't been a singing. It'd been a party, with both Amish and Englisch present. None of the men there had seemed to be someone he'd consider trying to convince to court Becky. He rubbed his aching head.

"You didn't drink last night, ain't so?" Daniel asked point-blank, maybe guessing where Jacob had gone. He stopped pitching hay into the feeding troughs and leaned on the pitchfork, spearing Jacob with an equally sharp look.

Jacob stared at him. "Nein." He never had, though most of the other teens in the back field had really put it away. Not that it was any of Daniel's business.

"Gut. Because I can't be responsible for you if you do."

With that thinly veiled threat, Daniel turned away, getting back to work. But Jacob could almost hear the unasked questions. Could see them in the rigidness of Daniel's back. How late had he gotten in? Had he taken a girl home?

He had no idea what time he'd come home. Home? Nein, to Cousin Daniel's. All he knew was that the party had started getting wild, and he'd left before the police had shown up.

Assuming the police had. He'd been to a party in Pennsylvania where the police had arrived with spotlights, loudspeakers, and sirens. A couple of his friends had been busted for possession. Jacob had been taken down to the station and tested for drugs. He'd been clean, since he didn't use, but it wasn't a scene he cared to repeat.

And as for the girl....

He hadn't taken one home. But the opportunity had been there. He'd probably talked with every girl at the party. Not that he'd searched them out. Several had even placed themselves strategically in his way to give him every chance to ask them if he could take them home. None had even tempted him.

There hadn't been a single one who'd intrigued him. Not that he was available, because he wasn't.

Maybe. After all, Susie didn't seem to be making an effort to remember she had a boyfriend. His cell phone hadn't rung since he'd arrived, and she hadn't written him a letter.

And then, there was the issue of his undefined relationship with Becky.

He'd fallen asleep last night thinking about her, about their sort-of date yesterday. By the time they'd arrived home, it had seemed as if he and Becky had formed a tentative friendship. After sharing her fancy coffee and talking, he looked forward to a different relationship with her.

If he'd known a long way to Daniel's house, he would have taken her that route instead of straight home. Anything to lengthen their time together. But he hadn't. And he hadn't felt comfortable asking Becky for that information.

Should he mention Becky to Susie when he wrote? It might hurt her to think that he was making friends with another female. He intended to return home to marry Susie. Nein, he shouldn't mention Becky. Better not to worry Susie.

But a friendship with Becky—jah, that would be a good thing.

Jacob whistled as he milked a cow. He could hear Daniel and Grossdaedi as they worked somewhere in another part of the barn. When at last he heard the bell summoning them for the morning meal, he all but ran to the house, feeling almost like a little kid expecting a surprise.

He washed up and found his place at the table, grinning at Becky when she came into the room with her boppli. But she avoided his gaze, keeping her eyes down.

When she sat without a word to him, even ignoring the "Gut morning" he extended to everyone, Jacob's heart crash-landed somewhere in the vicinity of his toes. Had all the progress they'd made been only in his imagination?

Or, had she heard him coming in late last night and assumed the worst, as Daniel had? He thought he'd been quiet when he'd snuck into the dawdi-haus.

He certainly hadn't stood under Becky's window and tossed pebbles at it, though the thought had crossed his mind. He'd dismissed it as being inappropriate for friends.

Right now, it seemed as if friendship didn't even factor into the equation.

Jacob tried to put on a neutral expression, hoping the rejection that had hit him so hard didn't show.

Rejection wasn't a feeling he had a lot of experience with.

He didn't care for it so much.

❧

Jacob would reject her in the light of this new day. Somehow, Becky knew it. Dreaded it.

Sure, he'd been nice to her after he'd heard the unkind remarks her cousin Ben had made, and he'd been kind to her at McDonald's, but she knew that after he thought about it, he couldn't possibly continue to associate with her.

Better to distance herself now so that she wouldn't be as hurt when it happened.

Still, it was hard to ignore his cheerful greeting. To not look up at his sky-blue eyes and almost feel warmth and sunshine.

She refused to meet his gaze, knowing that she'd reveal her silly schoolgirl crush.

Because if he hadn't rejected her after hearing what Ben had to say, or meeting Kent yesterday, he certainly would if he knew she *liked* him.

She didn't even want her parents to know. Especially since Daed had sent Jacob after her yesterday. He'd already guessed too much. And by sending Jacob—well, that could mean he approved.

She couldn't let Daed get his hopes up.

After the silent prayer, she fastened her gaze on her bowl of steaming oatmeal and kept it there, even when her sister passed the brown sugar.

The toe of someone's tennis shoe nudged her ankle. Becky jerked her feet back under her chair. She hadn't thought she had them too far in front of her. And with this wide, wooden table separating her from the other side....

Nein, it had to have been Jacob. Neither Daed nor Grossdaedi would resort to such a thing.

The bump came again, a bit firmer this time, pushing her foot a little to the right. Becky frowned and darted a glance under the table. Jah, Jacob's dirty white sneakers were in view.

She dug her spoon into her oatmeal.

The shoe retreated.

A bit disappointed that he'd given up so quickly, Becky lifted her filled spoon and took a bite, half hoping that Jacob would make another effort. Although, how she'd respond if he did, she wasn't sure.

Maybe nudge his foot back. Her face heated at the thought of it.

But he didn't make another attempt.

A few minutes later, Jacob pushed his bowl away. "May I be excused? I'll get the fire started in the shop, Daniel."

"Jah, that'd be fine. You want coffee first, ain't so?"

"Nein. Maybe you could bring a cup out when you kum."

Out of the corner of her eye, Becky saw Daed nod, and then she heard the scrape of Jacob's chair against the wood floor.

The door slammed.

Becky spooned another bite of oatmeal into her mouth.

"What's going on, Rebekah Rose?" Anger tinged Daed's voice.

Rebekah Rose? She hadn't heard her full name in years. "I'm, uh...." Becky dared to glance up.

"I will not have you being deliberately rude to a guest in my haus."

Becky jerked back. And the last time she'd been scolded? She didn't care to venture a guess when that had been. "Sorry, Daed."

"You need to take that cup of coffee out to the blacksmith shop and apologize to Jacob. Finish your breakfast, then get out there."

At least she wouldn't be wearing her heart in her eyes. Her secret would be safe for another day.

Daed shoved his chair back. "And I want to see you wearing a smile when you get out there. This unhappiness has gone on long enough, jah?"

A smile? She didn't think she remembered how.

⤜⋅⤛

Jacob packed the forge with crumpled newspapers and pieces of kindling, getting a small fire started. Then, he cranked and listened for the whoosh as the fire caught.

Daniel came into the shop and hung his coat on a hook next to Jacob's. He brought the bucket of coal closer. "Seems like you're learning here, Jacob."

"Jah." Maybe so. He glanced around. "You forgot the coffee?"

Daniel smiled. Shook his head. "It's coming."

Jacob's eyes flickered back to Daniel's. Surely, he hadn't asked Becky to bring it out.

Daniel avoided his gaze. "Ah, there's that sound we were looking for. Hear the roar of that fire, Jacob?" He hefted the bucket in his arms and poured the black chunks around the sides. "Ser gut." He lowered the now empty bucket to the floor.

The door opened, and Jacob glanced that way, not at all surprised when Becky appeared, carrying two cups of coffee. She handed one to Daniel. "Daed."

He nodded.

Another couple of steps, and she stood in front of Jacob. Silently, she held out the mugful of black coffee. Then, her mouth moved to form what he'd call a fake smile. Her eyes made it clear she didn't mean it. And the grin faded quickly. "I'm sorry for being rude."

Jacob accepted the coffee, then glanced from Becky to Daniel and back. "You went to McDonald's and got that fancy coffee, ain't so?"

A twinkle appeared in her eyes, brightening them. "Not this time."

"Maybe next, jah?"

"Jah. Maybe so." She backed up a step, not smiling, but at least she still looked at him with a light in her eyes. He could have gazed into them all day long.

Daniel stepped up beside her. "You tell your mamm you're needed out here in the shop today."

Jacob broke eye contact and turned away, frowning. What was Daniel up to? Did he think he could get them together by making them spend time working side by side?

Chapter 13

Becky couldn't remember the last time she'd helped her daed in the blacksmith shop. Back before she was old enough to quit school, for sure. After she'd finished her schooling, she'd needed to be in the house to prepare for marriage and to stop being such a tomboy.

But now? She couldn't think of a reason why Daed would need her. He had Jacob out there helping, and, as he'd said before, the shop was no place for a young lady.

Something had changed. Maybe he'd given up on the idea that she needed training in household chores, and....

And what?

It was the unknown that concerned Becky.

Was Daed giving up on the prospect of her ever marrying?

When she went inside and told Mamm, her mother hesitated a bit before giving her consent. "We can care for Emma, and I'll send Abbie to get you if she needs your attention," she finally said.

"Danki." Becky ran upstairs to her bedroom, where she changed into an older dress and put on her oldest pair of tennis shoes. She knew from experience that she would get dirty and would want a hot shower as soon as she came in. What did Jacob think about blacksmith work? Daed had said that his folks didn't have a blacksmith shop, so he was a novice.

But Daed had also said he was "ser gut."

Becky dashed back downstairs and out the door, then started to run toward the blacksmith shop. She stopped when she saw a buggy without a horse waiting outside. Daed did farrier work only on occasion.

Besides, it would be improper for a maidal to arrive all out of breath. How many times had her parents warned her that young ladies shouldn't run? Too many times to count.

She slowed her motion to a more respectable pace and made her way into the shop.

Jacob stood over by the fire, holding a piece of metal into the blaze, then pulling it out, looking at it, and putting it back in. She spotted Daed on the other end of the shop, holding up a horse's leg and looking at the shoe, she guessed. Amos Kropf stood beside him, pointing at something and talking.

Why had he brought his horse to Daed? Her onkel David was the farrier.

Surely, Daed hadn't called her out to spend time with this man in the shop. Would he be so cruel? Besides, how could he expect her to focus on Amos Kropf when Jacob was in the building?

Maybe Amos Kropf's horse required special shoes that Onkel David didn't carry normally. Daed did make the shoes for Onkel David, who kept only a few sizes on hand. Special orders came to Daed to measure and fit.

Jah, that might be why Amos Kropf was here.

He certainly wouldn't have come to talk to Daed about courting her.

Becky tried to repress a shudder as she surveyed the older man. His hair had already started graying, and his beard had grown shaggy, reaching almost to the bottom of his neck.

Her future husband, if what Annie had told her was true.

Another tremor shook her, and she decided to stay as far away from him as she possibly could. She headed in Jacob's direction.

"How can I help?" She kept her voice hushed, hoping it wouldn't carry.

Jacob nodded toward the handle. "Could you turn that a bit? I don't think I've got the fire hot enough."

⌖

Jacob didn't like Daniel's asking Becky to work in the blacksmith shop. It just didn't seem right for her to be out here. He especially didn't like how that older man standing next to Daniel had locked his eyes on her as soon as she'd walked across the room, looking at her with what Jacob could only call lust. He felt the same protective anger well up inside him that he'd felt when Kent had approached her at McDonald's.

He wanted to tell Becky to go back to the house.

But it wasn't his place.

Becky took hold of the handle on the forge and slowly turned it. If Daniel had mentioned what it was called, Jacob couldn't remember. But that didn't matter. What did matter was making the hook that Daniel had told him to make in accordance with the detailed instructions he'd provided.

Instructions that Jacob prayed he'd remember, despite Becky standing so close to him.

Ach! And Daniel had told him to be careful so he wouldn't get burned. Why had he asked Becky to come out here? If he had any inkling of Jacob's growing attraction to his daughter, he certainly wouldn't have asked her to work out here.

He pulled the piece of metal out of the fire and looked at it for a moment, catching the orange-red hue that Daniel had stressed. "Gut, Bex. Danki." He reached for a hammer and laid the metal on the anvil, stopping for a second to cough. Would he ever get used to the thick, cloying smoke?

Becky stood there and watched him pound that piece of metal. Surprisingly, it turned out to be very good. At least he hadn't embarrassed himself in front of her.

"Hello, Rebekah."

The man who had been at the other end of the shop now stood beside Becky, his eyes fixed on her.

Becky shot Jacob a frantic glance that he couldn't quite interpret before she looked at the man. "Hello. How are you?"

"Gut. Gut. Can't complain." He gestured behind him. "My buggy horse is lame. I think he has a loose shoe."

And he'd brought the lame horse to Daniel? Jacob frowned, confused. Daniel had said he did very little horse work. His brother David worked as a farrier.

Becky looked in the direction of the horse, nodded, then looked back at Jacob.

Jacob glanced at the now cooled piece of metal. He didn't know quite how to handle this. Should he continue working, as if this man weren't here ogling Becky?

That would be unkind.

Of course, to just stand there listening to a conversation that clearly didn't include him would be wrong, too.

With a shrug, Jacob set down the hammer, put the metal aside, and walked over to join Daniel, trying to ignore the look of betrayal Becky gave him as he turned away. He wished he could reassure her that he'd be right across the room keeping an eye on things. He needed to find out who this stranger was and what business he had with Becky. And the only one who would know, besides the man himself, would be her daed.

With a frown, Daniel poked at something on the bottom of the horse's foot. "Seems to be a stone under here. No wonder this horse is lame."

"Who is he?" Jacob whispered, hoping Daniel had heard him but the stranger across the room hadn't. "I don't like how he looks at Bex."

Daniel's lips tightened, then he spoke. "Amos Kropf. He's approached the bishop about marrying our Becky." He dislodged a pebble from the horse's hoof and tossed it aside.

"You can't be serious."

"He came the other day and asked my permission to court her."

Jacob's eyes widened, and he stared over at the man, who'd stepped even closer to Becky. "You said nein, ain't so?"

"Becky is old enough to make her own decision." Daniel's voice indicated nothing.

Jacob shifted. Frowned. Glanced again at Becky and this Amos Kropf, then looked away, horribly aware that this would be yet another thing he couldn't control.

Whom Becky allowed to court her would be none of his business. But he still didn't like the way Amos Kropf looked at her. Inappropriate, especially for a man who appeared old enough to have a daughter her age.

"You could stop it."

The voice was so low, Jacob didn't know if he'd imagined the words or if Daniel had actually spoken them.

Not wanting to appear befuddled in case he had imagined them, Jacob didn't acknowledge them.

Daniel straightened and walked away from Jacob, back toward Becky and that man. "Looks like your horse is gut to go, Amos. A rock had gotten lodged in there."

"Danki for your help, Daniel."

"Anytime." Daniel pulled his watch out of his pocket and glanced at it, then wordlessly slid it back inside.

As if somehow summoned by the action, a car pulled into the parking lot and stopped next to the buggy.

"I'd better be going. I'll see you later, Rebekah." Amos shuffled his feet as he turned away.

Becky dipped her head.

⋘⋙

Amos Kropf finally led his horse out of the shed as the new customer came in. Becky was glad for the interruption that had prompted him to move out of her personal space. She hadn't wanted to be rude by backing away as he'd kept getting closer and closer, and it had taken great effort to restrain herself.

"Becky, could you refill our coffee cups?" Daed asked as he strode toward the door to greet the new customer. "And tell your mamm that Amos Kropf and his kinner will be joining our family for dinner. I expect she'll want you up at the haus to help prepare an apple pie or two."

"Daed?" Becky choked on the words. She swallowed. "His whole family, too?"

"Jah."

Jacob gave her a sympathetic look but then turned away, going over to the forge and cranking it to make it hotter.

She was on her own. The last thing she wanted to do was make her special apple pie for Amos Kropf. Her recipe had won a blue ribbon at the county fair last fall, and even though pride was a sin, Becky still felt some.

She'd made her pie for Jacob the day he'd arrived. And he hadn't even tasted it.

It'd be a sin to purposefully ruin the pies to mislead Amos Kropf and make him think that she couldn't cook.

Especially since she wanted Jacob to believe she could.

Jacob bumped his shoulder into hers and handed her his coffee cup. "He's gone. You can go now."

Becky nodded, grateful that Jacob suspected she'd lingered because she didn't want to talk to Amos Kropf while he hitched up his horse. That was the absolute truth.

"Maybe you'd want to make your escape to McDonald's for that fancy coffee again tonight, ain't so? Or maybe you could suddenly remember a dinner appointment with a friend?" Jacob hesitated for a couple of seconds. "I could take you to one of the restaurants in town."

Ach, if only he would. Dinner out with Jacob would be wonderful. Gazing into each other's eyes across the table...talking, laughing, falling in love...or maybe it would only feed her crush. Not a good idea.

"I wish I could, but nein. Danki." Becky walked away, collecting Daniel's empty cup as she passed. "I'd best go clean up and get to work."

"Maybe some other time, then."

Becky glanced over her shoulder at him. "Maybe so." Probably not.

Her stomach churned the whole way to the house. Mamm looked up in surprise when she came in. "Done so soon? What'd he need you for?"

Becky shrugged. "I don't know. All I did was crank a bit, then he sent me up to tell you that Amos Kropf and his kinner are joining us for supper. And to help you make a couple of apple pies."

Mamm frowned. "But it's Mary's birthday." Heaving a sigh, she picked up a wooden spoon and stirred whatever she had cooking in the pot on the stove. "Go on and clean up. Then you can feed Emma and kum help. I'll get the pies started."

"First they want a refill of coffee."

"They need one of those Englisch coffeepots down there." Mamm turned away and reached up into the spice cabinet for something. "Maybe you could suggest plugging one into the generator. Hurry back."

Becky filled the cups, her heart heavy. Would she have the right to tell Amos Kropf nein, or would she be forced into a marriage with him? No one had mentioned whether the bishop supported it or not, but since Amos Kropf had approached Daed, she could only assume he did. And that Daed had agreed, hence the supper invitation.

How many kinner did he have, anyway?

Chapter 14

Jacob's morning passed with increasing activity in the blacksmith shop. Daniel gave him jobs that kept him busy, but he now wished for Becky's help. They could have used a third person. No matter how long a job would take, many of the customers hung around the shop to talk while they waited for Daniel and Jacob to finish. And sometimes they stayed even after they'd paid for the completed work.

The dinner bell rang, but with customers still in the shop, Jacob lingered to help Daniel finish up.

He knew at least one thing: if he could talk Becky into joining him for an outing, then her parents would watch Emma. They seemed to have no hesitation stepping in when Becky was needed elsewhere—or when she disappeared, as she had yesterday.

Becky needed to be in front of the other men of the community—and she needed to smile and laugh—if she was to have any hope of marrying better than Amos Kropf.

He'd start asking every day. Eventually, she had to give in.

And he'd make sure that all the men saw how wonderful, fascinating, and domestically skilled she was. He didn't know how they could miss it.

He'd treat her with utmost respect so that no one would see her as loose.

"This is going to take a bit longer than I thought," Daniel said to the elderly man who had a bushy beard that reached almost to his waist. "Would you like to join us for lunch, Bishop?"

Jacob straightened, his eyes narrowing. This man might be the bishop forcing Becky to marry Amos Kropf.

The man shook his head. "Nein. I'm sure my frau is wondering where I am. I'll kum back this afternoon."

"We'll get you fixed up." Daniel turned to Jacob. "You run up to the haus and tell Leah I'll be there shortly."

The day had warmed, dispensing the morning chill. Jacob grabbed his coat and carried it up to the dawdi-haus. He'd take a moment to put it away before going into the main house.

Maybe he'd take the time to wash up over there first, too. Get some of the grubbiness off before he saw Becky. Even his face felt caked with soot from the morning's work. A shower would be wonderful.

"Jacob?" A voice intruded his thoughts.

He turned to see Becky holding the dinner triangle. She must have been about to ring it again.

"Where's Daed?"

Jacob grinned at her. "He'll be up shortly."

"Gut." She stood there, staring at him with a strange look in her eyes. Betrayal? Pain? Longing? Maybe a combination of the three. He wasn't sure.

Something in his heart hurt. He moved toward her and reached out to touch her cheek. "Bex?"

A shutter closed over whatever the expression had been. "You have mail."

❦

Becky had planned to tell him that she had changed her mind. That she'd take him up on the offer to take her out for dinner and deal with the flack for shunning Amos Kropf later.

But the daily mail delivery had put a stop to that fantasy—more specifically, the plain white envelope addressed in flowery script to Jacob Miller and bearing the name of Susie Chupp in the upper left-hand corner.

Or maybe it was the stamp with hearts on it in the top right-hand corner.

Or the "I miss you" written on the back flap of the envelope.

Either way, it was a brutal reminder that he had a sweetheart back home.

To her shame, she'd been tempted to throw the letter in the fire and pretend it had never arrived.

Instead, she'd held it and stared, studying this Susie's handwriting. What words had she written to him?

Jacob now froze in front of her, a scant foot away, his eyes searching hers. His hand dropped to his side. She didn't know what he'd been reaching for. "A letter? For me? Is it inside?"

Ach, why couldn't she have kept her mouth shut? The letter was in the front pocket of her apron. How was she to explain to him why she hadn't put it with the rest of the mail? And, worse, that she'd left the letter from his mamm inside the house?

His mamm wasn't her competition. Susie, on the other hand, was.

Her face burned. She pulled the letter from her apron pocket and handed it to him without a word.

Jacob gave the envelope a dismissive glance before his eyes returned to hers. Searching.

She took a deep breath. Released it.

Jacob stepped back. "I'll be right in for lunch. And Daniel should be there directly."

He went into the dawdi-haus, and she heard him whistle as he shut the door behind him.

Becky stood there a moment, staring at the closed door. Her life seemed like a spiral of dirty water going down the drain. A deep whirlpool, going faster and faster, out of control. If only Jacob had been reaching out for her. To rescue her, maybe. If only she could cling to Jacob to save her from the madness of being courted by Amos Kropf, which apparently would begin tonight.

What a frightening turn her life had taken.

If only Jacob could have been the one to love her in spite of herself.

Instead, he was a flirt, with absolutely no intentions of following through.

Right now, he was probably bent over the letter, poring over every word penned by his Susie.

Or maybe he was laughing over the gullible Missouri girl falling for him.

A tear crept out of the corner of her right eye. She brushed at it and turned away.

A buggy moved down the drive toward the road. The bishop raised his hand but drove on by. He must have been the last customer, which meant that Daed would come out of the shop any moment.

She didn't need Daed to see her acting like a little lost puppy, waiting for Jacob to reappear.

Becky brushed at her eyes again, squared her shoulders, and went inside.

∾§∾

Jacob tossed Susie's letter onto the bed, hung up his coat, and went to wash his hands. He'd save the letter to savor later in the day, when his chores were done. Something to look forward to.

He figured the letter explained the look of betrayal in Becky's eyes, but not why she would feel abandoned. She knew about Susie. He'd been straightforward about their relationship from day one.

If anything, Becky was the "other woman." He really should ask Susie for a break so that he could think. Ever since that run to McDonald's to fetch Becky, something had changed. Jah, he needed to think about his relationship with Susie. Though how much thinking he'd do, daily tempted by Becky, he didn't know.

He didn't understand why it hurt him so much when she felt pain. Why the confusion about his feelings for her? It should have been cut-and-dried. Susie was his future.

Maybe.

Jacob rolled his shoulders and strode toward the door.

Going into the shared kitchen in the main house, he found the family already gathered around the table, except for Daniel, who stood drying his hands with a towel. Jacob nodded toward him, then slid into his seat, his eyes searching Becky's face.

She raised her eyes to meet his, tears shimmering in their depths. Then, just as quickly, her glance lowered.

He hoped that she'd seen his silent apology but feared she hadn't.

It shouldn't have mattered so much, but it did.

Jacob sighed. He knew that he should have been keeping his distance from Becky, but instead, he'd been seeking her out, trying to talk to her, reaching out to her.

As curious as he was as to why, the prospect of finding the answer scared him.

Chapter 15

Becky needed contact with someone who loved her. She picked up Emma, even though the baby seemed completely content lying on her back in the cradle and kicking her feet at the string of bells Mamm had strung across the rails. Becky swaddled her in a sling that had been a boppli gift from her great-aunt Martha. A gift that Becky appreciated and used quite often. It was a handy way to carry Emma when she was fussy or if Becky needed to go somewhere. Right up next to the body. Whoever had thought of that was a genius.

Once the baby-bearing sling was in place, Becky started the kitchen chores. Mamm had already rolled out crusts for the pies, and when she brought out some dried apples from their fall harvest, Becky realized she was making schnitz pie. Relief washed over her to know that she wouldn't have to bake her special apple pies. She didn't want to go to all that work for Amos Kropf. Not right after making them for Jacob.... Ach, she shouldn't go there, but it still hurt that Jacob had refused a piece. Maybe he didn't like it.

There was something wrong with him if he didn't. Everyone liked apple pie. Right?

"I thought we'd have fried chicken tonight," Mamm whispered with a glance around the kitchen. "It's Mary's favorite, and we do have plenty of hens."

Becky nodded, but she could never stomach killing a chicken and eating it the same day.

That didn't really matter, though, since she wouldn't be able to eat a bite of anything with Amos Kropf at the table. The way he looked at her made her feel dirty. Cheap.

It reminded her of how she'd felt after Kent's lies had circulated. The way she still felt when she got around some of the young men.

Ach, if only she could go out with Jacob tonight.

But he'd hesitated for a few seconds too long when he'd asked, as if he might not have meant it. And then, there was that letter to consider. She should have thrown it in the fire. If only this Susie didn't exist.

She started peeling the mound of potatoes her mother had placed beside the sink, setting the peeled spuds onto a sheet of newspaper.

"The schnitz pies just went in the oven," Mamm announced. "I'm going to kill the chickens." She touched Becky's shoulder and stood still a long moment, her hand resting there comfortably. Then, she pulled Becky into a sideways hug. "If you care to talk, I'm willing to listen."

Tears burned Becky's eyes, and she struggled to keep from flinging herself into Mamm's arms and crying out all her woes—her hopeless feelings for Jacob, her deep dislike of Amos Kropf, and her willingness to be a maidal all her life if Jacob wouldn't have her.

But emotions were something Becky had thought she'd gotten under control. At least, until Jacob had arrived. She'd cried more over her mistakes in the past several days than she had since Kent's rejection of her and Emma, and since the lies had begun.

Mamm lingered a moment, gave her another squeeze, then released her. "I'll be right back. When you see Katie, ask her to bring in the laundry, okay? I asked her to get the gifts for Mary ready. But I'm thinking we'll celebrate her birthday either before the Kropfs arrive or tomorrow. It really isn't a gut time for company."

That would be the only negative thing Mamm would say about Daed's having invited Amos Kropf and family to supper.

The door shut behind Mamm. Becky shifted the sling and the now sleeping Emma, growing heavy at her side.

She sighed and picked up the next potato.

Jacob looked up from the forge, disturbed by the sudden squawking of chickens. Daniel didn't seem to be paying much mind to the racket, but Jacob worried that something was bothering them. He decided to check it out, so he put down his things. It could be a fox. "I'll be right back," he told Daniel.

Daniel nodded, and Jacob made a beeline toward the chicken coop. Leah, holding an ax in one hand and a chicken in the other, was headed toward a stump in the yard.

Jacob stood there watching for a moment. Should he offer to help her kill the chicken? He felt a bit disappointed that it was Leah and not Becky, but then he realized that Becky would be in the house, away from her mamm's eyes. He wasn't sure where the grossmammi spent her days, but she certainly never seemed to show up in the kitchen except at mealtimes. Odd. His grossmammi loved to cook.

No matter. If Becky was alone, maybe he could talk with her.

And a couple of cookies sounded right good. A cup of coffee, too.

Whistling, he strode toward the house, opened the door, and paused to wipe his feet before entering the kitchen. There she was, wrapping up a bundle of something into a damp newspaper.

"Hey, Bex. Got a minute?" He stopped beside her at the sink and reached for a bar of soap.

He didn't look at her as he soaped up, but he sensed her freeze and then stiffen.

He wanted to ask her to walk with him again, but then his nose caught a whiff of something sweet, and he realized that the scent came from the oven. She probably wouldn't want to leave whatever was baking unattended.

"Jah." Her reply was belated.

"Gut. I could use a cup of coffee and maybe a cookie or two. Take a break with me?"

Becky hesitated. "Nein. I need to slice the potatoes." She picked up a knife and turned away.

She must be an expert at rejection.

Jacob frowned and poured himself some coffee.

"Mamm said you and Daed need one of those Englisch coffeepots in the shop."

Jacob lowered the cup without taking a sip. She had to be teasing.

He turned to face her. "If we had a coffeepot out there, then I wouldn't get to see your pretty face so much." He added a wink. Surely, that would make her smile.

Color crept up her neck, and she shifted again, adjusting a blue thing that hung from her shoulder. He saw Emma asleep inside.

"Is that getting heavy for you?" Jacob put the cup down and stepped toward her.

"Jah. A bit."

"Here. Put the knife down. I'll help you."

He waited while she laid the knife down and turned to face him. Then, he put one arm under her sleeping boppli and, with the other, gently eased the contraption off of her. "Want her in the cradle?"

"Jah." She rolled her shoulders and neck.

Jacob eased Emma into the cradle and folded the blue blanket-like thing as best he could. Then, he moved toward Becky again. "Want a massage?"

Her eyes widened. Color shot into her cheeks. "Nein. Danki."

"Relax, Bex." He could feel the tension radiating from her as he went past, reaching for the cookie jar. He lifted the lid and pulled out two cookies, hesitated, and went for a third. They were chocolate chip with walnuts. His favorite, and he hoped to tempt Becky to take a break.

He set the cookies down on the table, putting one at her place. Then, he poured a second cup of coffee for her. "Kum, Bex. You did say you had a minute." He aimed a grin in her direction. "Please?"

After a moment's hesitation, she nodded and lowered herself into the chair. "Did you open Susie's letter?"

Jacob's smile froze. Died. "Nein. Not yet." Did she feel the need to remind him of Susie every time they were alone together? How would she react if he told her he wanted to take a break with Susie, to sort out the confusing whirl of emotions coursing through him, and to possibly pursue a relationship with her?

He reached across the table for her hand, intending to do just that. His fingers grazed hers. Sparks ignited.

The door opened. Closed with a bang. In his peripheral vision, he saw Becky's mamm enter the room.

She paused, surveying the scene. "What's going on?"

Her tone didn't sound judgmental, but Jacob suddenly considered the impropriety of his actions. He pulled his arm back, stood, and spun.

"I'd best be getting back to the shop." He snatched up his cup of coffee and the cookies and exited the kitchen as fast as he could.

⊰⊱

Becky's skin still tingled from Jacob's touch. Her face burned with embarrassment at Mamm's interruption, but thankfully, Mamm went to work without another word.

Becky picked up the knife, noticing that her hands trembled. She hoped that she wouldn't accidentally slice one of her fingers. She took a potato and pushed the knife through it with a force that might have caused the wooden cutting board to protest if it could talk.

Why couldn't Jacob leave her alone?

And, more important, why did she have to respond? Why hadn't she jerked away and run from the room? The way he continually reached for her, he probably believed that she really was as loose as Kent claimed. And then what? He'd try to lure her up into the dark recesses of the barn loft?

Becky froze and swallowed a sob, the knife suspended just millimeters above the potato.

Ach, God. How much are You asking me to bear? I can't go through this a second time.

But then again, which was worse? Jacob giving her attention that made her feel loved and wanted, or being forced to endure unwanted advances from Amos Kropf, a man who might be her future husband?

Why did she always have to fall for the guys who "loved them and left them," as she'd once heard some Englisch girls say? It seemed to fit.

The knife slammed against the cutting board again. This time, Mamm turned around. "Daughter, if you keep that up, you're going to dull the knife. Send Katie out to the kitchen. I think you need to go to your room and spend some time in prayer."

Becky hesitated a moment, wanting to talk back. But maybe being alone was exactly what she needed. And maybe she could take that big family Bible upstairs and do some reading, too. Sometimes, she yearned to go deeper—something forbidden by their Old-Order Amish Ordnung.

But then, once, she'd caught Mamm with a Bible study guide. She'd quietly shut it and hadn't acted bothered at all. She'd only said something about them all having their own private vices.

And they did. After all, Daed carried a cell phone. He said it was for business, but Becky had seen him use it for personal calls.

She quietly put the knife down and left the room with a glance at the sleeping Emma. She found Katie pushing a dust rag around the gas light fixtures in the living room. "Mamm wants you."

"Okay." Katie balled up the dust rag and walked toward Becky. "You like him, ain't so?"

She hadn't specified who "him" was, but Becky knew. She stared at Katie for a moment, wondering if her sister had come into the kitchen while she and Jacob had been sitting at the table and he had touched her hand. Or maybe she'd only heard them talking. Katie's gaze revealed nothing.

Becky swallowed. Hard. "He has a sweetheart."

Katie's grin was crooked. "She needs to be worried. He's into you."

Stunned by the Englisch words, Becky watched Katie go past, then turned and ran up the stairs. Could it be true? Might Jacob really like her that way? Her bedroom window faced the blacksmith shop. For a long while, she stood there, staring out, hoping for a glance of Jacob. He didn't come into view.

Finally, she turned away. Going into her parents' room, she found Mamm's small Bible. She settled down on her parents' bed and opened the Book.

She didn't know how long she'd sat there reading and praying for peace and understanding, as well as a reprieve from the evening's plans, but finally a shadow crossed the door, and Mamm stepped in. "You'd best kum down now, daughter. Amos Kropf is here."

Chapter 16

Jacob helped Daniel put away tools in the blacksmith shop, then flipped the sign in the window so that it read "Closed." Not that the sign seemed to matter much. Everyone around town appeared to know the hours, and those who came when it was closed just had to go up to the house. Daniel would help them, even if only by taking their items and writing them on the list of projects to do the next day.

Still, Jacob could have used several more hours out here. Since he'd left the kitchen, he'd been mentally kicking himself for his inappropriate actions toward Becky. How dare he have asked her if she wanted a massage? It was a good thing she'd refused his forward offer. How could he face her again? Yet he didn't want to keep his distance. The dinner with Amos Kropf loomed like a menacing storm. The way that man looked at Becky...it was just wrong.

A strong instinct within him screamed to stake some sort of claim on Becky tonight and send this Amos Kropf packing. If only he could. But that would be unfair to Becky, not to mention Susie, to whom he'd already made a promise. And not when Becky did need a husband—someone who would love her, cherish her, appreciate her, and take care of her.

Someone like him.

His stomach clenched.

He'd be writing Susie at his first opportunity to ask for that break.

Noticing the Kropf buggy parked in front of the house, Jacob slammed the door to the blacksmith shop on his fingers and yelped.

Daniel turned to look at him. "Something bothering you, Jacob?"

Jacob glared. Daniel should know full well what bothered him.

Daniel crossed his arms over his chest and studied him. "Care to take a walk?"

It wouldn't do any good. Jacob would still be conflicted over the situation.

He shook his head. "Nein." If Amos Kropf was in that house, ogling his Becky.... "His" Becky? When had she become his?

Daniel nodded his head toward the fields, apparently not taking Jacob's answer as final. "Kum." He started walking away from the house and toward the fields.

Jacob shuffled his feet in the gravel for a second. Then, with another glance at the house, where unwanted company waited, he hurried to catch up with Daniel.

"What's on your mind?" Jacob didn't want to give Daniel the opportunity to drag confessions and secrets from him. If he could control the conversation, he would.

Daniel sighed. "I don't like it, either. Amos Kropf and Bishop Sol have apparently been talking about this for some time, since I got a visit from both men. Amos wants to marry her before the young men kum down for the swap, and he won't even wait until wedding season. As soon as possible, he said." He kicked at a clump of dirt, breaking it up. "Bishop Sol wanted to take Becky out and talk to her, prepare the way for Amos's proposal. But I can't do that to her. She needs to have some choice in the matter."

"Jah." She needed more than some choice.

"They are pushing. Hard. They really aren't even allowing me a decision. Becky is, uh...a disgrace, I guess. But Amos, well, it's been said that he's abusive. I just can't in gut conscience allow my daughter.... I love her, you know."

"Jah, I know you do." Jacob nodded.

"So." Daniel glanced at Jacob. "What are your thoughts?"

Jacob chewed his lip. Was that supposed to be a nice, tactful way of asking his intentions? He scratched the back of his neck. No way would he tell Daniel about how he'd offered to give Becky a massage. He simply had to get his raging hormones under control, that was all. At least until he was free to pursue her the way she deserved.

"You like her, ain't so?" Daniel asked, not waiting for Jacob to formulate an honest answer.

"Jah." Jacob hoped his shrug appeared nonchalant. "What's not to like?"

Daniel looked down. "I want better for Becky. I want her to have a choice and to marry for love, like her mamm and I did."

"Only fair." Jacob nodded. That was what he wanted, too.

Daniel shook his head. "I just can't see him being her choice."

"Nein." He'd better not be.

"You got any ideas how to run Amos off?"

Ach, he had ideas. But none of them was worth mentioning.

Daniel glanced around, apparently making sure they were alone. "Nein? Gut. I do."

⋙

Becky closed the Bible and slid it back into the top drawer of Mamm's dresser, being careful not to bend the cover. Then, she straightened the coverlet on her parents' bed, erasing all evidence of her having sat there. Not that they minded, but it would postpone her going downstairs. After checking in on Abbie and Mary, who were playing quietly in their room with their dolls, Becky went to her own room and peeked out the window at the blacksmith shop. Then, she noticed Daed and Jacob walking out in the field, deep in conversation, it looked like. Maybe discussing the crop they'd be putting in soon.

Not able to think of anything else to keep her upstairs, Becky walked slowly into the hallway and down the staircase without straightening her hair, washing her face, or doing anything else to freshen up. Why bother? She didn't want to impress Amos Kropf. Just Jacob.

She found the Kropf family in the kitchen with Mamm and Katie. Amos sat at the long kitchen table in Jacob's seat, downing a cup of coffee. His kinner were lined up awkwardly against a wall, looking uncomfortable and unhappy. Some of them looked plain mad.

All buwe. Becky counted—seven kinner. And the oldest one didn't look all that much younger than she. He'd probably be in his rumschpringe in a year or two. Studying him, Becky's eyes widened. She remembered him from when she was in school. He was only a year behind her. So, he would be in his rumschpringe now.

The youngest one looked about three. He was a cutie.

But still, how could she be a mamm to this family when the oldest child was almost her age? What could Daed be thinking?

She aimed what she hoped looked like a smile in the direction of the kinner, but it probably looked more like a grimace. "Welkum."

She got a couple of grunts in reply. Communicative bunch.

"Care for more coffee?" She glanced at Amos Kropf's cup, almost half full. "Maybe a warm-up?" Turning for the coffeepot, she cast a desperate glance at Mamm, silently begging for help. Though what Mamm could do to help the situation, she didn't know.

Maybe she should be turning to God. *Lord, help me out, here. Help him to realize I'm not the frau he wants....*

She grabbed the coffeepot and turned, almost running into Amos Kropf, who had stood up while her back had been turned.

"Rebekah." He stepped in closer, talking the whole time. Becky had no idea what he was saying. She couldn't focus. It sounded like a bunch of nonsense. She stood there, uncertain, for who knows how long, holding the coffeepot and staring at his bushy, grayish-brown beard. He leaned toward her, and she caught a whiff of garlic on his breath. Ugh.

She couldn't do this. She couldn't do this. She. Couldn't. Do. This.

The door opened, and Daed came in, whistling.

Whistling!

Becky stared at him in disbelief. Didn't he realize what he was doing?

"Welkum, Amos!" Daed shook Amos's hand. "Right beautiful weather today, ain't so?" As if he hadn't seen the man all day.

Becky shook her head. Ignoring the chatting men standing by the stove, she refilled Amos's coffee cup, then filled a cup for Daed. After putting the pot back on the stove, she went over to speak to the kinner.

She'd just finished making small talk with all seven when the sound of buggy wheels crunching in the gravel drive caught her attention, and she turned to glance out the window. Who could it possibly be this close to dinnertime?

"Ach, that must be your beau, Becky. You'd best run and get ready, jah?"

Becky swung around and stared at Daed in disbelief. He winked at her, then nodded toward the other room. "Don't worry, we'll take care of Emma."

Becky darted from the room, relieved. But the relief was short-lived. When had Daed arranged a date for her? And with whom?

⤍⥤❦⥢⤎

Jacob's stomach churned as he drove the buggy from the shed to the house. Funny how this date with Becky affected him. He didn't remember being this nervous with Susie the first time. Of course, Susie had pretty much made all the arrangements. She'd decided they'd go out and had told him to pick her up down the road, out of view from her house. She'd wanted him to take her to eat at her favorite restaurant and then go riding. Susie was the life of the party, as he'd heard an Englischer say once. He'd been flattered by her attention.

Jacob hoped Becky wouldn't be upset that Daniel had set this up. Her daed had even offered him money to take her out. Unbelievable. He'd refused it, of course. He could do this little thing for her.

He gladly would have roped the moon for her.

And if it meant eliminating Amos Kropf from the picture, well then, all the better.

Since he'd always picked Susie up down the road, Jacob didn't know whether to go inside and wait for Becky or to stay outside and let her come to him.

He set the buggy's brakes and sat there a minute, then decided he'd go in.

He wiped his sweaty palms on his pants and climbed out of the buggy. As he approached the front door, he remembered the day he'd arrived, when he'd stared up at the beautiful girl who'd come to the door. She hadn't seemed too happy to see him, but he'd been intrigued, in spite of his fears.

That fascination had only grown.

As he reached the door, it swung open, and Becky appeared, strands of her blonde hair coming loose from her kapp. She didn't look mad. Just relieved. Maybe embarrassed. And scared.

"Bex, you okay with this?" He studied her, hoping she'd say jah.

She shook her head, then frowned and nodded. After a quick glance behind her, she whispered, "I'm confused."

Jah, he could relate. Still, he grinned and tilted his head toward the buggy. "Kum. I'll explain it to you over dinner."

She took a couple of steps, then hesitated. "I don't want to kum between you and your Susie."

Jacob blinked, then looked down. He'd jumped at the chance to go out with Becky, not giving Susie a moment's thought. The letter she'd sent hadn't even factored in. It still waited, unopened, on his bed. Half a world away. Maybe more.

Becky looked around and then shut the door behind her. "I do want to get away from Amos Kropf."

"Kum schnell."

She nodded, and together they hurried to the buggy.

Becky climbed in without assistance, then turned to look at him. "Where are you taking me?"

That was the big question in Jacob's mind, too. Where was this taking him?

Chapter 17

Becky tried to control her trembling as she perched next to Jacob in the buggy. She hoped that he wouldn't take advantage of her by spiriting her away to an isolated spot. She wouldn't have the strength to fight him off. But somehow, being alone with Jacob seemed less scary than facing Amos Kropf and his seven kinner across the dinner table.

Jacob had done nothing wrong except flirt shamelessly with her.

Of course, that was how Kent had begun, too.

She swallowed and turned to look at the man sitting next to her. As she watched, his expression changed from thoughtful to mischievous.

"Where am I taking you? Ach, I thought maybe McDonald's. We could share another of your fancy coffees, ain't so?" He shot a grin in her direction.

"A cappuccino does sound gut, jah." McDonald's would be busy, so they wouldn't truly be alone. And it wasn't likely that Kent would interrupt them again.

Jacob leaned over close enough that his shoulder bumped hers. "I'm teasing. You tell me where you want to go and how to get there, and I'll take you. Daniel said there are a few places to eat in town." Jacob turned the horse out into the road.

"McDonald's will be gut."

Jacob pulled closer to the edge of the road as a car sped past them. "Nein. We'll stop later for your fancy coffee if you'd like, but this is a...a date."

"A date? Because Daed told you to take me out? Probably paid you to? I'm grateful he gave me an out from dinner at home with Amos Kropf, but there's no reason to pretend this is a real date." Becky heard her voice quiver. Tears burned her eyes. Ach, why couldn't she turn off the waterworks?

Jacob's gaze turned thoughtful again. His brows drew together, and his forehead wrinkled. "Ach, Bex. Nein. Your daed didn't pay me. And, if you remember, I offered to take you out when we talked earlier today."

"How did Daed know that?"

A muscle flexed in Jacob's jaw. He shook his head. "I don't know. I didn't go talking about the intricacies of our relationship to him." His fingers slid over her hand, leaving tingles in their wake. "I'm going to be asking Susie for a break."

For a moment, Becky's heart stopped. She stared at Jacob, eyes wide, hope building, cresting, then breaking, like the ocean waves she'd seen in pictures. "A break?"

"Jah. I need to think about some things before I commit." He glanced at her. "Let's not talk about that. Are you hungry now, or would you like to drive around some first?"

She hated the distrust that instantly flared, and she slid as far away from him as she could. "Where do you have in mind?" Looking around, she noticed a house not too far off. She could jump; they weren't going fast. She wouldn't be alone with him in some secretive place. Never again with a man until she said her wedding vows.

Jacob shrugged. "I'm new here, Bex. Show me around the district. Where did you go to school?"

"School?" Why did he want to see her old school? It wasn't like he'd be attending.

"Jah. Take me on the getting-to-know Bex tour. Where does your best friend live? Did you ever work outside the home? What is your favorite restaurant, or do I know that already?" He bumped her shoulder again. "Tell me about you."

Jacob was interested in her past? Warmth flooded her. "Turn here. The schoolhouse is down this road." She slid a bit nearer to him, close enough that his arm pressed against hers.

Or maybe he was taking flirting to a whole new level. She eased away.

❦

There was a smile hidden inside her somewhere. Had to be. Jacob glanced at Becky, wishing she'd slide closer to him again. He considered wrapping his arm around her and pulling her nearer, but, considering how skittish she seemed, he decided he'd better not.

Probably best not to make any moves until he dispelled the confusion in his own mind.

Though he probably wouldn't be able to do anything about the temptation to tease her. He didn't want to be so attracted to Becky, but he couldn't help it. There was something about her that called to him. He couldn't keep from flirting.

He had to prepare her for someone else.

He felt a twinge in his heart. And he frowned.

Just not Amos.

Jacob studied the set of the horse's ears. To be totally honest, he wanted Becky. For himself.

And if he married her....

Jah, that would be his ultimate goal. To win Becky's heart.

"There's the schoolhouse." Becky pointed to a nondescript white building. 'We usually walked across the fields to go to school, because it's faster that way. My best friend, Annie, is the teacher. I wanted to be, but...."

Sadness crossed her face.

She didn't need to explain. Her silence said it all.

"Your Emma is a joy." He said the first thing that came into his mind, hoping it would chase her unhappiness away.

Her eyes brightened. "Jah. She is."

Jacob pulled the buggy up to the schoolhouse. "Can we see inside? Where did you sit?" He hopped out and went around to her side, then reached up to help her. "Kum, show me around."

She pulled back. "The building is probably locked."

"We could peek in the windows, ain't so?" His fingers grazed her waist. "Kum."

Becky narrowed her eyes and scooted out of his reach. She stared at the school. Jacob glanced back at it, too. Plain and white, with windows in the front and around to the side, low bushes beside the front steps, and a volleyball net peeking out from around the corner of the building.

He looked back at Becky. That was definitely fear in her eyes. He didn't see anything to be scared of.

"It probably looks just like your old school." Her voice trembled.

Jacob wouldn't beg. He swallowed his disappointment. Why did she keep rejecting him? Walking around a schoolhouse seemed so safe, so innocent. He wished he could understand her.

He opened his mouth to question her, but then comprehension flickered. After Kent, she had good reason to be wary of a man's physical attentions.

After a long look at Becky, he went back around to his side of the buggy and climbed in. He made a clicking sound to the horse, disengaged the brake, drove back to the road, and turned the buggy back the way they'd come.

Time to go to town, have dinner, and hope that Becky would relax a little.

She'd forgotten how isolated the schoolhouse was and didn't know how to explain her fear to Jacob. How exactly would she tell him that the idea of being alone with any man scared her?

Jacob hadn't spoken one word since they'd left the school, but he'd pointed the horse toward town, so apparently their date wasn't over. Did he still want to learn about her? She didn't know. Taking a chance, she nodded toward a house on the right side of the road. "That's where my friend Annie lives."

Jacob glanced in the direction she indicated. "Tell me about Annie. How did you become friends?"

His voice was quiet, kind, and calm. It sounded like the voice Daed used when he spoke to a frightened horse. But at least the topic was safe. And a moving buggy didn't involve empty buildings, low bushes, and dark, private places. Becky relaxed. "Annie and I were playmates ever since we were wee boppli...."

Hours later, after dinner and a long conversation at her favorite restaurant, which was followed by cappuccinos at McDonald's, Jacob drove the buggy up to Becky's house, now dark. She couldn't remember when she'd talked so much or had so much fun on a date. Never before had a man shown so much interest in who she was. But then, this wasn't a real date. She climbed out of the buggy. "Danki for taking me out tonight, Jacob. I'll always be grateful." She turned and headed toward the house.

"I enjoyed it, Bex. We'll have to do it again sometime." His voice came from right behind her, stirring the hair on the back of her neck.

She spun around, surprised that he'd followed her, and stumbled slightly. His hand grasped her elbow, steadying her. "Easy there."

She backed away, mistrust growing again. "I'm not inviting you in."

She could barely see his nod in the darkness. "I didn't expect you would."

"What do you want from me, Jacob?" She rammed her back into the railing on the side of the porch steps.

Jacob's gaze held hers. "Friendship. Trust. That'll do, for starters." He smiled. "Gut nacht, Bex. I'm going to take care of the horse and buggy. I'll see you in the morning." He reached out and pushed a cluster of loose hair under her kapp, his fingers lingering on her cheek. "Sleep tight." Then, he turned and walked back toward the buggy.

Chapter 18

Jacob wanted to sing as he took care of the horse and secured the buggy in the shed, but, respecting the lateness of the hour, he settled for a low hum. His date with Becky had gone well, all things considered. Her skittishness at the beginning had settled into something he would have called companionable comfort. He'd enjoyed getting to know about her favorite foods, preferred pastimes, and other simple things that made her who she was. He hoped she'd liked learning more about him, too.

But they hadn't touched on her recent past or her hopes and dreams for the future. Both seemed to be taboo subjects at this point. And he still hadn't earned a genuine smile from her.

Jacob snuck into the dawdi-haus, hoping not to disturb its elderly occupants. He avoided the squeaky step as he went upstairs to prepare for bed.

After turning on the gas light in his room, he knelt to say his prayers, a childhood habit he clung to, then stood up and crawled under the covers in the chilly room. The letter he'd tossed on the bed so many hours before stopped him in surprise. It almost felt like seeing a blinking neon light in Amish country. Susie would be furious if she ever discovered her message had received so little care.

He fingered the envelope, studying it, trying to see it through Becky's eyes. His calluses caught on the edge of the flap. He turned it over, carefully slid his finger along the flap to disengage it, and pulled out a single page, folded into thirds.

Drawing in a deep breath, he smoothed out the paper. Unlined green stationery with a faint background image of two girls collecting flowers in a meadow—definitely a feminine print. He'd expect nothing less from Susie. Totally unlike the plain, white lined paper his mamm used.

He closed his eyes, visualizing the gold chain she wore around her neck to let him know that she could leave the house without her daed noticing it. At the bottom hung an ornate heart-shaped locket, in which she'd put a picture of herself on one side and one of Jacob on the other. Jewelry and graven images were both forbidden in their Ordnung, but that never stopped Susie. She'd secretly purchased one of those cell phones that took pictures and used it often. He had a cell phone, too, but he'd never snapped a picture of anything, except his foot once, by accident.

He smiled as he remembered the day that photo had been taken. It had been the last day of summer, and Susie had worn a pair of tight blue jeans with a revealing shirt that had nothing but tiny little straps going over her shoulders. He'd been in jeans and an unbuttoned shirt. Of course, those now hung in his closet at home. He hadn't packed his Englisch clothes when he'd come to Missouri. After all, he planned to join the Amish church. Susie wasn't so sure she wanted to remain Amish, another reason his daed was opposed to her. Maybe he could see Susie trying to lure him away.

That last day he'd seen Susie before leaving Pennsylvania, she'd worn her tight jeans and a fuzzy sweater, and she'd brought along her boom box. It had looked so odd set up on the barn floor. She'd danced while he'd sat on a hay bale with most of their friends, drinking pop and talking.

He missed his friends the most. More than the Englisch clothes, the freedom to drive cars, the music...everything. They used to get together every Friday and Saturday night. Sometimes, after their chores were finished, they'd go fishing. Maybe he'd make some friends around here, but so far, he'd met only Becky's cousin Ben and his friends, and he hadn't connected with any of them. But maybe some of his friends from home would be part of the arranged swap Daniel had mentioned. Josh Esh would volunteer, for sure. After all, he'd wanted to come with Jacob in February. And maybe Matthew Yoder would come. For some time, Matthew had been chafing at the lack of farmland in Lancaster County. Jacob relaxed on his bed, his thoughts still on his friends at home, but the crinkling of the letter drew his attention again. He opened his eyes, rolled onto his side, and began to read.

Dear Jacob,

I can't believe you are gone to Missouri. I hope you've had a gut trip. Your mamm gave me your address since I hadn't heard from you yet. I tried to call your phone, but I keep getting your voice mail. Are you avoiding my calls?

Ach. He'd never even thought to check his phone since he'd arrived. But no matter. He didn't know of any place to charge it here. He'd try to remember to check his messages tomorrow. And he'd need to ask Daniel about someplace to plug the phone in. Although, why bother? Might be better to make a clean break from Susie.

Timothy Shultz asked to take me for a ride the other night. I agreed, since you aren't here to take me. We had fun, and I thought maybe I should consider asking you for a break.

Relief flooded him. God had this Susie issue under control.

We could see other people until you get back. That way, I won't be stuck at home without a date. Though you're still my sweetheart.

Write soon!
Ich liebe dich,
Susie

Jacob folded the letter and dropped it on the floor beside the bed. Seemed he wasn't the only one considering a break, even if Susie's reasons were entirely different. Well, maybe not so different. Perhaps she needed to think, too. Timothy Shultz had always been sweet on Susie, making eyes at her long before she'd set her attentions on Jacob. Timothy hadn't waited long to make his move.

Strange thing was, Jacob didn't mind one bit. Not since he'd decided to ask her for a break, anyway. And Timothy was nice. He'd make a good husband for Susie. And maybe he'd be a strong enough lure to keep her from jumping the fence.

Jacob hadn't been strong enough for that. Susie had figured she could take him with her.

He felt a weight slide off his back knowing he no longer had a girl back home in Pennsylvania to worry over. Although, maybe the break was unofficial until he wrote back and agreed to it. He wasn't sure.

Maybe soon he'd have a girl in Missouri, Lord willing.

Though he'd assume nothing. After all, he'd thought they'd made progress before, only to have Becky turn into an ice princess overnight.

Jacob sat up to extinguish the gas lamp, then collapsed back onto his pillow, thinking again of Becky.

His stomach clenched as he tried to imagine her wearing revealing Englisch clothes like Susie's. He couldn't see it. Becky didn't seem the type. And he liked that about her.

❦

Becky helped Mamm get breakfast on the table, setting the jams and jellies next to the basket of sliced bread. Jacob, Daed, and Grossdaedi came in to wash up. Jacob pressed something into her hand as he passed behind her. A folded piece of paper. She slid it into her pocket, but as she did, she remembered the letter from his mamm still sitting on the hutch. She picked it up and put it near his place at the table, hoping he wouldn't say anything about her tardiness in delivering it to him.

Daed sat, but he didn't have the usual twinkle in his eye. His typically jovial attitude seemed to be missing. Instead, he frowned at the table, his shoulders slumped as if he carried the weight of the entire Amish district on his shoulders. Becky studied him, hoping for some clue as to what ailed him, but he avoided her gaze. She hoped he didn't think she'd gone and invited Jacob in the night before. Maybe the lateness of the hour when she'd snuck inside disturbed him. But then, wasn't he the one who'd arranged the date in the first place?

Perhaps he hadn't realized she and Jacob would stay out so long.

Of course, she never would have dreamed that, either, nor that she would have such a good time.

She'd try to get out to the blacksmith shop later. Maybe Daed would tell her what bothered him.

Breakfast was eaten in near silence, then Grossmammi retired to the dawdi-haus to work on her quilts. Katie, Ruth, and Abbie set to work doing the dishes, as they always did before school, and the men returned to the blacksmith shop or the barn. Becky needed to do laundry. She headed for the gas-powered washer but had barely started work when she noticed Mamm standing there, observing her silently.

Becky began to feel a bit uneasy. "Did you need something?"

Mamm shook her head. Frowned.

"You're scaring me." Becky dropped the pair of pants she'd been holding into the laundry basket.

Mamm laid her hand on Becky's arm. "I'm not sure what is going to happen. Amos Kropf didn't take your leaving very well at all. He got nasty with your daed and threatened to send the deacon out."

"I don't want to make things difficult for you and Daed." Becky swallowed. "I don't want to marry him, but if it means—"

"Ach, Becky. Nein. You mustn't think that. We'll weather whatever comes. There is no way your daed would allow anyone to bully him into giving you up to that man. There's talk of some Amish moving to Arkansas for cheap farmland. If need be, we'll go, too."

Becky nodded. At least she knew what was wrong with Daed now.

Mamm pulled Becky into a hug. "I need to run to market. I'm taking Mary with me today." She started to move off, then hesitated, her eyes searching Becky's face. "Did you have fun last night?"

Did she hear a bit of hope in Mamm's voice? Heat rushed to Becky's cheeks. She didn't give an answer. But then, Mamm didn't really expect one, anyway. Details of courtship were traditionally kept secret.

Not that she and Jacob were courting.

He had a girl. He'd said he wanted friendship.

Sure, he'd said he would be asking Susie for a break, but that sounded a lot like what Kent had said when she'd gone to tell him about her pregnancy and caught him with another girl: "Surely, you didn't think you were the only one I was seeing!"

And then, he'd insisted she was the one who was loose. Except he'd used a much harsher word.

She'd made a horrible mistake.

She wouldn't make it again.

The laundry had been hung out to dry before Becky remembered the note Jacob had given her that morning. She pulled it out of her pocket and settled down on a porch step to read it.

The note was on a fancy piece of stationery, not the plain white paper Mamm used to write letters to distant family. And the handwriting matched the address on Susie's envelope yesterday. Extremely feminine.

Why would Jacob give her Susie's letter to read?

She scanned the message quickly, then started over to read it more slowly. Ach, Jacob must be heart-broken, having been dumped by his Susie like that. But the closing sentence and the "I love you" in the sig-nature confused Becky. Why would Susie sign it like that after breaking up with him? She seemed flighty. It sounded like she wanted to keep Jacob dangling.

Becky turned the page over, searching for some clue as to why Jacob would have given his letter to her.

Bex, I thought you should know. You aren't coming between us.

Jacob

She stood up and refolded the letter, sliding it back inside her pocket. Maybe it was time for that visit to the blacksmith shop. Daed and Jacob would surely enjoy a cup of coffee and a couple of cookies.

❦

Jacob's mind was not on his work. Instead, he tried to imagine Becky's reaction as she read Susie's note. Would she understand what he was trying to say? He reached to pick up a rod but jerked his hand back immediately after touching it, dropping the hot metal. It fell to the ground with a clatter. He'd forgot-ten to put on his work gloves.

Daniel appeared at his side instantly. "Let's see." He reached for Jacob's palm and studied it. "Probably need to get on up to the haus and get some burn salve on it. Doesn't look too bad, though. Here, dip your hand in this cold water for a bit to soothe it first." He pointed to a bucket of rainwater standing in the corner, then flexed his own hand. "You need to be careful out here. Did I tell you I lost most of the feeling in my hands because I've burned them so much?"

"Nein." That didn't sound too pleasant. Jacob plunged his hand into the water, not liking the idea of being unable to feel Becky's soft cheek when he touched it.

"Have your mind on something else today, Jacob?" Daniel's voice held a teasing note.

Jacob swallowed. He glanced at Daniel and gave a brief nod.

Daniel smirked. "Need I ask what? Or who?"

Heat surged up Jacob's neck, and he answered in Englisch instead of Deutsch, "No, sir. You don't."

Daniel opened his mouth, but before he could say anything, the shop door opened. For a moment, the person in the doorway stood with her face in the shadows and the bright sun behind her, but Jacob recognized the dress Becky had been wearing that morning. A moment later, she headed in their direction, and he noticed she carried two cups of coffee and something wrapped in a napkin.

"Daed? Is everything okay?" Becky handed a mug to her daed, then glanced at Jacob, her gaze sliding to his hand submerged in the bucket. Her eyes widened. "Did you get burned?"

Jacob frowned. "Not bad." He pulled out his hand and fluttered his fingers but couldn't hold back a wince.

"Kum to the haus. I'll put some salve on it, jah?"

"I'll be fine."

Becky set down whatever was wrapped in the napkin on an anvil and placed the other mug beside it. In the next moment, she stood beside him, reaching out for his hand. "Let me see."

He didn't want to appear wimpy in front of Becky, but the truth was that the burn hurt worse than any pain he'd ever experienced, except maybe her rejection. He started to pull away, but her soft hands cradled his before he could. Jacob's breath hitched. He hoped she hadn't noticed.

Too much to hope that her daed hadn't. Jacob saw the smirk deepen on Daniel's face.

"Take him on up to the haus and get him taken care of, Becky." Daniel turned away as the crunch of tires sounded outside of the shed. "Jacob, as soon as you're bandaged, kum back out. There are still things you can do. Maybe this time, you can keep your mind on the job."

Jacob nodded and moved away from Becky. He strode over to the still open door and stood aside long enough for an Englisch man to come through, then headed toward the haus.

Becky hurried ahead of him. "I'll get everything ready. Just wait in the kitchen."

"Jah." Jacob watched her skirts swirl around her ankles as she dashed away.

The kitchen was empty when Jacob arrived, so he sat down at the table. A few moments later, Becky bustled in and set a shoe box on the table. "Hold out your hand and rest it on the table," she said gently. Then, she went to the windowsill, where an aloe plant sat in a ceramic pot, and snapped off one of the long, pointy ends.

A few seconds later, her free hand grasped his trembling fingers, holding them still as she squeezed the gooey stuff out of the plant and onto the burn. Next, she wrapped a gauze bandage loosely around it. She dropped the roll of gauze back into the box as Jacob stood. "Danki, Bex."

She backed up a step. "Jacob, I...I read Susie's note."

"Jah." He'd wanted her to.

"I'm sorry. That must hurt." Her forehead wrinkled a little.

Jacob shrugged. "Not so much. I told you I would be asking her for a break."

"I thought you were just saying that."

"I never just say things." Jacob reached out with his unburned hand and let his fingers slide over her cheek, down to her chin, touching the corner of her mouth along the way. "I wanted to think about things before I committed to anything." He'd said that on their date, but it needed repeating.

"What things?" There was a definite catch in Becky's voice, but she didn't pull away from his light touch.

Jacob grinned. "You. Me." He leaned forward and kissed her cheek. "Us."

Chapter 19

Becky's fingers rose to touch her cheek as she watched Jacob stride from the room. He didn't look back, not even as he paused to close the door behind him. Maybe now she'd find out what it was like to be courted by Jacob Miller.

Once, when she was at the home of an Englisch friend, they'd watched a movie on the television box that sat in the corner of the living room. In the movie, after a boy kissed a sixteen-year-old girl on the cheek, the girl had squealed. Becky wished she could squeal like that. Maybe it would let out some of her bottled-up emotions as an alternative to tears.

The door opened again, and Jacob stepped back inside. "Hey, Bex. What are you doing Friday night?"

Becky blinked, pulling her hand away from her face. She hoped Jacob hadn't noticed her childishly touching the place where he'd kissed her. "I don't know. Reading, maybe." She'd recently bought a new book but hadn't started it yet.

"There's a frolic at your cousin Ben's haus. I'll take you."

Becky sucked in a breath. "Ach, nein. Jacob, I.... Nein." She would not go there. Not even for Jacob. So much for finding out what it would be like to be courted by him. That was a quick death of that dream.

Jacob advanced toward her but stopped a couple of feet away. "Why not, Bex? I know Kent lied about you, and your reputation suffered a beating, but sometimes the best way to get past that sort of thing is to face it with your head held high. You know, as the Englisch say, 'Don't let them see you sweat.' I'll be there; I'll stay right by your side. Promise."

"Jacob, maybe you don't know what goes on at some of Ben's parties." Though he should. He'd been to one already.

His mouth quirked. "I know. Trust me. But this one is supposed to be nothing more dangerous than a bonfire with hotdogs and s'mores, and maybe a volleyball game. It's Ben's birthday." He hesitated, his expression softening. "And if it does turn out to be something you're uncomfortable with, we can leave."

Becky thought for a moment, tempted. But then, memories flooded back from the last time she'd gone. *"No one will miss us, Becky. Kum. We'll be back before they even know we're gone."*

She hadn't stayed around to hear that version of what Kent had said. It had taken everything for her to keep from slapping the boy who'd whispered to her. Would she ever get over this embarrassing nightmare? Wasn't it enough that she'd shamed herself and her family? Did they have to force her to relive her mistake every time she ventured out?

Becky shuddered, forcing her mind back to the present. Her attention focused on the man tempting her now, and she straightened her posture. "Nein."

Jacob sucked in a deep breath as a wounded expression flitted across his face, then disappeared so fast that she wondered if she'd imagined it. He spun around and headed for the door, making no move to touch her or tease her. She almost wished he would.

Over his shoulder, he said, "No need to give your answer now, Bex. Take some time to think on it first."

Thinking on it wouldn't change her answer. Jacob might not be Kent, or any of the other boys who looked at her with lustful eyes, but he was still male, and his smooth talk rivaled Kent's, for sure. She would not be lured into his trap.

Becky moved to the window to watch Jacob stride back to the shop, and she turned away only after he disappeared inside. What had she been doing before Jacob had come in and confused her emotions? Her gaze landed on the boxful of medical supplies. Ach, had she really been so bold as to go out to the shop in search of Jacob, carrying coffee and cookies as an excuse?

Had she expected him to pour out his hurt and dismay over being dumped by Susie for this Timothy and cry on her shoulders? He'd hardly do that. But still, poor Jacob had been upset enough to reach for a piece of hot metal and burn himself. And Daed had told him to keep his mind on the job. He didn't know that Susie had just broken his heart.

Never mind that Jacob had turned on the charm after she'd bandaged his hand, saying he wanted to think about "us."

And he'd kissed her cheek.

Warmth washed over Becky again, and she almost smiled.

Almost.

Instead, she frowned at the realization that swept over her. She snatched up the box and marched out of the room. Ach, Jacob was just like all the buwe. He had to have a girl on his arm. And if it couldn't be his Susie, then, for now, the next best thing was Becky.

Because, after all, who did Becky have?

Nobody.

And that was the absolute truth of it.

Maybe marrying Amos Kropf would not be such a bad thing after all. Even though her parents had offered to move the family so she wouldn't have to, she would hate to disrupt their lives.

Tears welled in her eyes. Impatiently, she wiped them away with her knuckles. She would grin and bear whatever was best for her family. And for her daughter.

⁓

As Jacob strode back into the blacksmith shop, he caught Daniel's wink. He wasn't sure if it was directed toward the man he'd been chatting with or toward Jacob because he had spent a few precious moments alone in the kitchen with Becky.

She'd actually seemed receptive to him—at least, until he'd brought up the idea of attending her cousin Ben's party. Then, that solid barn wall had been erected so fast, it'd crushed his toes, as well as scraped his heart. Would he ever get past her defenses?

Pain from more than just a burned hand ate at him. Becky was a master of rejection, and it still stung him, even though he'd experienced it every day since coming here. What would it take to get her to open up to him, to accept him? For her to agree to be courted by him?

Still mulling over his questions, Jacob picked up the cup of coffee Becky had left on the anvil, took a sip, then set it aside, out of the way of his work. The bundle wrapped in a napkin still waited there, too, so he picked it up, and the contents shifted in his hand. He peeked inside. Cookies. Four of them. They appeared to be oatmeal raisin. Jacob didn't know when Becky had baked them, or even if she had. Perhaps they had been one of Leah's baking projects yesterday.

He set the cookies down next to his coffee, then moved over to the crank to get the fire going again. Daniel was spending less time telling him what to. Must mean he was catching on. And he actually found himself enjoying the work.

It'd be something he could do to support Becky, if their relationship went that far. He glanced out the open door toward the fields. How far did Daniel's land extend? Did he plan to give a portion of it to Becky when she married?

Not exactly questions he could ask at this point. He and Becky were hardly ready to discuss a future together. The present was uncertain enough.

He shook his head and grinned. And he'd thought nothing would ever come between him and Susie.

He'd need to take this relationship slow and steady. Make certain that Becky would be his one and only.

The trouble was, did he have time? With the bishop and Amos Kropf pushing for Becky to marry now, would he and Becky be forced into a decision neither one of them was ready to make?

The fire burning fiercely now, Jacob reached for the project he'd been working on. The customer left, and Daniel wandered over and watched Jacob work for a few moments, then gave him an approving clap on the shoulder and disappeared out the door.

Several minutes later, Jacob heard the familiar clip-clop of a horse coming down the lane. Putting down the hammer, he peeked out the window to see the man Daniel had referred to as the bishop. He might be there to have some work done, but since he came so close on the heels of the failed dinner with Amos Kropf, Jacob doubted it. This wouldn't be good.

He wiped his unburned hand on his work apron and headed outside to look for Daniel. To his relief, he spied the older man coming back from the house.

"Welkum, Bishop Sol. What can we do for you today?" Daniel approached the bishop, shooting Jacob an indecipherable glance.

The bishop looked at Jacob, his expression dismissive, then turned his gaze back to Daniel. "Can we talk?"

"Jah." Daniel didn't invite the bishop to walk or ask Jacob to leave. But when the bishop remained silent, he nodded toward Jacob.

Jacob took that as his cue to disappear. For a second, he stood there in indecision. Should he go for a walk, get back to work, or head up to the house? Since he'd just come from the house a few minutes ago, he didn't figure that to be such a good idea.

Back to work it was.

Inside the shop again, Jacob took another sip of his coffee, now lukewarm. He eyed the cookies but didn't think they would agree with him, his nerves in a tangle the way they were. If only he dared creep to the doorway and eavesdrop on the two men. He suspected they would be talking about Amos Kropf and the date that hadn't happened with Becky.

Knowing he'd probably get caught, he went back to work, trying the method Daniel had shown him to curve the end of a piece of metal.

After a while, he heard buggy wheels crunch over the gravel, and Daniel returned to the shop. Jacob eyed him, wondering how the talk had gone but not daring to ask. Judging by his expression, it hadn't been too bad.

Still, Daniel didn't seem inclined to share what they had discussed. Instead, he busied himself looking at the work Jacob had accomplished. "Ser gut, but you need to smooth it out a little bit. Here, let me show you." He headed back to the forge.

Jacob impatiently raised his eyebrows and trailed Daniel to the fire. "The visit from the bishop...?" Maybe a gentle prod would do the trick. More like a broad hint.

As he waited, thunder rumbled, and the skies opened up. Rain pattered down outside, and inside the shop, water started dripping from a few holes in the roof.

"I guess I need to fix the roof. A job for tomorrow, ain't so?"

"Jah." Jacob tapped his foot on the blackened floor.

Daniel nodded toward the lever, indicating Jacob should stoke the fire. "The bishop, he didn't realize our Becky had other options. He's willing to wait a bit before marrying her off."

Jacob's heart soared, relieved he'd have time to try to win Becky over. But then he shivered with a sudden chill. From the rain? Probably not. Other options—that meant him. And if that didn't work out.... Ach, he wouldn't think that way.

There was no reason why it shouldn't.

❧

Becky immersed herself in greenhouse work in an effort to keep her mind off both Jacob and Amos. She destroyed spiderwebs with a broom and began to clean up for spring planting. She loved working out here, especially on rainy days, when the sound of water hitting the glass panes overhead seemed much what she imagined an Amazon rain forest to sound like. Mamm had ordered the seeds they needed, so their work would begin in earnest as soon as the package arrived.

When Becky's stomach rumbled with hunger, she squared her shoulders and headed for the kitchen. Time she started lunch, not that she was in a hurry to see Jacob. But Mamm and Mary should be home soon, and Mamm would be expecting to find the meal under way. Maybe Mamm would be home by the time she finished peeling the potatoes.

After she'd made her decision to marry Amos Kropf, her heart had died, the direct opposite of how completely alive she felt in Jacob's company. Now it was just numb. Accepting, but not happy.

If she wouldn't be allowed to stay with her parents as a maidal, then marriage to Amos Kropf would solve everything—if she could resign herself to the emotional prison. She pushed a nudge of doubt to the background. She'd be out from under her parents' roof, Emma would have a daed, and her parents would no longer bear the shame and disgrace of having a daughter who was an unwed mother. The unmarried men who had lustful thoughts about her would be forced to look elsewhere. What could possibly be wrong with that picture?

Other than the fact that she'd be married to a man as old as her daed. A man who had a son almost as old as she was. A man who was believed by most to have abused his former wives, maybe even killed one of them. The last one had died falling down a set of stairs. Suspicious, as far as Becky was concerned. But that wasn't the worst of it.

He was a man she didn't love.

Tears burned her eyes. She angrily brushed them away.

She would not cry.

After all, she could find things wrong with Jacob, too. He frequented parties—well, at least one—and hung out with her cousin Ben. Granted, nobody had told him about the singings where the good Amish teens went. Becky was so far out of the loop, she didn't know, herself.

If Ben had called the upcoming gathering at his house a "frolic," then maybe it would be safe. And maybe Jacob was confused about where to get acquainted with people. After all, he was new to the community.

If Mamm didn't need her, she'd run down to Annie's house after school let out and see if Annie could tell her where the legitimate singings would be held. In case Jacob would like to know.

And Becky could find out if Ben's get-together would be a true frolic, or if he was just calling a party by a different name.

Chapter 20

J acob pulled his watch out of his pocket and glanced at the time. Almost five o'clock. Someone should be ringing the dinner bell soon. He strode to the shop door, glad to see that the heavy rain had lightened to more of a drizzle. When they'd sloshed through the mud to the house for the noon meal, Daniel had joked about it being fine weather for ducks. Leah had put a large plastic tray by the back door where they could leave their shoes. His mamm did that back home in Pennsylvania, especially during the winter and early spring. Homesickness struck. He missed Mamm's daily hugs. He didn't get any hugs here, but he should have expected that.

The rain had transformed the Ozark world even more. When he'd arrived in Seymour, the trees had been bare and broken, coated in ice, but now they were turning green, with leaves a little bigger than a squirrel's ears. Wild jonquils were beginning to bloom along the roadsides and scattered in the yards, and wild violets made a beautiful ground cover. Both were sure signs of spring.

The transformation amazed him. Even more amazing was the dramatic transformation his own life had undergone—from pursuing Susie to pursuing Becky, and with greater passion; from hating the blacksmith trade to thoroughly enjoying the work;

from harboring bitterness toward his daed for send-ing him here with duplicitous intentions to fully for-giving him.

Jacob's stomach rumbled, and he glanced toward the house, hoping somebody would appear soon and summon them to dinner. But then, he caught move-ment out by the road. It was Becky, scurrying home through the light rain from wherever she had been.

An image came to mind of Susie dashing away from his buggy after he dropped her off down the lane from her house. Was Becky running home after a date with a bu?

His heart clenched with unexpected jealousy, and, without thinking, he stepped out of the shop and started running toward her. Surely, she hadn't gone out with Amos Kropf. Daniel had made his opinion known about that match. At least, to Jacob. And ei-ther he or Leah certainly would have spoken to Becky about it.

His stomach churned. But, as he neared her, he forced what he hoped would be a happy expression onto his face. He didn't want to scare her. "Bex."

She looked up, rain running down her face in rivulets. The black bonnet she wore over her kapp was soaked, but then, so was the rest of her. Mud coated the bottom third of her dress.

"Ach, you're going to get sick."

She waved his concern away. "I'm fine. I went to visit with Annie. She told me it really is a frolic at Ben's. And the singing will be held at her haus on Sunday night."

Relief filled him. She hadn't been with another man. And she'd been able to get the information on where the singing would be. Not another party. He didn't intend to go to another of those; he'd finished with that scene. "Does that mean you'll go with me?"

She frowned.

Jacob stepped nearer and cupped her chin with his hand. "You know, it takes more muscles to frown than to smile."

"I've heard that before." Becky shrugged. And didn't smile. "I don't know, Jacob. No one would expect me there. And I really don't fit in. Never have. You'd be so much happier without me along. Really." She stepped out of his reach, causing his hand to drop away. "Not to mention, you'll meet some nice girls. My friend Annie...."

Jacob edged closer, reaching out to touch her upper arm and gently tug her toward him. "Are you saying you aren't interested in me?"

Her mouth dropped open, and she stared at him. "Nein, I...uh...."

"Then, you're interested in being courted by me?"

She dipped her head, but not before he saw the blush staining her cheeks.

He moved his hand to trace the curve of her cheek. "Please go with me, Bex." His hand slid around to the back of her neck. "Please?"

She shivered under his light touch. Or maybe it was from the chill of the rain. He wasn't sure. "Jah. I will."

Jacob smiled. "Gut. Danki, Bex."

With one finger, he raised her chin, then wiped some of the rainwater away, not that it did much good. Her tongue peeked out and licked the moisture from her lips. Jacob's gaze fixed on her mouth. She must have noticed it, because she leaned ever so slightly toward him, as if offering an invitation.

An invitation he certainly wouldn't refuse. He edged closer and gently brushed his lips against hers before she had a chance to reconsider her actions. Or maybe she hadn't realized what she'd done.

He pulled back and stared into her eyes, searching, then lowered his head again just as the dinner bell rang. Confident they were out of view of the back porch, Jacob didn't step back. Gently, he tugged her the rest of the way into his arms, deepening the kiss. A few seconds later, he broke the kiss and wrapped her in a hug.

"That was amazing." He sucked in a breath. "You'll have fun. At the frolic, I mean. I promise."

⊷❦⊷

Emotions churned through Becky so fast and hard, she could barely sort through them. She wanted to pull Jacob back and kiss him with all of her pent-up longing, but at the same time, fear that he could be another Kent gnawed at her. Was this just a different approach to get the same thing?

How badly she wished she could wrap her arms around him and hug him back, but she didn't dare. Instead, she stood there in the shelter of his arms while her thoughts and feelings warred within her. Wishing he'd kiss her again and never stop. Wanting the strength to pull away and run. Ach, she was so confused.

Jacob's embrace felt so strong, secure, and even safe. Something she'd never felt when Kent had held her. But then, had he ever held her just because?

After the too-brief cuddle, Jacob pulled away, ending their moment of closeness. "I heard the dinner bell, I think. But now we're both soaking wet." He grinned at her. "We should sneak in the front and get changed, ain't so?"

"Jah, for sure." She moved toward the house, then stumbled when she noticed Daed standing in the doorway of the blacksmith shop, watching them. Shame coursed through her. Would she never learn her lesson? What must Daed be thinking? He'd be ready to put Jacob on the next bus out of town.

Jacob caught her hand, steadying her. "Are you alright?"

She glanced at him. "Daed," she whispered.

He looked toward the blacksmith shop, then raised his hand in a wave. To Becky's dismay, Daed waved back. So much for pretending he hadn't seen.

Becky trembled, and Jacob's grip on her hand tightened. "It's okay, Bex."

"Nein. After Kent...I shamed him. I've given up the right to liebe." Ach, she hadn't intended to say that.

And she'd used the word *love* in relation to him. How could she have been so dumb?

That might explain why Jacob seemed to be taking his precious time in responding. Maybe she'd stolen his voice away.

"Not that 'Ich liebe dich.' I mean, uh...."

"Careful, Bex. You're going to hurt my feelings." He drew in a breath. Exhaled. "There is only One with the authority to deny the right to love. And He refuses to do so."

Becky blinked at him. She couldn't think of a thing to say in response to something so profound.

They'd reached the house, and he led her around to the front. For a charged moment, they stared at each other. Jacob's gaze flickered to her mouth, lingering for an eternity, then moved away. "Go on, now. Get changed. I'll see you in the kitchen." He grinned at her, then headed toward the dawdi-haus for his own fresh set of clothes.

Was it bad that she wished he would have kissed her again?

∽❖∽

Jacob whistled as he took off his muddy boots and left them in the tray by the door of the dawdi-haus, then headed upstairs to his room.

He couldn't believe Becky had allowed him to hold her—not only hold her, but kiss her, too. And that kiss had been knee-weakening. He'd be dreaming about it at night, for certain. It had taken only a second or two for her to respond, and then she'd returned his kiss with a passion and abandon that had surprised him.

Even though the dinner bell had been rung, Jacob decided to take a shower. If he made it quick, he wouldn't be all that late. That rain was cold, chilling him to the bone. And Becky had been out in it longer than he had.

He was on his way back downstairs, his body clean, his hair towel-dried, when he remembered that Daniel had stood by the shop and watched him make a move on Becky. Would he find a bus ticket on his breakfast plate the next morning? He hoped that the cues he'd picked up from Daniel so far were accurate—that he was, in fact, matchmaking. And that the kiss they'd shared would be a major step forward rather than a strike against him.

After all, Daniel certainly hadn't come charging at him like an angry bull seeing red, leaving Jacob bruised and battered three counties over. Nein. He'd just stood there.

Still, Jacob wished that Daniel had gone back inside the shop, because his spying had certainly made Becky uncomfortable. And the knowledge that someone might be watching from inside the house had been the only thing that had kept Jacob from kissing her again on the front porch.

He raked his fingers through his damp hair. Courting a girl he practically shared a roof with could get very awkward. Their relationship would not have the usual degree of secrecy, for sure.

But then, he wouldn't have to go very far to pick her up for a date, either. And he could see her almost as often as he liked. Definite benefits.

Only Becky hadn't agreed to a courtship. All she'd said was that she'd attend the frolic with him. But she hadn't denied her interest in him, either. Plus, she'd blushed when he'd mentioned courting. That had to mean something, right?

Jah. And he would take what he could get.

He would do his best to make sure that the frolic was an event she'd never forget.

If only he could get her to smile.

Seriously, what would it take?

Chapter 21

As the time neared for Jacob to take her to Ben's frolic on Friday, Becky's stomach roiled. She must have been out of her head to agree. Obviously, Jacob had caused her brain cells to pack up and leave for vacation, because she never would have accepted his invitation if she had given it serious thought.

Maybe getting sick would be a good thing, because then she would have an excuse to stay home. After all, her sister Naomi Joy had come home for a brief visit, brought by a driver she'd hired, and it would be nice to talk with her this evening. If Becky claimed to be sick, well, it wouldn't exactly be a lie. After all, Mamm had even commented that she looked a little green and had sent her out to sit on the front porch to get some fresh air. She planted her bare feet solidly against the warmth of the wood porch to still the porch swing so that it wouldn't cause her queasy stomach to be even more upset.

Maybe Jacob would notice that she didn't look so well and would go without her. After all, he'd have more fun if she wasn't there. He certainly didn't need her to hold his hand. And even though he had kissed her—just once, at the beginning of the week—when it came down to it, she was used goods, and he would never want to marry her.

But oh, that kiss. She shut her eyes and inhaled, reliving the pressure of his lips on hers. Wow. That was almost enough to make a girl believe in miracles and second chances.

God might still work miracles today, but Becky had never seen any, except for when Emma was born. And she didn't think He'd want to waste His time and abilities on her. What did God care about an Amish girl who had made a mistake, gotten herself shunned, and then had been accepted only grudgingly after she'd repented and joined the church? Did God hold the same reservations toward her that the rest of the community did?

Jacob's comment about God not withholding love made her wonder. She wished she knew where to find answers, which book of the Bible to search.

Whistling warned her of Jacob's presence moments before she heard his footsteps coming up the stairs. She opened her eyes.

He stopped before her. "Hey, Bex. Your mamm said I would find you here. I'm going to get cleaned up, and then I'll be ready to go."

"I'm not feeling so gut."

"Nerves, ain't so?" Jacob nodded without waiting for her reply. "Your daed said not to let you talk me out of it." Something about his smile looked sympathetic. Maybe it was his eyes.

Becky frowned and stared at the porch floorboards. "You go without me. Maybe I'll go next time." Most definitely not next time. Or ever. Ach, if only Daed hadn't told him not to allow her an out.

Jacob gazed at his work-blackened hands. "I'd really like it if you'd go. I can't make you, Bex, but... please?"

That "please" conveyed a mountain of unspoken feelings. Becky almost cried at the longing and loneliness she thought she'd heard. Was Jacob beginning to feel isolated here, so far away from his friends and family, not knowing anybody? That was enough to make her reconsider. Maybe he did need her, or he at least wanted the familiarity of a friend.

"Jah. Nerves." She took a deep breath. "Just nerves." That might have been the truth; she just wasn't completely sure.

"Gut." Jacob backed away, then hesitated. "I'll be praying for you to feel better."

"Danki." She set the swing in motion with her big toe, then curled her weak-kneed legs into the swing.

Jacob eyed her bare feet. "You should get ready too, ain't so?"

"Jah." She would. In a minute. When she could find the strength to make her legs work. Right now, they felt as if they were made of rubber.

Jacob nodded. His gaze flicked toward her lips, then away. "Listen. I...um, I should probably apologize for, um, kissing you without permission the other day."

She sucked in a breath. He was sorry for kissing her? And here she had just been thinking about how amazing it had been. Tears burned her eyes.

"I mean, I know I don't have the right to kiss you without a promise being made. But, well…. The intent is there."

The intent for a promise was there? Becky struggled to wrap her mind around his words. If only she could believe that.

But then, why shouldn't she be able to? Kent had never made such promises.

Jacob moved away another step, his shoulders slumping. "I'll be right back."

"You have my permission," Becky blurted out before she could change her mind. And then she wondered if he'd take advantage of it right at that moment. She almost wished he would. Yet another part of her already regretted her offer. She would be setting herself up for a fall. And it would be bad. Very, very bad.

His eyes searched her face and then lit up with a brightness she hadn't seen in them before. He straightened his shoulders and gave her a heart-stopping grin. "I'll pick you up in a few minutes."

She nodded, then watched him turn and jog down the porch steps and across the lawn. When he disappeared inside the dawdi-haus, she got up and went inside to get ready. Not that it'd take much. She'd need to take care of Emma, put on her shoes and socks, and grab her black bonnet. And maybe say a prayer.

It would be a frolic. Annie would be there. Jacob would be there. And the chances that Kent would be there? Probably next to none. Jah, she would have a good time.

When Becky went into the kitchen to check on Emma, she found Naomi Joy and Mamm sitting at the table.

Naomi Joy looked up and smiled. "Becky, we were just talking about you! I was telling Mamm that I'm looking to hire someone to help with Regina, who, as you know, will soon have a baby brother or sister. I wondered if you might consider doing it."

Becky blinked. "You want me to be your hired help?" But what about Jacob?

"Jah. You could just kum home with me tonight. Mamm said it'd be okay with her if you agreed."

"Tonight?" Ach, she sounded silly parroting her sister's words. "I promised to go to the frolic tonight." Even sillier was her excuse, considering her nerves. "I can't kum now. Maybe Katie could, and then I could kum some other time." Like when she was more certain of where she stood with Jacob. Or, when she'd gotten over her crush, if only partway.

"Katie is still in school," Naomi Joy reminded her. After a pause, she said, "Well, think on it, Becky. I want you, but you can kum when you're ready."

"Jah, I'll do that." Becky nodded, then lifted Emma out of her cradle. "Best go take care of her."

Upstairs, she gave Emma a quick diaper change and then settled into a chair to feed her. Jacob would just have to wait a bit.

Thirty minutes later, a sated Emma heavy in her arms, Becky selected a clean pair of socks and went back down to the kitchen, where she gently laid the boppli in her cradle again. Mamm and Naomi Joy had disappeared, but Daed and Jacob were both there, sitting at the table with cups of coffee and a plate of cookies. Becky covered Emma with her pink blanket, then went to the door to retrieve her shoes before she sat down to pull them on.

"You're teaching Jacob bad habits," Becky said. "He'll be expecting his future frau to keep his cookie jar full."

When Becky looked at Daed, he smiled and shrugged. "Jah. But you're...." He hesitated for a moment. "Any well-trained Amish girl would be up to the challenge, ain't so?" His eyes issued a challenge. Or at least seemed to.

Any well-trained Amish girl? Or her?

"You ready, Bex?" Jacob drained his coffee cup.

"Jah. Jah, I'm ready." Well, aside from her still-queasy stomach. And her out-of-control emotions screaming for her to kiss Jacob with all the passion bottled up inside her, then beg him for the right to be the frau keeping his cookie jar full.

Daed pushed himself to his feet. "Have fun, you two. Don't worry about anything, Becky. Emma will be fine. You just relax and try to enjoy yourself." He carried the two empty cups to the sink. As he left the room, he looked over his shoulder and added, "And don't forget to smile."

⋙⋘

Jacob wondered if Becky's smile function might be permanently broken. Her mouth didn't even flicker when Daniel issued that final directive. For a second, he considered using his thumbs to press those soft lips into a smile, but he quickly dismissed that idea. Touching her right now would be like putting a lit match to a piece of paper.

He needed to get her to the relative safety of the frolic. At least there, they wouldn't be alone, and she would have less need to be fearful.

"I have the buggy hitched and ready to go." Jacob nodded toward the door, trying to ignore the expression in Becky's eyes. It seemed to be a mixture of fear and anticipation, but it made him want to scoop her up and carry her off someplace where she would never be hurt again.

She nodded, then turned to peek in Emma's cradle once more, adjusting the blanket, before following him to the door.

"Maybe I should take you by McDonald's first for a fancy coffee, ain't so?" he teased. "Take the buggy through the drive-through?"

"That'd be out of the way." She pressed her lips together in a tight, thin line.

"Jah, but worth it if it'd make you happy."

"I'll be fine."

"Afterwards, then." Jacob offered his hand, but when she shook her head, he stood by and watched her climb into the buggy without help. Then, he went around to the other side, climbed up into the seat, lifted the reins, and guided the horse toward the road. "Aw, Bex, this isn't a death sentence. It's a birthday frolic. For your cousin. Loosen up."

Her hands curled into fists. He braced, expecting one of them to come flying in his direction. Though maybe he did deserve it. That comment was rather callous, now that he thought about it.

"I didn't mean that the way it sounded. I meant... um...." What did he mean?

She glared at him. "You meant I need to loosen up. And I suppose you've got that magic little brown bottle hidden away under the seat. All I have to do is reach under there, and.... You know, maybe you'd better let me out now." Her voice thickened.

Okay, that apology hadn't gone over so well. "Huh? What little brown bottle?"

He watched as she leaned over and reached her hand under the seat. She groped around there for a minute before he realized what she was talking about. His eyes widened in shock. "Nein, Bex. I don't drink, and I would never dream of asking you to." He flicked the reins, hoping she had never gotten drunk. Or even tasted the stuff. He hoped she'd never experienced anything so ugly. "I just want you to enjoy yourself." But maybe she'd already decided that she wouldn't have any fun. And if she had—well, there was nothing he could do. "Don't sabotage our evening. Please."

She straightened, her eyes brightening. "I'll try not to."

"Gut." Maybe there was some hope after all.

Jacob pulled into Ben's yard, which was already crowded with buggies. They were late, but there was nothing like making an entrance. With a smile, he hopped out of the buggy and headed around to the other side, surprised for a moment by the sinful pride that came from knowing he'd have the lovely Becky on his arm. But it wasn't for his own good; he'd be showing Ben and his friends that Daniel's Becky was someone worth spending time with.

God, forgive me for my pride, he prayed. *Help her to have fun.*

As Becky turned to climb down, excitement coursed through his veins. Without a thought, he reached up and grasped her around the waist, lifted her down, then swung her around in a circle. Her eyes widened, and she grabbed his shoulders, her hands twisting his suspenders. "Jacob!"

∾⊰∾

"Sorry." He put her down, the light in his eyes anything but apologetic. With an arm around her shoulders, he guided her toward the field, where she could see the bonfire already burning brightly.

Judging by the bounce in Jacob's step, Becky would say he couldn't wait to be out and around people. He must have been pretty popular back in

Pennsylvania. She wondered if Missouri would have a vibrant enough social scene to hold him.

She didn't think it would. His friends and family were all back there. He had no one here, except for her kin. No girl, no friends, no relatives. Though he did seem to be trying to make the best of it. Getting out to meet people would be a good thing.

Although with her at his side, maybe not so much.

As they neared the crowd of young people, Jacob released her, perhaps thinking better of the intimate gesture. Maybe, despite his words, he was ashamed to be associated that closely with her in public. He strode beside her, his walk turning into something that reminded her of a rooster strutting before the hens. As they entered the crowd, he held his hands high in the air, and some of the guys in the group came up and slapped them.

Becky stopped walking to watch the exchange. What exactly was Jacob doing? And how on earth was she supposed to act while her date made such a spectacle of himself? Ignore him? She'd seen other Amish men do this, but never anyone she was with.

Jacob was well ahead of her when another man came out of the crowd toward him. "Jacob Miller, is that you?"

The next thing she knew, both men had their arms around each other in a bear hug, arms slapping each other's back.

So much for thinking he had few friends. She didn't recognize the Amish man he was with, though, so she turned away to look for a quiet place to stand—someplace where she could observe the festivities and remain invisible.

Something she did better than most.

If only she'd brought a book along.

Would Daed be upset if she walked home early without Jacob? Would that be construed as being rude to his guest?

All she knew was that if Jacob had invited her on the rebound to help him get over his Susie, he didn't need Becky. He'd already forgotten about her.

She glanced over at the group of Amish young people and gasped as a man caught her eye. He raised his eyebrows, his mouth curling, and turned to say something to the person he stood with. The girl turned around and stared at her. Then, she whispered something to the man and laughed before nudging another friend and pointing in Becky's direction.

Becky let out a deep sigh. So much for Jacob's promise to stay right by her side.

Chapter 22

Jacob couldn't believe it. One of his best friends from Pennsylvania, Matthew Yoder, stood before him. When they pulled apart from their embrace, Jacob found it difficult to stop smiling. He wondered if Joshua Esh had come, too. "Hey, I'd like you to meet Becky." He turned to introduce her to Matthew. "Bex, this is one of my best friends—Bex?" She wasn't there. He looked all around. Not a sign of her. She must have found her friend—the one she'd asked about tonight. Annie. He'd catch up with her later, he supposed.

But maybe he should look for her now. He didn't want her to be alone. Why had she wandered away without telling him?

"Didn't take you long to find a new girl," Matthew commented quietly. His eyes narrowed but then brightened again a moment later. "I did hear Susie's been seeing someone else, though."

"Jah, she asked me for a break." Jacob nodded. But then, he hadn't written to acknowledge the break. He wondered again if it would it be official only when he did. He shrugged, making a mental note to write later that evening, if possible.

"She asked you?" Matthew's eyes widened. "I thought she was totally into you."

Jacob shrugged. "She said she didn't want to sit home alone. Besides, I was going to ask her for a break. I got here and met Bex." He glanced around again. Where was she? "Bex is amazing." He eyed a group of giggling females standing on the other side of the fire. He'd never met Becky's friend Annie. He had no idea who any of the girls were. He couldn't remember meeting any of them before—but he might have. He searched from face to face but didn't see Becky. The one he'd come with. The only one he cared for.

He needed to check on her, especially with her fears and her "reputation," according to Ben. "I really want you to meet her. But I don't see her right now. Want to help me look?" He hoped no one had her cornered while he spit insults at her. Though surely no one would be cruel enough for that. Behind her back, maybe. But not to her face.

Matthew raised his eyebrows. "Uh, jah. Blonde hair or dark?"

"Blonde. Blue eyes. Prettiest girl here. Stands about so tall." Jacob held up a hand slightly below his shoulder to indicate her height. How could he have lost her? He'd thought she was right beside him. He strode back in the direction he'd come. Where exactly had he let go of her? He wouldn't make that mistake again.

He and Matthew walked all the way back to the buggy, but still they didn't see her. As they retraced their steps back to the field, they caught up on news.

"Maybe she went inside to use the bathroom?" Matthew suggested when they neared the house.

Jacob shrugged. "Could be." He could have checked, but his instincts told him that wouldn't be where he'd find her. "Let's look in the barn first."

The lanterns cast a flickering glow across the barn, but that didn't stop some people from going in there, sitting on hay bales and talking or swinging from the loft on a long rope.

Jacob gave the big room a quick once-over. Not seeing Becky, he headed back to look in the chicken coop, the cow room, the horse stalls, and several other small rooms. There were lofts, too—some high ones—but he didn't see any sign of her there, either.

Surely she wouldn't have crawled into a loft to hide.

Another possibility hit him hard. What if she'd been overwhelmed when they'd arrived and had turned around to walk home? Without even saying good-bye? Ouch. He shut his eyes. What would Daniel say about that?

Even more important, what would he say to her when he found her?

That brought him back to his original question: Why would she leave without telling him? She had to know he'd be worried sick about her.

He looked around the barn once more, but she was definitely not in there.

"She's around someplace. Maybe she went to the haus for some reason," Matthew suggested again. "Or maybe she'll be back out by the fire now. Is this girl that important to you?"

Matt was a good friend to help him hunt like this. Kind of reminded Jacob of the time they looked for Mathew's little sister when she went missing. The child had been there one minute and gone the next. They'd finally found her sound asleep on the floor underneath her bed. They'd been pretty frantic by then.

"Jah, she's pretty special. She made me rethink my relationship with Susie."

"Avoiding the *l* word, though, ain't so?"

Jacob laughed. "Too soon to tell. I am interested in courting her."

"Whoa, really? This fast? You sure you aren't on the rebound? I mean, since Susie asked you for a break and all."

Jacob shrugged. "Not on the rebound. I told you that I was considering a break even before Susie told me about Timothy." He tried to push aside his concerns about Becky. "Well, like you said, maybe she's outside. She's definitely not in here. So, where are you staying?"

"The Stoltzfus family is putting me up, and they offered me a job in their carpentry shop. They have a haus full of kinner, but it isn't so bad. I'm sharing a room with their two buwe. Kind of reminds me of home." Matthew chuckled. "They told me that their pond is a gut spot for fishing. Care to check it out tomorrow?"

"Jah, that'd be gut. I haven't been fishing since last summer."

They walked out of the barn and headed toward the bonfire. As they passed a tree, Jacob noticed someone sitting there, leaning against the trunk. Becky. She watched the activities but made no attempt to join in. He grinned, relieved he'd found her, yet saddened that she wasn't with her friends.

"There you are, Bex! I've been hunting all over for you." Jacob crouched beside her. "Are you okay?"

She swallowed. "Jah."

"Why are you hiding? You'll never find any of your friends if you stay out of sight."

She shook her head. "I couldn't find Annie."

Was Annie her only friend? Jacob frowned. "Scared of what people might say, Bex?" He stood and held out his hand. "Kum."

After a moment's hesitation, Becky put her hand in his and allowed him to tug her to her feet. She glanced at Matthew and blushed. Jacob hoped she wasn't bothered by what he'd said.

"This is one of my best friends, Matthew Yoder from Pennsylvania," Jacob said. "He came down to be part of the swap. Matthew, this is Becky Troyer." He swung an arm over her shoulders and pulled her close.

"Nice to meet you, Becky." Matthew smiled. "You're right, Jacob. She is the prettiest one here. Maybe if you change your mind..." he teased.

"Not happening." Jacob grinned back at him and hugged Becky tighter.

He felt her wince, but she nodded to Matthew. "Nice to meet you, too, Matthew. Welkum to Missouri. Ach, look. There's Annie." She pointed in the direction of the buggies, where Jacob saw two girls walking. "Kum, I'll introduce you both."

She slipped out of Jacob's embrace and headed toward a black-haired girl. "Annie!" Jacob and Matthew followed her.

Annie stopped and smiled when she saw Becky. "You came!" She glanced behind her at Jacob and Matthew, her eyes narrowed in confusion. Then, a flush of what looked like anger flashed across her face, highlighted by the flicker of the fire. She straightened, her back stiff. "Shoo. Go sniff after some other girl. Leave Becky alone."

Jacob stared at her in confusion. Hadn't Becky said this Annie taught in the one-room schoolhouse? She certainly had the sternness necessary. He felt like a naughty boy being scolded. Nice Becky had a friend willing to look out for her, though.

Becky reached behind her and clasped Jacob's arm. After a second, she slid her hand down to grasp his. She shook her head. "This is Jacob Miller from Pennsylvania. The one I told you about. And this is Jacob's friend, Matthew Yoder."

Annie tilted her head and narrowed her eyes even more. She assessed Jacob, studying him as if judging his worthiness of her friend's attention. Jacob wondered what Becky had told Annie about him. He hoped it was good.

Annie finally smiled. "Nice to meet you both. Now, I must find Ben and tell him happy birthday."

"We haven't talked to him yet, either. We'll go with you," Jacob said. He turned to Matthew. "Have you met Ben?"

"Nein, not yet. I came with Joseph; he's one of the buwe I'm rooming with." Matthew looked around and pointed toward the fire. "He's over there. He was going to introduce me, but then I saw you first."

"I can introduce you around," Annie offered. "Both of you. Though Jacob might have met most everyone already."

That was probably true, though he didn't remember anyone's name. Except for Ben, and now Annie.

Jacob adjusted his hand so that his fingers intertwined with Becky's. He didn't intend to let her out of his sight again.

He supposed that the two of them would be fodder for gossip, but he didn't mind so much. He'd seen the looks sent their way and the cupped hands concealing whispers. He wasn't sure if the stir was because of Becky's attendance or because she and her beau were being so demonstrative, but he shrugged it off. He'd never seen the point in trying to keep relationships a secret, anyway. People always found out. Might as well be up-front and open about it from the beginning. And if it kept people from matching Becky up with men like Amos, so much the better.

"I see Ben, right over there." Annie pointed to the far side of the bonfire. Then, with a glance around at the three of them that came just short of saying, "Line up now, scholars," she led the way over.

Jacob resisted the urge to fall in line and march like a soldier. He wondered if Becky and Matt felt the same way.

Matthew glanced at Jacob, eyes narrowed, brow furrowed in concern. Jacob grinned and mouthed "schoolteacher." Matthew nodded.

Jah, she must be a wonderful teacher.

Ben saw them coming, and his grin widened but abruptly turned into a scowl. Probably because he saw Jacob holding Becky's hand.

Jacob heard a tiny gasp come from Becky and felt her give a small tug to release herself.

He held on tighter.

When Ben's eyes met his, Jacob lifted his chin, daring Ben to make something of it. *Just don't get involved with Daniel's Becky....* The refrain rose to the surface of his memory.

The way Becky tensed up beside him, he knew she remembered it, too.

"Proverbs thirty-one, Ben," Jacob said with a grin. "Might want to read it sometime."

Ben's eyes widened slightly, and he glanced quickly at Becky.

So did Jacob. Color flooded her cheeks, and she dipped her head. Beside her, Annie fixed her gaze on Jacob with something like respect shining in her eyes. A small smile appeared on her lips.

But her words were directed toward Ben. "Happy birthday."

Jacob, Becky, and Matthew chorused the words after her. Then, Jacob gestured toward Matthew. "This is one of my best friends from Pennsylvania, Matthew Yoder. Matthew, this is Becky's cousin, Ben Troyer."

"Nice to meet you, Ben," Matthew said.

Ben found his manners. "Nice to meet you, too, Matthew. Glad you could kum. Food's set up over there by the haus. You should have some cake. Mamm made my favorite. It's a white cake with Jell-O poured in."

"Sounds gut," Jacob said. "We'll see you later, then."

"Jah. I'm going to see about getting a volleyball game going." Ben nodded toward the net set up on the near side of the barn.

Jacob turned, still holding Becky's hand, and they headed toward the tables piled high with finger food. He couldn't hold back a grin. Ben had heard his message about Becky loud and clear. And, hopefully, that message would get around.

After filling their plates, he and Becky, along with Matthew and Annie, found a place to sit where they could watch the frolic yet still visit.

Jacob didn't know how much time passed while they sat and talked, getting to know each other better. Neither he nor Matthew went to join the volleyball game. But with the rosy glow of the sunset long gone, and Annie yawning, it was probably time to head home. Several Amish teens had already left.

Jacob stood and stretched.

"Time to go?" Becky looked up at him.

"Jah," Annie said, getting to her feet. "I'm going to go straight to bed. Our rooster has got his internal alarm clock off and has been crowing at awful early hours. Daed is threatening to make him our dinner."

Matthew chuckled. "I see Joseph over there playing volleyball. Guess I could work my way into the game until he's ready to go." He nodded toward Annie, then Becky. "See you later. Tomorrow, Jacob." He strode off.

"You ready, Bex?"

Becky nodded, helping Annie gather the paper dishes before she stood. "Jah. Just let me throw these into the fire."

Jacob trailed the girls to the fire, then found Ben to say good night. Finally, he tucked Becky's hand into the crook of his arm and escorted her out into the darkness where the buggies waited. He tried to remember where they'd parked and, when he couldn't, wondered how they'd find Daniel's buggy.

Becky didn't seem to have that problem. She led him right to it, taking the time to pat the gelding on the nose and hand it a bit of carrot. "Gut, Shakespeare. Did you have a nice visit with the other horses?"

Jacob laughed, amused at Becky talking to the horse as if she expected it to answer. "Shakespeare, huh? Why'd you name him after some playwright?"

Becky gave him a mischievous glance. "That is what Daed brought home from the library the winter he gave me the horse. A big, thick book."

Jacob shook his head. "And you actually read it?"

"It took me a while. Daed had to renew it twice."

"You still want to go to McDonald's for that fancy coffee, ain't so?" Jacob asked when Becky was settled in the buggy.

She shook her head. "It's awful late for a cappuccino. That would keep us up all night."

"I should have taken you there first." He quirked his mouth. "But you're right. Some other time. Besides, Matthew and I talked about going fishing tomorrow. How about you and Annie going with us?"

"I have too much work to do in the kitchen tomorrow. This weekend is a church Sunday, and we're hosting it."

Back home in Pennsylvania, the houses were designed with partitions that slid back to make one big room out of several smaller ones for church. Daniel's house wasn't designed that way. "Where will you hold it?"

"The barn." Becky shrugged as if to say, "Where else?"

"Well, you'll have some spare time, ain't so? I'll need you to show me how to get to the haus where Matthew is staying."

She was quiet a moment, then nodded. "I'll go with you and Matthew tomorrow, after the work is done."

❖

Jacob definitely affected her mind. Did she really think that she'd have time to go out and not only show him where his friend lived but also go fishing, when she had her chores to do and her baby to care for?

She wouldn't. Especially the day before church Sunday, when she'd be needed to help clean out the barn and make sure it was ready for the benches to be set up.

Though Daed would have Jacob out there helping to set things up, too. The whole family worked together, especially after the cooking was done.

In fact, she should have stayed home and helped out tonight instead of running off to the frolic. But she had enjoyed sitting and talking with Jacob, Annie, and Matthew. She'd even harbored brief daydreams of Annie and Matthew maybe starting to court, but she hadn't seen any sparks between them tonight. Nothing besides casual interest.

Had Annie and Matthew seen the attraction she felt for Jacob?

Probably so. Annie was pretty astute. She always figured out who was courting whom long before Becky did. Of course, Annie usually attended the frolics and singings.

At least, she had until Luke jumped the fence.

Becky thought this was the first frolic Annie had attended since then, but she wasn't sure.

She let her mind wander back over the evening. Ben had seemed so shocked when Jacob had shown up with her and called her a Proverbs 31 woman. She'd need to reread that chapter sometime, but it seemed that was his way of telling Ben that she was worthy.

Worthy.

She pulled in a deep breath, tears burning her eyes.

If only she could believe that.

Jacob reached out and let his arm settle on the back of the buggy seat. In a few minutes, his arm was wrapped around her shoulders, and he pulled her against him. "Want to go someplace and talk? I'm not ready to go back home yet."

Talk? Alone? Becky swallowed. Ach, but she was torn. She wanted to go talk, to hear him say what he really thought of her, convince her of her worth. But what if he couldn't? And the truth was, she was ready to go home. It was long past Emma's feeding time, but Mamm had probably given her some formula already. Becky couldn't use her boppli as an excuse.

Jacob's hand lazily traced figures on her shoulder.

If they were going to talk, then McDonald's would be a good place. But the sensations she felt didn't have much to do with wanting to talk. Besides, they were already going the opposite way. Becky swallowed. "Nein. I need to get home. Emma might need me." She shrugged, instantly ashamed of her lie.

She felt Jacob's chest rise and fall with the breath he took. "Jah, probably so. Then, I'll be looking forward to tomorrow."

His hand brushed against the bare skin of her neck. Accidentally, she was sure. But still, she shivered from the contact.

She needed distance—physical and emotional. Ach, if only she could bring Susie up again. But then, why not?

She did want to know if Jacob had decided to court her on the rebound. He'd said he'd wanted a break, but maybe he was just trying to save face after being dumped by his Susie.

She gave him a sidelong look. "Does it bother you, Susie dating Timothy?"

Jacob's fingers froze. His hand moved off her shoulder. After another moment, he slid his arm from the back of the buggy seat and grasped the reins with both hands.

Ach. Why couldn't she leave well enough alone? Jacob probably thought she yanked him like a yo-yo, though she felt the same way inside.

For a moment, she heard nothing but the rumble of buggy wheels and the clomping of horse hooves. Then, he finally spoke. "Does it bother you, being courted by me? Is that why you keep bringing up Susie?"

❦

He'd probably sounded harsher than he intended, which would explain why she'd winced. But he'd said he wanted to court her; he'd told her that he wanted to think about them as a couple, and that the intent was there to make a promise. Why did she insist on asking about his former love?

Jacob expelled his breath with force. Nein, he hadn't been in love with Susie, not really. Though what it would have been called, he wasn't sure. Puppy love, perhaps? One thing he'd learned is that an instant flash of attraction doesn't mean love. He had courted Susie, which had been all her idea. Come to think of it, she was the one who had brought up marriage and talked about it as if it were a decided fact. And he'd gone along with it, never giving much thought as to whether they should take that step. They had always disagreed about whether to join the church—Jacob wanted to be a member of the community and not an outcast, and Daed would have shunned him, even if the church wouldn't have, if he'd left before baptism.

Susie wanted to leave the Amish. She'd chafed at the rules. She'd even gotten her hair cut super-short and styled it in spikes colored redder than her natural strawberry blonde. At home, she'd hid it under her prayer kapp, and Jacob didn't know if her parents had ever found out she'd cut it. He'd hated her new hairstyle. Begged her to grow it out.

Jah, with hindsight, he could see why Daed was set against Susie. Especially now that Jacob had met Becky.

Sweet, quiet, steady, dependable Becky.

The type of woman any good Amish man would dream of marrying. The kind he could take home to Mamm and Daed without being ashamed. Daed would be thrilled to know about Becky.

He opened his mouth to say something else when Becky stayed quiet. But he didn't know what to say. Always Susie between them.

His heart stuttered as he wondered if Daed and Daniel might have planned this out in advance. Knowing how Daed had wanted him away from Susie enough to lie about the reasons for his trip, and knowing how Daniel had tried his hand at matchmaking, he wouldn't be surprised. But then, how could they have known? Hoped, maybe. But they couldn't have known for certain that he would be attracted to her.

He glanced at Becky, surprised to hear a sniff. Her face was turned away from him, but it didn't take much imagination to realize she was crying. Or trying not to.

She hadn't answered his questions. Ach, he must have been harsher than he'd realized.

But then, he hadn't answered hers, either.

And he still didn't know what to say. Could he explain Susie's pushiness and rebellion in a way Becky would understand?

Chapter 23

J acob drove the buggy down the driveway and
parked it in the barn. Becky tried to keep the tears
from falling, but every now and then, one crept out
of the corner of her eye, ran down her cheek, and
dripped off her chin.

Jah, Jacob was on the rebound. He didn't say it,
but then, he didn't have to. He'd answered her question with a question. And she couldn't answer him
without betraying her heart.

Jacob engaged the brake and hopped down from
the buggy, coming around to her side before she had a
chance to gather her skirts enough to turn sideways.
The next thing she knew, he had lifted her down and
pulled her into his arms. His strong hug felt comforting. Warm. Safe.

His chest rose as he drew in a breath. "Bex,
I'm sorry. Susie and I...I mean, I...um, nein. It didn't
bother me when Susie asked for a break. I planned
to ask her for one, anyway, and I...well, as far as I'm
concerned, Susie and I are over. And now I'm wondering whether I ever loved her. I think not. After all,
would I be here courting you if I'd been in love with
her? Nein, I'd be hopping on a bus back home and
trying to win her back, ain't so?"

She supposed that made sense. Relief washed
through her.

His hands flattened against her back, pulling her nearer. "I haven't written to tell her about you, but I'm sure she'll be just as pleased that I found someone as I was to hear she did."

Becky blinked. "You're going to tell Susie about me?" Not a good idea. She couldn't imagine how Susie would react to that news.

"Jah. Why not? I'm not ashamed of you." He lifted a shoulder in a carefree shrug.

Why not? Men were so clueless. She could think of a million reasons why not.

Number one on the list was the phrase "Ich liebe dich" that Susie had written at the end of her letter.

But how could Becky tell him that? She pulled away from him. "I need to go."

He released her but still blocked her way. "But you didn't answer my question, Bex. Do you want to be courted by me? Simple answer. Jah or nein. Pick one."

Simple answer? If only he knew that it was anything but simple. She studied the dirt by their feet, wanting to say "Jah." Truly, she did. But she couldn't think of how to say it without sounding breathless with longing. She couldn't give him that power. He'd end up hurting her, destroying her dreams—dreams that had only dared to peek out of the ground since being nurtured by the warmth of Jacob's attention.

But she couldn't say "Nein," either. That word would sound the death knell of their relationship, for sure.

And she was still torn up inside over so many little things. What would Daed say if Jacob started courting her? On second thought, that wouldn't be an issue. Daed seemed to be treating Jacob more like a son every day.

The biggest question was, How did she know she could trust him?

Words. All words.

Jacob seemed to pick up on her hesitation. He sighed and stepped out of her way. "I'm going to pretend you didn't give me permission to kiss you. Because no promises can be made as long as one of us is uncertain." His voice sounded flat. Resigned. With every bit of life drained out of it.

Guilt ate at her. She hadn't meant to make him feel bad.

"Gut nacht, Bex. I'll see you tomorrow."

⤜⋆⤐

Ach, that hurt. He'd been anticipating their good-night kiss almost the whole way home. Instead, they hadn't kissed, and it seemed they were back on shaky ground. That solid barn wall had resurrected itself, leaving his heart battered and bruised.

After unhitching Shakespeare and putting him up in the stall, Jacob snuck into the dawdi-haus and upstairs to bed. Turning the gas light on in his bedroom, he decided to take a few minutes to write that note to Susie before saying his prayers and crawling into bed. It wouldn't take long.

Thinking of Susie triggered another thought, and he dug into the dark recesses of his suitcase until he found his cell phone. Flipped it on. Low battery. Yeah, he'd figured that. But he hadn't figured on having so many missed calls.

He'd ask Daniel about charging it up tomorrow.

He turned the phone off, slipped it into his pants' pocket, and dug into the suitcase again, looking for the plain white paper and stamped envelopes Mamm had sent with him when she'd given him orders to correspond.

He needed to write another letter home, too. Mamm had sent him at least three letters that he hadn't answered. Other than the letter he'd written when he'd first arrived, he hadn't sent anything home. So much for being a faithful son.

His family would be sleeping now. But what had they done that day? Grossmammi had probably fried up some apple fritters. His stomach rumbled. Best not to think of food at this hour.

He decided to put off writing to his family until he'd written to Susie and officially ended that relationship. It was done. Finished.

No matter what happened with Becky.

Dear Susie,

Danki for your note. Glad you are doing well. I had a gut trip down to Missouri. Cousin Daniel has a blacksmith shop and has been teaching me.

He also has a daughter named Becky. I think I'm in love with her. I've never felt this way before. So I'm glad you asked me for a break.

I wish you the best with Timothy.

Jacob

He slipped the letter into an envelope, addressed it, and pulled the plastic strip off the flap to seal it. There.

And now, to write to Mamm and Daed. They would want to hear all the details of everything he hadn't shared in his first letter, from the hot, smelly, dirty job as a blacksmith to the lack of apple trees on Daniel's property, on down the list to his growing attraction for Becky. He might even tell them about her hesitation where he was concerned, so they would know that it was possible nothing would come of their relationship.

He tapped his pen against the paper.

Dear Mamm and Daed,....

⸎

It was still dark outside when someone shook Becky's shoulder, rousing her from her troubled dreams. "Rise and shine," Mamm said cheerfully. "Lots to do today, daughter."

Becky wanted to roll over, bury her face in the pillow, and go right back to sleep. But Katie was already out of bed and bustling around, and even though Mamm had left the room after waking her, she would return if Becky didn't make an appearance in a short while.

She rubbed her gritty eyes. That was her reward for crying herself to sleep, then shedding more tears during Emma's 2:00 a.m. feeding.

Her bleak situation didn't look any brighter this morning than when she'd stumbled to her room last night.

As long as one of us is uncertain....

She didn't know how to take that. Her feelings were certain; she just didn't know how to express them. Or even why he wanted to court her. She was the one with the past. He must not be thinking clearly, because he wouldn't want her if he was.

Jah, he was the one who was uncertain. At least, he should be.

Which ultimately meant that she would be wise to guard her heart.

Any hope she'd been cultivating had just gotten a bad case of frostbite.

She put her dress on, securing it with pins, and roughly pulled her hair back and up, smashing her kapp down on top of it. Then, leaving Emma asleep in the crib, she hurried downstairs.

She tried not to let it bother her when Jacob strode in with his usual, cheery "Gut morning, Bex."

Just as if her dreams hadn't been squashed like a bug underfoot.

Chapter 24

Jacob noticed that Becky looked tired, but that didn't seem to slow her down at all. Even though she yawned, she still worked circles around him as he helped the family get the barn ready for Sunday services. He didn't know how clean they expected the barn to be, but he did as he was told. In addition, he helped carry in the benches and spread around copies of the Ausbund.

It was mid-afternoon before things slowed enough for Jacob to work up his courage to approach Becky about the fishing trip they'd planned. He hoped she'd still go with him. Even if she didn't, he still needed directions—not necessarily from her, but it'd give him an excuse to talk to her. Maybe the chance to touch her soft cheek.

He shoved his shaking hands into his pockets as he followed her to the barn door. One of his hands bumped against something hard. Ach, his cell phone. He frowned and changed course to talk to Daniel. He watched Becky scurry away.

Daniel looked at the phone and whispered, "You'll want a place to plug that in, ain't so?" He glanced around and leaned forward, as if afraid the mice would overhear. "I have mine on a charger in the shop when the generator's running. Do you want to go back and turn it on now, or can you wait until Monday?"

"Monday's fine." Jacob slid the phone back inside his pocket. "But if you don't mind, I'll put it out in the shed now so I don't forget to charge it."

"Ser gut." Daniel nodded. "What are your plans for this afternoon?"

Jacob shrugged. "Becky and I had talked about going fishing with some friends, unless you have something else for me to do." And if Becky hadn't changed her mind. They hadn't exactly parted on good terms last night.

"Nein. Fishing's fine. Go on, then. It's a gut thing you're doing, getting Becky out like this." He clapped a hand on Jacob's shoulder. "She's learning to live again."

Was she? Jacob didn't know.

Daniel sighed. "Haven't seen her smile since she got involved with that Englisch bu."

Jacob hadn't seen a difference there. He had yet to see her truly smile. Even so, he nodded, then went to look for Becky, stopping first in the blacksmith shop to drop off his cell phone. Becky had gone back to the house a little while ago to take care of Emma. At least, that was what she'd announced moments before she'd left. He swallowed hard as he entered the kitchen, trying to force the lump in his throat down to his stomach.

He had every reason to be afraid of her response. He steeled his heart for her rejection.

Becky leaned over the cradle, gently placing the boppli in the center of a soft knitted blanket. She folded the edges up over Emma, cooing as she did so. The boppli stared up at her adoringly.

Jacob cleared his throat.

Becky straightened and faced him. "Ach, Jacob. I didn't hear you kum in."

He nodded. "Jah." He glanced down again at the boppli, who was now staring at him, unblinking, as if she understood he wanted to spirit her mamm away. It almost made him feel guilty. "Uh, are you free to go fishing?"

Her mouth opened and shut. Then, she nodded. "Let me tell Mamm that we're leaving."

She wasn't going to refuse? Joy burst upon him like morning sunshine.

"I should pack a picnic supper, ain't so?" she said.

His eyes widened. He hadn't thought about supper, but it would probably be past the dinner hour when they got home. His stomach rumbled just thinking about food. He nodded. "Maybe we should take Emma with us, too. That way, you won't have to worry about her." And she wouldn't be able to use her as an excuse to cut the evening short.

⌘

Weak. That's what she was. She should have refused and cut herself loose while she had the chance. But nein. She had to go and accept. Like she couldn't get enough of Jacob. She had to soak up every bit of his attention to store away in her mind and remember someday.

If only she'd been able to say jah to him last night. One simple word. Just jah.

She pulled in a breath and opened her mouth to say it now, but the word wouldn't come out. She almost choked when it lodged in her throat.

With a sigh, she moved past Jacob to the gas-powered refrigerator, then opened the door and took out an assortment of picnic items: peeled and cut carrots, celery sticks, sliced cheese, meat, and bread. From the shelf, she took down a wicker basket and began filling it with the food. "Should I pack enough for Matthew, too?"

"Jah. And for Annie, if you think she can join us."

Becky knew she wasn't good enough for Jacob, even if he seemed to think so. But Annie would be. Maybe this would be an opportunity for Jacob to get to know Annie better. She nodded, suddenly glad that her voice had gotten stuck. But her next thought hit her like a blow: How could she stand by and watch Jacob and her best friend—her only friend, really—fall in love?

She wanted him for herself.

She'd lose Annie as a friend.

"How can I help?" Jacob still stood there by the cradle, looking lost.

She wanted to tell him to pull her into his arms and hold her like he'd never let her go. Instead, common sense took over. "Choose a few apples." She pointed at the bowl of fruit in the middle of the kitchen table. "Or bananas, if you'd rather."

"Apples are great." Jacob selected four and put them in the basket, nestled beside the sandwich supplies. "Do you want your sling?" He glanced at the hook by the door where it hung.

"Jah, maybe so."

He lifted it down, then nodded toward the door. "I'm going to get your horse and buggy ready while you finish up. I'll be right back to help."

"Danki." Becky stood and watched as he left the kitchen again, this time with a bounce in his step, as if he was happy about going fishing and seeing his friend again.

Of course, she would be if she were in his situation.

She went into the other room and found a couple of old blankets to spread on the grass. It might be a warm spring day, but it would still be chilly for Emma without some protection from the cold ground.

The blanket was where Becky would sit, as well, watching Jacob have a good time with his friend. Her heart sank at the thought that he'd invited her only because she knew the way to the home where Matthew was staying rather than because he really wanted her along.

Matthew had mentioned the pond on the farm where he lived as a good place to fish, since the family he stayed with kept it well stocked. Jacob loaded the supplies he'd borrowed from Daniel, including fishing poles and lures, into the back of the buggy. It would be great to visit with Matthew and maybe get to know Becky a little bit more, without putting the pressure of a date on her. Especially since she didn't seem certain about wanting him to court her. Fine. He'd settle for being just friends for now.

Sometimes, he wondered why he didn't just give up, since she didn't seem to be more than mildly interested.

But she gave him just enough tiny morsels of encouragement to keep him trying, like today, when she'd agreed to go fishing with him.

But then, Daniel thought Jacob was helping Becky. He almost laughed. What Daniel saw in him, he surely didn't know.

Jacob heaved a sigh, rubbed his eyes, and went to get Shakespeare out of the stall. A nap sounded good. He and Becky had been out pretty late last night, and on top of that, he'd stayed up even later writing those letters and then taking them out to the mailbox before he forgot to send them. Maybe after supper he could stretch out on the ground and rest. If he happened to fall asleep, well, Matthew would still be there. Becky would be safe with him.

Jacob hitched the horse to the buggy, released the brake, and drove to the house. After resettling the brake, he went inside. Becky had set the basket and a couple of blankets on the table beside the sling and a small diaper bag. She reached into the cradle and wrapped her boppli in her pink blanket.

"Ready?"

She stood there a moment, her brow wrinkled as if weighing her options, or maybe looking for a good reason to refuse. Jacob felt hope drain out of him. If she said nein, he'd...what? Ask Daniel for that promised ticket home?

Nein, he wasn't ready to give up yet. God help him, he did want to make Becky his bride.

He'd renewed this resolve every time he'd seen that Amos Kropf on the property that week. He'd been hard-pressed not to run and protect her every time the man had appeared.

"Jah, I'm ready."

Whew. Jacob refrained from wiping his brow. That would have been too dramatic, and she might have been offended by his sarcasm. "Gut. Let's go, then." He picked up the basket with his right hand and tucked the blankets under his left arm. Then, he watched as Becky put on the sling, lifted Emma out of her cradle, and picked up the diaper bag. He turned and held the door for her, and together they walked to the buggy, where he loaded everything into the back. He held Emma while Becky climbed in and then handed the boppli up to her. Becky secured the sling.

Boppli were lots of work.

No wonder she looked tired. She probably needed a nap, too.

As they rode down the road in silence toward Annie's house, Jacob wished for a renewal of the friendship he'd struggled to develop with Becky. He couldn't see what he'd done wrong. He'd asked for an answer to a simple question. Nothing difficult in that. Then, he'd corralled his wild emotions long enough to put a halt to the physical side of their relationship until Becky was sure how she felt about him. Maybe that had been the wrong thing to do. Perhaps kissing her senseless would have clarified the matter.

Women. Such confusing creatures.

He glanced at Becky, then pulled the buggy to the side of the road and reined in the horse. He owed it to himself to try to understand, to fix the problem if he could. "Bex, are you angry with me?"

Chapter 25

Becky stared at him. Was she angry? How could he ask that? "Nein. Not angry."

Hurt, jah. But not angry.

Jacob glanced away and looked down the road, maybe checking for oncoming traffic, then looked back at her. "What did I do?"

That settled it. Men were clueless. How could she spell out everything he'd done? Did he think that her heart didn't need protecting? That, after Kent's rejection, she was just a dry sponge ready to soak up all of his attention?

Okay, she was. But still. He didn't need to know the power he had over her. She had to think of herself here. And he couldn't possibly be sure about his feelings for her. He didn't know her story.

She swallowed. Hard. "What, you expect me to just throw myself in your arms and be grateful for every scrap of attention you pay me? I'm not your dog."

Jacob blinked. After a long silence, he frowned. "You think I treat you like a dog?"

"Look, if you're interested in Annie, just say so. I'm willing to talk to her about you. I'll even say gut things."

He had the sense to look confused. "You think I'm interested in Annie?"

"Isn't that why you wanted to invite her?"

He shook his head. "How did we go from my treating you like a dog to being interested in Annie?"

It didn't seem like such a leap to her.

His lips parted, and he stared at her, then shook his head again. "I'm sorry if it seems I treat you like a dog. I don't know what I did to give you that impression, but I'm sorry. As for Annie, nein, I am not even remotely interested in her. I've told you that it's you I'm interested in. I just thought maybe you would be more comfortable if she were with us. And, since she isn't seeing anyone, I thought Matthew might be interested." Jacob shrugged.

Okay, now she was the one rendered speechless. How could she have been so far off target? He'd wanted to have her friend along to help her feel more comfortable. That was so sweet.

He waited a beat. Or two. "Are we gut, then?"

She shook her head. "You said you were uncertain." She hoped she didn't sound as pathetic as she felt, begging for that needed scrap of attention.

Jacob furrowed his brow and blinked again. "I did?"

"Jah, last night."

His eyes widened. "Ach, nein. I said that promises couldn't be made as long as one of us was uncertain."

She shrugged. The repetition hurt just as much as it had last night.

He caught her gaze and held it. "I'm certain, Bex. You're the one who needs to decide."

～※～

She fell silent again. Jacob studied her, the curve of her cheek, the set of her mouth, and the way she avoided looking at him. Jah, she needed to decide how she felt about him. Had Kent done this to her, made her so fearful? Was it possible that her reticence was not a judgment of him but a revelation of the condition of her hurting heart?

She pulled the boppli closer to her side. Out of the corner of his eye, Jacob noticed movement, and he glanced behind the buggy to see a car approaching. A bright-red one.

It looked suspiciously like the one Kent had been driving when he'd left McDonald's that day. The car flew past, too close to the buggy, undoubtedly exceeding the speed limit.

Jacob flicked the reins and pulled out behind it. He should have found someplace more secluded than the side of the road. That had been unsafe. Besides, they had so much more that they needed to say to each other. He supposed that would be a conversation for another day.

He took a glance in her direction. "You let me know when you decide. Until then, I'm here."

She nodded but didn't give him the affirmation he longed for. Couldn't she forget herself long enough to say, "Jah, I'm interested in you, too"? Or maybe, "Jah, I want you to court me, Jacob"? Or, well, just anything?

Except "Nein." He didn't want to hear that.

Instead, she twisted her skirt with her hands. Must be a nervous habit.

Lord, help her to relax.

"Annie lives there, jah?" He pointed toward the house they approached, recognizing it as the one Becky had mentioned on another drive.

"Jah."

He pulled into the driveway and parked the buggy. "Will she come out, or will you need to go in?"

"I'll go in and make sure she can go."

He nodded. "I'll hold Emma, then." He reached over and lifted the sling off her shoulder, careful to support Emma so that she would not fall out. "Hurry back."

Becky slid out of the buggy and darted toward Annie's house. Jacob watched as she disappeared inside the front door without knocking, though she did call a greeting. Then, he turned his attention to the boppli in his arms. Emma was still wide awake and stared up at him. He swallowed. "Your mamm is a sweetheart, ain't so? But she needs to learn to smile. Can't you make her smile?"

He ran a finger over Emma's cheek. She blinked. Then, her mouth widened into a toothless grin.

Jacob couldn't help but grin back. Ach, if Becky smiled like that, his knees would liquefy, for sure.

He didn't know how long he sat there as he and Emma cuddled and grinned at each other, but Becky finally came back outside with Annie, who climbed into the back of the buggy. "Hi, Jacob."

He tried to wipe the foolish grin off his face. Who would have known a boppli smile would be so contagious? "Annie. Glad you could join us."

"Jah, it'll be fun."

Jacob nodded. He handed Emma back to Becky and waited while she secured the sling again, absently wondering what their children would look like if she ever got around to saying jah.

᪐

An hour later, with dinner finished, Becky watched as Jacob stretched out on a blanket. Matthew stood closer to the water, stringing a fishing rod. Annie handed her the container of celery and carrots as she loaded the leftover food back into the basket.

Jacob squirmed. Maybe trying to find a comfortable spot. "That was ser gut, Bex."

She glanced at him, but his eyes were shut. He opened them briefly and looked up at her. "Want me to cuddle Emma while you finish up?"

She shrugged, lifted Emma out of the sling, and laid her in the crook of his arm, wishing she dared to fill that spot herself. Emma didn't know how lucky she was. Instead, Becky picked up the basket and carried it to the buggy.

Annie followed her. "Pennsylvania sure has some gut-looking men," she said. "Jacob will make a great daed for Emma."

Becky felt the heat flood her cheeks. "You think so?"

"Isn't it obvious?" Annie turned back to look at them. "If it wasn't a sin, I would envy the way Jacob looks at you." She fanned her face with her hand. "I wish someone would look at me that way."

"Matthew is cute, too." Becky glanced over at the man walking down to the bank of the pond. His hair was light brown, or maybe dark blond, and it curled slightly at the ends, a length nearly too long for the Amish look. He'd need a trim soon.

Annie shrugged. "Jah. But there's nothing there. Not like the attraction between you and Jacob. Matthew might end up being a friend."

Becky turned and looked back at the blanket. More specifically, at the man lying on it. Annie thought the attraction between her and Jacob was obvious? Really?

"I know you like him." Annie wasn't going to let it go. "And it's so sweet the way he talked you into courting again. Isn't it great that he's interested in you? You won't be forced to marry that horrible Amos Kropf!" She shuddered.

"Jah." Except that Becky still wasn't sure what would happen with Amos Kropf. He'd been out to the farm a couple of times this past week and asked to see her, but she'd managed to avoid him, disappearing into the attic when she saw his buggy coming and not reappearing until it headed away down the lane after he'd talked with Daed awhile.

"When are the rest of the men from Pennsylvania coming down?" Annie asked.

Becky shook her head. "I don't know. But I hope there'll be someone for you."

Annie shrugged. "Maybe." She grabbed Becky's arm and tugged her farther from the buggy and the men. "So, is it hard to trust Jacob after what Kent did? I'm afraid of being abandoned again, since Luke jumped the fence. I need a man I know will stick around. And you...well, your situation is so much worse."

Becky looked down and lowered her voice. "Jah. It's hard. I can't trust him. Or, maybe it's that I can't trust myself."

Chapter 26

Jacob woke up to water dripping on his face. He opened his eyes and saw Matthew holding a line full of fish over him. Sputtering, Jacob turned his head. "Knock it off!" The sun setting behind Matthew created a colorful background for the fish display. The boppli was still curled up at Jacob's side, sleeping. Becky and Annie sat near him, talking quietly.

Carefully, Jacob moved his arm from beneath Emma's head and lowered her gently onto the blanket, then sat up. "What'd I miss?"

Becky looked over, expressionless, but Annie grinned at him. "Oh, we were just sharing our deepest, darkest secrets. Don't you wish you knew what we had to say about you?"

Jacob laughed. "And I had to sleep through it."

Matthew nudged him with his foot. "The fish were biting gut, too."

"Hmm. Maybe I'll get some fishing in next time." Jacob stood, leaving the boppli sleeping on the blanket, and moved closer to Becky. He dropped next to her and put his arm around her shoulders, hugging her loosely. "So, what'd you say about me?"

"Maybe you don't want to know," Becky said.

Jacob blinked. Was she teasing him? He slid his hand down to her waist and tried to sound threatening. "I have ways of making you talk."

203

"Ooh, maybe Annie and I need to take a walk," Matthew joked.

Fiery red flooded Becky's cheeks, and she shifted away, but not enough to dislodge his arm.

"Nein. Stay," he told her.

She must not be comfortable with that type of teasing. Well, what good Amish girl would be? He knew he shouldn't have embarrassed her like that. He got to his feet again. "Let's take the fish up to the Stoltzfuses' haus and then go to McDonald's for some of Bex's fancy coffee."

Matthew looked confused. "Fancy coffee?"

Annie pushed herself to her feet, too. "Cappuccino. Becky's Englisch boyfriend got her hooked."

"Englisch boyfriend?" Matthew raised his eyebrows.

Oops. Jacob needed to explain Becky's situation in case Matthew thought she was two-timing. He frowned and glanced at Becky, who sat mutely and looked even redder. He wasn't doing a good job of making her comfortable. "The point is, it's gut."

"Too bad we didn't go yesterday. They have free frappe Fridays," Annie said.

"This sounds like a whole different language." Matthew shook his head.

Jacob bent to pick up Emma. "Jah, like I said, fancy coffee. And it sounds like you're hooked, too, Annie." He cuddled the boppli in one arm.

Annie shrugged. "Maybe so. Can't help it when you hang around Becky."

Jacob laughed and held his other hand out to Becky. "Kum, Bex."

She put her hand in his and allowed him to pull her to her feet.

~∻~

Becky was glad that theirs wasn't the only Amish buggy hitched at the post this time. Jacob held the door open for her and Emma, Matthew, and Annie, then followed them into the restaurant. Becky saw the Zook family sitting at a booth, eating a late supper.

Jacob held her hand as they placed their orders at the front counter. Then, as they moved to the side to wait for their cappuccinos, Becky felt the skin on the back of her neck prickle. She glanced around. Kent's green eyes were locked on her. He stood from where he'd been sitting and strutted toward them.

Ach, not now. Not here.

Becky held Emma closer and tightened her grip on Jacob's hand. She wanted to draw from his strength and confidence. If only she had some of her own.

"So, is that the brat?" Kent asked, peering at Emma. Becky caught the whiff of alcohol on his breath. This could get even worse than she'd feared. "Doesn't look anything like me." Jacob stiffened beside her.

She hadn't noticed Kent's car in the lot, but then, she'd been paying more attention to Jacob and her friends.

If she kept running into him here, she'd have to give up her favorite drink and stay away. That wouldn't be so bad. She'd gladly stop drinking fancy coffee if it meant never having to see Kent again.

She shifted Emma, using a hip to help support her. "She's not a brat. She's a boppli."

A sneer crossed Kent's lips. "A boppli. Don't you know you're in America now? You need to speak

English, not whatever that is you talk." He poked a forefinger in Jacob's face. "I remember you. Chakob Miller. Still haven't gotten enough of Becky yet, huh? You could hang with me. I could introduce you to some girls who really know how to have fun."

"I think it's time for you to go," Jacob stated.

Becky glanced down and saw his free hand forming a fist.

Ach, her nails were digging into his skin. She eased her grip, not wanting to draw blood.

Kent nodded toward Annie. "Luke got smart and dumped her. She was a cold fish, anyway."

Wait a second. How would Kent know if Annie was a "cold fish"? Anger flashed in Becky's mind. She sucked in a breath and opened her mouth to lash out at him.

"Shut up, Kent." Annie's voice sounded strong, but the Englisch words coming out of her mouth shocked Becky. She'd never heard Annie say anything like that before.

Becky mentally repeated the words. *Shut up.* Maybe she'd find the courage to say them. Someday.

She wished Kent would just go away, but he didn't seem inclined to. He inched closer, the stench of alcohol growing stronger.

"Never could say that about Becky. But I'm sure you know that. At least she could—"

Becky stumbled as Jacob released her hand and shoved her behind him. She blinked, stunned to see him getting in Kent's face.

"I think you've said quite enough." Jacob's voice sounded dangerously calm.

"Gonna make me stop, farm boy? Go ahead. Make me." Kent puffed out his chest.

"Hey, break it up!" someone yelled from behind the counter.

Something bumped Becky's arm, and she glanced over to see Matthew holding a cappuccino in each hand. He nodded toward the door. Annie was already going out, carrying her frappe and another cappuccino. "Kum. You could get hurt in here."

She walked a few steps toward the door.

"You're drunk." Jacob's voice dripped with disgust. "Leave her alone. Haven't you done enough?"

Something crashed behind Becky and she looked back. The display of Happy Meal toys had toppled, but she hadn't seen who had run into it. Jacob and Kent circled each other.

Matthew moved behind her and nudged her with his forearms. "Go. Now. Before the boppli gets hurt."

Becky gasped and rushed toward the door.

"Break it up!" Becky heard again as the door shut behind her.

⤬

Amish are pacifists. Amish are pacifists. Amish are pacifists. Jacob said it over and over in his head as he and Kent moved in a circle and glared at each other. How much was Becky expected to take? Would she have to "turn the other cheek" forever?

Kent had to be stopped. And, sometimes, the only way to stop a bully was to stand up to him.

What had Becky ever seen in this jerk?

Kent swung, his punch grazing the side of Jacob's head. Poor aim.

Jacob could have leveled him. Easily.

Amish...are...pacifists.

Still....

The manager—at least, that's whom Jacob assumed he was—hurried out from behind the counter. He grabbed Kent and nodded at Jacob. "Get out of here."

Jacob obeyed and rushed out the door after Becky, Matthew, and Annie, glad that he'd been saved the embarrassment of getting into a public fight. He could hear the man yelling at Kent and threatening to call the police and bar him from the establishment. Maybe Kent had caused problems there before.

Jacob shouldn't have gotten in Kent's face. He'd been in the wrong.

But it had been to protect Becky's honor.

And Kent would have deserved it if Jacob had flattened him.

He would have won, no contest.

But, praise be, someone had stopped them.

Jacob jogged toward the buggy and unhooked the horse from the hitching post. He climbed in and flicked the reins. "I think it's time we got home."

"Jah. Some of the Englisch are not so nice here, either, ain't so?" Matthew said from the backseat.

Jacob shook his head. "Not so much."

They were barely outside of town when a red car flew by them and screeched to a stop up ahead, completely blocking the road.

The horse reared. Jacob tightened his grip on the reins and prayed that the animal wouldn't bolt. Thankfully, he managed to get it under control.

On second thought, it might be better if the horse would bolt, taking them to safety.

Jacob drew in a deep breath. What now?

Chapter 27

N ein, nein," Becky whispered as Jacob got out of the buggy. The door of the car flew open, and Kent jumped out, yelling curses at Jacob, pointing his fingers, and jabbing the air in his direction.

Jacob rolled his shoulders and neck, then moved into what appeared to be a relaxed stance. He said something to Kent, but whatever it was seemed only to fuel the Englischer's anger, as his gesturing became wilder, more out of control.

Matthew sighed heavily from the backseat and muttered something that Becky couldn't discern. Then, he climbed out, too, and led the horse to the side of the road, where he stood and held him by the harness.

Becky watched as Kent approached Jacob, still gesturing wildly. "Why is he doing this?" She curled her fingers into her skirt.

Annie placed a hand on Becky's shoulder. "It'll be okay. Jacob tried not to fight."

Becky's hands shook, and tears singed her eyes. "Not Jacob. Why can't Kent leave me alone? I was such a fool."

"Jah. But we all make mistakes. It could be worse. Kent could be insisting on his rights as Emma's father. Or he might have married you."

Becky blinked back tears. "Both of those would be worse."

She glanced back at the road in time to see Kent shove Jacob.

Jacob staggered, but he didn't move to shove Kent back. Instead, he said something, though too quiet for Becky to hear. Didn't he understand that this was not a time to demonstrate the Amish way of "turning the other cheek"?

Kent shoved Jacob again, but when he still didn't retaliate, Kent stepped back a couple of steps, then lunged, knocking Jacob to the ground. Kent raised his fist, still yelling insults.

Ach, if only she didn't have the boppli strapped to her side. Becky struggled to loosen herself, then shoved Emma into Annie's arms and climbed out, racing over to where the two men rolled on the ground.

"Nein! Kent, stop!" She jumped on his back, pummeling him. "Stop! Jacob, why don't you defend yourself?"

He didn't have to answer. She knew why. But, ach, she wanted him to fight. He could whip Kent.

"Hey! Hey, stop it, Becky!" Kent rolled away from Jacob, leaving him lying there in the dirt, blood dripping from his mouth and dribbling down his chin. His left eye looked red and puffy.

Kent stumbled to his feet and pulled her into his arms. But it wasn't a comforting sort of hug like Jacob's. It was more controlling. Harder.

She shuddered and tried to escape.

"See, Becky, he won't even fight for you. I will. I just did. Take me back." He leaned forward and tried to kiss her, but she twisted her head away. His lips grazed her cheek instead.

"Look, I'm sorry for the way I treated you about the kid. I was wrong. And you aren't like any of the others. You're the best thing that ever happened to me. Please, Becky? I'll try to do better this time." His grip tightened around her right arm so hard that she feared it would leave marks. "Let's get out of here." He propelled her toward his car.

As if that feeble apology would make up for everything! Her ruined reputation, a boppli out of wedlock, her foolish mistakes.... It didn't even begin to scratch the surface.

Besides which, she didn't even like him anymore.

"Let me go." Becky desperately wanted someone to help her. She glanced back at Jacob, then toward the buggy, where Annie and Matthew seemed frozen.

She looked at Jacob. Why wouldn't he help her?

"I can't leave Emma," she pleaded.

"Let Annie babysit. Come on."

Kent dragged her toward the car as she tried to dig her feet into the ground to halt their progress. Difficult to do with tennis shoes on hard, packed dirt. "Nein, Kent. Nein. You're drunk. Don't do this!" Couldn't anyone hear the fear in her voice? Her desperate pleas for help?

How could she live with herself if he—

"The maidal said nein." Jacob's deep voice interrupted her panicked thoughts.

Becky lost her balance and fell when Kent released her and whipped around. She'd have a bruised hip, for sure.

Though her injuries were nothing compared to Jacob's.

"Gonna fight now, Chakob Miller?" Kent's mouth curled in contempt. He swung at Jacob.

This time, Jacob ducked to avoid him, then returned the punch.

His fist collided with Kent's diaphragm.

Kent spewed the contents of his stomach all over the ground. He doubled over, clutching his midsection, as tears streamed down his cheeks. Then, he fell to his knees in the road, gasping for breath like one of the fish Matthew had caught earlier.

Red and blue lights flashed behind them.

⌒⌒

Jacob didn't know whether to help Becky to her feet or to put his hands over his head. He started to turn when a stern voice came over the loudspeaker. "Everybody freeze!" That settled it. He put his hands up over his head.

His stomach threatened to expel its contents, like Kent's had done. Why had he succumbed to temptation and punched Kent? He should have stuck it out and clung to his commitment to nonviolence. But he hadn't. And now, the police were here. He'd failed. He'd failed Becky, he'd failed himself, and he'd failed God.

Lord, forgive me.

A police officer approached and shone his flashlight directly into Jacob's eyes. "Who are you?"

"Jacob Miller."

The flashlight's beam swung toward the buggy, illuminating Annie and Matt before turning back and landing on Becky, sitting in the dirt, then Kent, who was also still on the ground, gasping for air.

Jacob wished he dared go help Becky up. She shouldn't be sitting there in the dirt. He avoided her gaze. Too bad it had come to this.

"Ah, Kent Johnson. We had a complaint about you once already tonight. Seems you're not done getting into trouble. The person who reported you said you were drunk and disturbing the peace." The light flashed back to Jacob. "You're the new Amish man James mentioned. Not high, are you?"

"Nein."

"Can you walk a straight line?" With the toe of his boot, the police officer scuffed a mark in the dirt.

"Jah." Jacob lowered his arms and stepped on the line.

"Who are your friends?" the officer asked as Jacob followed the line.

"Becky Troyer, Matthew Yoder, and Annie. Sorry, I don't know her last name."

The officer's partner got into Kent's car, which was still running, and moved it to the side of the road as Jacob finished walking the scratched trail.

The one holding the flashlight on Jacob nodded. "So, you haven't been drinking?" The police officer moved closer, as if to do a sniff test.

"Only water and tea. And I just had some of that fancy coffee." He wasn't sure how fresh his breath smelled.

The officer's eyebrows rose. "Fancy coffee?"

"Cappuccino," Becky said. "From McDonald's. May I get up?"

The officer walked over to the buggy and peered inside, then came back looked down at Becky, still sitting in the dirt and rubbing her hip. "Who are you?"

"Becky Troyer."

"Daniel's daughter?"

"Jah."

The officer nodded. "You can get up. Tell your dad that Troy said hi. You are all free to go." He turned to Kent. "And as for you, Mr. Johnson, I think I'll take you for a ride to the station. My partner will drive your vehicle back. I know your dad would prefer that over having it towed."

"Thank you, sir," Jacob said, but his heart still pounded like crazy. He turned and walked over to Becky, reached down, and grasped her hand to help her up.

She started to move into his arms, but Jacob held up a hand, stopping her.

⤚⟡⤙

Jacob had frowned all the way home, and he hadn't said a word—not when he'd dropped off Matthew, then Annie, and certainly not while he'd been alone with her and Emma afterward. He'd maintained the silence all the way up to the house.

Becky's thoughts had been in turmoil for the duration of the trip. Was Jacob angry with her? Upset that she'd gotten out of the buggy to help him? Maybe that had damaged his pride. But it had looked like he wasn't about to do anything other than let Kent beat him up, and so she'd needed to jump in!

Ach, she shouldn't have worried that Jacob wouldn't protect her. He had when it had mattered most. But what must he think of her now?

He was probably disgusted that she'd ever gone so far into the world to want to date a guy just because he drove a fancy red car. That was pretty shallow.

Jacob released the reins and vaulted down, then came around to the other side of the buggy. He reached up to take Emma and helped Becky down, handing Emma back to her when she was ready. Then, he went around to the back to get the picnic basket, quilts, and diaper bag.

And, still quiet, he followed her into the kitchen.

Mamm and Daed looked up from the table, where they were sitting. Mamm's eyes widened as she took in Becky and then Jacob, and she sprang to her feet. "What happened to you? Are you alright? Becky, your dress is all torn and dirty. And Jacob...?"

"We ran into Kent," Becky started to explain, "and—"

"I'm sorry, Daniel. I failed," Jacob interrupted her, dropping into a chair. "I'm so very sorry."

Becky laid Emma down in her cradle and went to get an ice pack. Jacob's eye was almost swollen shut and had turned an ugly shade of purple.

"I'm going to get a warm washcloth," Mamm said. "We need to get you cleaned up."

Tears crept down Jacob's face as he spilled out the story. "I'm thinking maybe you should make arrangements to send me back. I shamed you and your family."

Becky froze, standing there beside the table, the ice pack in her hand. "Nein, Jacob. Don't say that." Maybe that was why he'd been so quiet on the way home. She'd been proud of him, and he'd been beating himself up.

Daed nodded slowly. "Jah. Jah, you shamed us." But then, a grin lifted his mouth. "I'm thinking you did a gut job protecting my Becky, and maybe we'll just keep you around a bit longer." He eyed Jacob sternly. "So long as you behave yourself."

Becky let out the air she hadn't realized she'd been holding in. She looked up as Mamm hurried back into the room and went to Jacob. Becky stopped her. "I'll do it, Mamm."

Jacob looked at Becky with furrowed brow and pursed lips, as if she was the last person he wanted touching him. But then, he shut his eyes. Acceptance, maybe, though he must not want to even see her. Or, maybe his eyes just hurt. He didn't make any effort to stop her as she gently wiped the blood off of his strong jaw and removed the dirt from the rest of his face. An occasional tear still made a track down his cheek, and Becky wished she had the nerve to kiss each one away. But Mamm and Daed were right there in the room.

And even if they weren't, his swollen, split lip looked much too sore to kiss.

Some blood had run down his neck, so Becky moved the washcloth to wipe that up, but Jacob grabbed her hand, stalling her. His eyes flew open.

"I can handle it, ain't so? I'll just go take a shower—if you don't think I'll disturb them." He motioned toward the dawdi-haus, where Grossdaedi and Grossmammi slept.

Daniel waved his hand in dismissal. "Go on. Gut nacht, Jacob."

He nodded, stood, and went outside. A moment later, Becky saw the horse and buggy headed away from the house toward the road.

She hoped that this didn't mean he was driving out of her life.

Chapter 28

J acob drew in a deep breath, then pushed open the door to the police station. He walked up to the desk in the middle of the room. It looked different from the police station back home, but this was a small town and probably didn't see much crime.

The dispatcher fixed his gaze on Jacob's eye, which by now was badly bruised. Jacob had seen his reflection in the glass door on his way in.

"How can I help you?"

Conscious of how awful he must look, Jacob swallowed, wishing he'd thought twice before making this trip. Maybe he should have showered first. "Uh, is Kent Johnson still here?"

The man behind the desk slowly stood. "Yes. He's in a holding cell. Why?"

"May I talk to him?"

"Who are you?"

"Jacob Miller. I need to apologize."

The dispatcher narrowed his eyes. "You're the one who fought with him? I wouldn't worry about it. That boy has been asking for it for a while. He finally got what he needed. About time someone stood up to him. Just because his daddy is on the city council...."

City council? Was his daed some kind of important person? "Please?" Jacob rubbed his thumb against his forefinger.

"Alright. If you insist. I'll have to pat you down to make sure you aren't carrying."

"Jah." How much humiliation would he need to bear? It didn't matter. He deserved every bit of it. He knew better. All his life, he'd had it drilled into his head that violence was not the answer. And yet....

"Put your hands here." The man indicated a file cabinet.

Jacob nodded and complied, then tried not to flinch as the officer frisked him.

"Come on." The man walked away from the desk and turned a corner. He stopped at the first of two small cells. It had a concrete floor and a stainless-steel toilet with no seat on one side, two built-in cots on the other. Kent sat hunched over on the bottom bed. He still looked a bit sick.

"You have company, Johnson," the officer said, then looked at Jacob. "I'll leave you out here, if you don't mind."

Jacob swallowed. "Let me in."

"Leave him out."

The dispatcher grunted. "I think you've kind of given up any say here, Johnson. Your dad said to throw the book at you. That would be disturbing the peace, driving under the influence, assault—"

"I don't want to press charges," Jacob interrupted him.

"I do." Kent glared at him.

The officer sighed and banged the door with his fist. "Doesn't change anything. I'm not letting you in. You got fifteen minutes."

Jacob stepped forward and grasped the bars. His fingers tightened around them until his knuckles turned white.

He stood there for a long time in indecision. He could hear the officer talking in the other room—on the phone, probably, since no one else had been there when he'd arrived.

Kent began to fidget. "Go ahead. Say what you came to say, then get out of here." He didn't look up.

"I...I'm sorry. Violence, it isn't our way. I was wrong to react the way I did. I had no excuse for it, except that I didn't want you to take Bex—I mean Becky. Please forgive me." Peace washed over him. He relaxed his grip.

Kent sniffed, his upper lip curling in contempt. "I expected you to fight. I wanted you to fight. But I guess even more than that, I wanted to beat you. I wanted Becky to go with me." He raked his fingers through his hair as a vulnerable look crossed his face. "I'm jealous of you, you know. You have her. I don't." It must be the alcohol talking. Surely, Kent wouldn't admit to this if he were sober.

"But you did." And that still goaded Jacob.

"I thought she was like all the other girls, that once we got started...I thought she was on the pill. How was I supposed to know she was a virgin? None of the other girls ever complained. And she got pregnant the only time I...uh...." Kent's face flushed.

Jacob frowned, wondering if she'd been forced. It sounded like it.

"She took it so hard," Kent added.

It was good that the officer had kept Jacob out here instead of allowing him inside the cell. He chewed his lip to keep from saying anything he might regret later. The metal bars bit into his fingers when his grip tightened again.

"Said she was saving herself for marriage," Kent continued. "I told her it wasn't a big deal." He shrugged, but then his expression changed. Hardened. "I suppose you think I owe you an apology. You're probably the one she saved herself for. I always knew she'd marry one of her kind. But I'd hoped to convince her to become one of us. To move in with me. Get away from her too-strict father."

"Yet you said the boppli wasn't yours...and ruined her reputation among the people." This Englischer's thinking sure was mixed up. Jacob's mind struggled to process everything that Kent had dumped in this information overload.

"I wasn't ready to be a dad. I was only nineteen—way too young to settle down. Besides, I offered to pay for an abortion. Even offered to take her into Springfield for it. She wouldn't have been ruined if she'd agreed. She's the one who refused. She made her choices." His lips curled.

Jacob flexed his jaw.

"Time's up." The officer stepped around the corner, jingling some keys as he approached.

It was probably time to leave, anyway. Jacob's temper had already risen to the boiling point. He forced himself to calm down. To turn and walk out. He'd said what he had come to say.

The officer led the way back into the main room, where the police officer who'd drawn the line in the dirt stood waiting. The one who'd said his name was Troy.

"Came to apologize, did you?"

"Yes, sir." A time like this called for Englisch. Jacob's shoulders slumped with fatigue, and he stifled a yawn. He dreaded the drive back home. His left eye throbbed, and he wished he'd taken a couple of pain pills.

Troy sat on the corner of the desk. "Feel better?"

Jacob shrugged. "A little. I still need to apologize to Becky and to God."

Troy nodded. "Might want to start with God. And then, forgive yourself. Did you talk to Daniel already?"

Jacob nodded.

"And my guess is, he forgave you. Daniel's a good man. Got a reputation around here for being upstanding. A man of integrity."

"I'll try not to shame him again."

Troy stood and walked over to Jacob. "I know you will, Jacob." He clapped him on the shoulder. "Go on home and have that talk with God. You'll be alright."

⌘

Becky had seen Jacob return home almost two hours earlier. He'd parked the buggy and put the horse in the barn before heading into the dawdi-haus. She was almost asleep when she heard what sounded like hail hitting the bedroom window. She rolled over, wondering if Katie expected a beau. Not quite fifteen, she wasn't old enough for courting, but Becky knew that the buwe looked Katie over. Yet her sister slept. She would have been awake and fully dressed if she'd been expecting someone.

The light taps continued steadily, with a short pause between each one, as if someone was deliberately causing them. It was probably no one, nothing; maybe a branch brushing against the house. Becky slipped out of bed and peeked out the window just to be sure. Her eyes widened when she saw Jacob standing there in the moonlight. She opened the window and leaned out.

"Jacob? Where'd you go? Are you alright?" She hoped she hadn't awakened Katie or Emma. She glanced back at the beds to make sure. Neither one stirred.

He shook his head. "Meet me in the kitchen."

Becky slid the window shut and grabbed her clothes. She shed her nightgown and climbed into her dress as quickly as she could, then padded downstairs in her bare feet.

Jacob already waited in the dimly lit kitchen. She felt the heat of a blush as she recalled the time she'd told him she wouldn't invite him in. Daed never locked the doors. Jacob could have walked in anytime he wanted.

He shoved a mug of hot chocolate toward her. There was no way he would have had time to make it after rousing her, so he must have been down here a few minutes beforehand. He cooked? There seemed to be no end to his talents. She studied his bruised face. "Do you want ice for your eye?" She wished she could fix it.

"Maybe later. Sit."

So, was he courting her? The pebbles thrown against the window would certainly indicate as much.

"I think we need to talk. First of all, let me start by saying I'm sorry."

She shook her head as she sat. Ach, not courting. But she was glad he was finally talking. "Nein. I'm sorry for goading you into it. I wanted you to stand up to him."

Jacob nodded. Like he'd known.

Becky lowered her eyes, ashamed. His sin was her fault. *Lord, forgive me.*

"I'm going to ask you a question. Don't go telling me this is none of my business. Tonight made it my business, ain't so?" Jacob studied his mug. "What exactly happened between you and Kent?"

Becky swallowed. "What do you want to know?" She didn't want to tell him about that. She had to live with her mistake every day. But still, if there were any hope of a future between her and Jacob, she'd have to open up.

Though if she told him, he would dump her so fast, her head would spin.

"I went to the police station to talk with him." A muscle worked in Jacob's jaw. "He said he offered to pay for an abortion. The way he talked, it kind of sounded like he forced you to...uh, lie with him." He drew in a sharp breath.

"Ach." Heat rushed to Becky's face. How could she tell Jacob about this? She'd never shared it with anyone. Not her parents. Not even Annie.

Jacob leaned forward and grasped her hand. His eyes held hers. "Did he, Bex?"

She tried to draw strength from his pleading glance. "It was my fault. All my fault. I shouldn't have dated an Englischer. Their ways are so different from ours. He said it was expected, and I thought maybe he was right." She shrugged one shoulder. "He insisted, but I didn't know...I never dreamed that.... I told him nein, but he said it was too late and just did it."

She'd cried the whole time. Just remembering the awful experience made her want to sob again. Ach, the humiliation. She blinked the tears back.

"I'd wanted to find out on my wedding night. It was only that once. I broke up with him afterward. I figured if I didn't tell, then no one would ever know."

Jacob's jaw flexed.

She silently pleaded with him to forgive her for her past mistake. Instead, she saw his expression harden.

She lowered her head. "Our sin has a way of finding us out, ain't so? About three months later, I couldn't deny the horrible truth anymore." She sighed.

"I thought maybe he'd marry me. I never expected the humiliation of what happened instead. And then I had to go home and tell Daed and Mamm."

Becky could still see her parents' faces when she broke the news to them. The disappointment in Daed's eyes, and Mamm's tears, had hurt more than any of Kent's accusations.

"I had to have a kneeling confession in front of the people. And they shunned me for six weeks for my sins." Tears rolled down her cheeks. Ach, that was an awful memory.

And now, she had to tell the shameful story to a man she was falling in love with.

Jacob's fingers stroked her hand. Silence stretched between them.

Becky studied the mug in front of her, still full of the hot chocolate he'd made. It was probably cold by now. She hadn't touched it. After a minute, she looked up at Jacob, wishing she could read his thoughts.

If only he'd say something like, "I'll marry you, Bex. I'll be Emma's daed."

Of course, if she'd already agreed to let him court her, that might have been the next step.

But her fears had kept her from agreeing. Fears that once he knew the awful truth, he'd dump her.

She wasn't worthy. Not of Jacob.

⎯⎯✤⎯⎯

Jacob struggled to control his emotions. It sounded to him like Kent had raped her. Maybe not forcefully, but if she'd said nein and he'd done it anyway, that was rape, as far as he was concerned.

Maybe it was good that he'd found this out after the run-in with Kent, or he might not have stopped with a punch. Nein, it would have been far worse. He might have been in prison for murder.

Vengeance is mine; I will repay, saith the Lord.

Why hadn't Becky told the church that she had been raped? The community would have looked upon the whole thing differently. But then, maybe she hadn't known. She'd said it was her fault. And she wouldn't have expected a date to rape her. But why hadn't Daniel told them? Maybe he didn't know that part of the story. The church would have rallied around her to support her and not shunned and condemned her.

It was just wrong. In so many ways.

If only he knew how to explain to her that it hadn't been her fault. But the words wouldn't come.

Not when all he felt was fury that anyone would do this to Becky. That she'd had to pay the high price.

This explained so much.

She pulled her hand out from under his and got up from the table. "I'll understand if you don't want to court me. Annie is a much better choice." Her voice wobbled.

And, with a muffled sob, she hurried toward the door.

Jacob sprang to his feet and ran after her, not paying any attention to the chair that crashed to the floor behind him. "Bex, wait!" He grasped her arm and pulled her backward against his chest. Her shoulders shook. Wrapping his arms around her, he moved toward a different chair. He sat down and pulled her into his lap, letting their tears mingle as they soaked his shirt.

Probably not his brightest action. But he wasn't about to shove her off. Instead, he snuggled her nearer. He needed to hold her, to offer what comfort he could give, while he searched for the words to say.

A floorboard creaked. Jacob looked toward the doorway. His heart pounded.

Chapter 29

"E verything alright in here?" Daed's voice broke into the stillness. He sounded hesitant, like he knew he shouldn't be peeking in on a courting couple—not that she and Jacob were courting.

Ach! Caught in this compromising position. Her face heating, Becky squirmed out of Jacob's lap and, without looking at him, went to pick up the chair he'd knocked over.

Daed stood in the doorway. "I heard a crash and came down to check it out. Didn't realize...." His face colored.

Jacob stood. "We were just talking. I thought maybe I should hear the story about what happened between her and—and that Englischer."

Daed nodded, then backed up.

Jacob shook his head. "Nein. Stay. We need to talk with you about this. I made enough hot chocolate. Would you like some?" He moved to the stove.

For a second, Daed looked as if he thought he hadn't heard right. Becky remembered her own similar reaction.

"Nein, I wouldn't want to intrude."

But he already had. Becky stared at a scuff mark on the floor. And she had no idea what might have happened if she'd stayed on Jacob's lap. They might have kissed, if his lip wasn't too sore. But that moment was forever gone.

She heard Jacob draw in a sharp breath. "She was raped."

Ach, there was nothing like Jacob's bluntness. Hadn't the man ever heard of tact?

She didn't have to look up to know that the color had washed out of Daed's face. He collapsed into a chair.

And that word—that ugly word—had Jacob just used it in relation to her? He couldn't have. She hadn't been raped. It was her fault—she was the one who'd agreed to date an Englischer.

"Nein," Daed whispered. He shut his eyes. After a moment, he opened them wide and shook his head. "We need to get her to the hospital."

"Not tonight, Daniel." Jacob set a mug in front of Daed. "When she conceived Emma."

Daed straightened and glanced at Becky, his gaze softening. "Ach, Becky." His eyes filled with tears. "I didn't know. We didn't know. Things would have been so different." He shook his head again, and his gaze hardened as he looked back at Jacob. "How do you know this?"

Becky frowned. How dare they talk about her as if she wasn't there? She glared at Jacob. "It wasn't—"

He silenced her with a look. "It was. You said you told him nein, and he did it anyway. That is rape."

"But he is Englisch."

Jacob shook his head. "That is an Englisch law."

An Englisch law? Did Jacob mean that she had broken the law? Did the Englisch really have laws about such private matters? Her knees buckled. She swayed and grasped the table for support, then reached for a chair, instead. Maybe if she sat down....

Becky missed the chair and fell, her left elbow banging the back of it on her way down. She landed on the floor, and her bruised hip took the brunt of the impact. She bit her lip to keep from crying out, then grasped her throbbing arm.

Jacob instantly crouched beside her. "You okay, Bex?"

For a moment, she considered waving him away and just staying on the floor. It would be so much easier not to have to move, judging by the pain radiating from her already bruised body. She swallowed. "I'm fine. Just missed the chair, is all." She scrambled to her feet, ignoring his outstretched hand.

"You could have told us, Becky." Daed's hand smoothed his blond beard, his gaze accusing. "We would have understood. You know that. I've been supportive of you all the way through this."

Jah, he had been supportive. But how could she have told them something she was too ashamed to admit to herself?

A cry from upstairs kept her from commenting.

She glanced at Jacob. Now that he knew the truth, rejection would surely follow.

But she wanted him to state his undying devotion to her. Fighting tears, Becky whirled and hurried from the room as fast as her sore legs would carry her.

⤲⤳

Jacob watched her go, wishing that Daniel hadn't interrupted and that Becky was still sitting on his lap. But then, they wouldn't have had the previous conversation, and Daniel needed to know.

Daniel sat and stared into his cup of hot chocolate, just as Jacob had seen him do with a cup of coffee when he was stressed or thinking of a response. He'd hated to bother his cousin, but this truth needed to be told. Becky deserved nothing less than that.

After a few moments, Daniel reached for the cup and took a sip. A look of disgust crossed his face, and he put the mug down again. "Becky didn't make this." It wasn't a question.

Jacob considered his own mug. Cocoa and hot water—weren't those the main ingredients? Maybe he should have read the directions. But he'd wanted to have a hot drink ready for Becky, even though she hadn't touched hers. Probably a good thing. He took a cautious sip and almost spit it out. Ugh. It really was nasty.

"If Becky didn't say...rape, then how did you find this out?" Daniel got up and dumped the contents of his and Becky's cups into the sink and then rinsed the mugs.

"The way both she and that Englischer worded it when I talked to them individually about it."

Daniel nodded and turned toward him. His lips still curved down, and there was no trace of light in his eyes. Jacob hated being the one who'd erased the smile.

"I will be having a talk with the bishop about this. With a year gone by, I'm not sure how he's going to want to handle telling the people. He may tell the truth, or he may decide to leave things as they are. He might say that there's no point in upsetting the apple cart."

As far as Jacob was concerned, this apple cart needed upsetting. The church needed to apologize to

Becky for shunning her, for treating her as an out-cast. For not coming alongside her and helping.

"I would imagine something will be said, though." Daniel pursed his lips, his gaze remaining thoughtful.

"One more thing." Jacob frowned at his still full mug, searching for some measure of courage. "You and Daed. Did you work this out in advance to get me away from Susie? Hoping that I would fall in love with Becky, maybe?" He hated asking. It put everything he'd been taught about confidentiality in courtship to shame. But then, everything was pretty much out in the open, anyway. Might as well lay it out there and see what Daniel had to say.

Daniel hesitated. Even got up and poured a glass of milk, taking the time to sip it slowly. Finally, he came back to the table and sat down, shaking his head. "Nein. Your daed didn't say much of anything. He did mention that he thought you were on the verge of making a serious mistake, so he was signing you up for the swap of Amish buwe. He wanted you to kum down in hopes that you would see the error of your ways. He didn't say what the 'serious mistake' might be."

Jacob nodded.

"Your attraction to my Becky, though...that was pretty plain." Daniel took another sip of milk and swallowed. "Most young men shy away, knowing Becky's history, and that she is part of a twosome, having a daughter already."

"I know now is not the time, especially consider-ing what she just said. But, when the time arrives—if it arrives—do I need to talk to the bishop first before approaching Becky about marriage?" At home, the bishop wanted to be approached first, and then he would talk to the girl, preparing the way. Would it be the same here?

Daniel hesitated, then reiterated a reminder. "Becky has a boppli. You'd be an instant daed."

"Jah." He'd thought of that. Looked forward to it. Emma, and more boppli in God's time.

Daniel nodded. "Then, you talk to the bishop first. He likes to be kept informed. And he'll require you to go through instruction and join the church before you are published. Always there's plenty to do before a wedding. We'll plan for December, jah?" Daniel grinned and slapped Jacob's back, as though the matter was settled.

Maybe it was—at least as far as the two of them were concerned.

A December wedding. It sounded good to him. Now, to convince Becky. To win her heart.

Could he recruit her friend Annie to help him?

⤜⊰⊱⤛

After the church service, Becky helped the other women set out food for the meal. She hurried to slice the pies and cakes and arrange the cookies that had been brought for the noon potluck. Annie joined her, armed with knives and pie servers.

Becky didn't feel very social. She'd had a rough night, tossing and turning, reliving every moment of the evening's conversation with Jacob and Daed. She muttered a greeting to Annie, then looked down, carefully cutting into a chocolate cream pie that Mary Zook had made. Right now, Becky just wanted to grab a fork and eat the whole thing. Maybe it would make her feel better.

"You're quiet today. Something wrong?" Annie rearranged the desserts so that they were placed alphabetically—cakes, cobblers, cookies, and then pies. Like anyone would notice. Or care.

"Bothered by thoughts last night. Running into... well, you know." She hadn't meant to spill it out like that. Jacob's bluntness must have affected her.

Annie nodded. "Jah. Did Jacob demand answers?"

"Not 'demand' so much as ask for them."

A soft laugh escaped Annie's lips. "Of course. He needed to know."

Becky turned the chocolate cream pie tin in a circle, studying it from all directions. Maybe nobody would miss it if she took it and disappeared. There were a lot of desserts.

"He is gut-looking. And if it weren't for you, I'd definitely be interested. But, Becky, Jacob sees only you. When are you going to realize this?"

Becky turned the pie in another circle without answering. That chocolate pie was hers, all hers. She could almost taste it.

Annie groaned. "Don't look now, but...." She shivered. "I've got to go. You, too. Run." With that, Annie twirled and hurried toward the house.

That Annie was too dramatic. Or maybe not. Becky peeked over her shoulder to see Amos Kropf approaching at a fast clip.

"Rebekah. Kum, take a walk. I want to talk with you."

Chapter 30

Jacob and Matthew made their way toward the long tables laden with food for the noon meal—homemade bread, cold meats, salads, vegetables, and more. Jacob's stomach rumbled just looking at the spread.

Men always went through the line first, while the women and children waited, but they never seemed to mind. Jacob smiled as he remembered Mamm saying that she always sampled the food while she set it out. So, in reality, the women ate before the men. Jacob scanned the group of women but didn't see Becky.

Then, a movement caught his eye, and he looked at the field beyond the blacksmith shop. Becky walked that way with a man who grasped her upper arm. She didn't seem to be resisting.

For a second, Jacob felt as if his heart had been physically ripped from his body. He stared at the couple. No wonder she'd rebuffed his efforts. She had a beau that neither he nor Daniel knew anything about.

Unless it was the bishop. Daniel had said he would talk to him, but Jacob had figured it would be on Monday. Sunday wasn't a day for business. But another glance at the food table revealed the bishop filling his plate at the head of the line. The other ministers were lined up behind him.

Could it be Amos Kropf? Jacob scanned the crowd. He wasn't certain, but the man talking with

Daniel looked like Amos. Considering how much the man had visited Daniel recently, it seemed to Jacob that they would be all talked out.

Jacob sighed. After one last look, he turned his back on Becky and her beau. He didn't want to see them or witness any more of their tryst. She'd made her choice. And, clearly, Jacob didn't factor in. She must have laughed to realize that she had Daniel and Jacob completely fooled. And that she'd won his heart.

No wonder she hadn't agreed to let him court her.

But why couldn't she have simply explained that she was seeing someone else? She wouldn't have had to say who.

Matthew nudged his arm and said something. Jacob nodded automatically, though he had no idea what his friend had said.

He stared at the spread before him, wondering how he could force a bite down. How could he have completely ignored all the ways in which Becky had told him she wasn't interested?

Looking back, he could see it all so clearly now.

Matthew speared a slice of roast beef with a fork and slid it onto his plate. "Isn't that your Becky?" He nodded with his chin toward the field.

Jacob didn't want to look, but he couldn't keep his eyes from going in that direction. Becky and her beau walked farther out into the field. "It would appear that she's not my Becky."

Matthew bumped Jacob's shoulder with one fist. "You deserve better."

Jah. Maybe so. But that was no consolation.

❧

Becky tried to disengage herself from Amos's grip, but he didn't seem inclined to let go. Even a sharp jerk of her arm failed to dislodge his hand. She would probably have more bruises to match her hip by nightfall.

All the way into the field, Amos expounded on the many failures of one Jacob Miller from Pennsylvania. He'd been seen fighting with the Englisch, as well as riding a bicycle through Seymour. That was clearly against the Ordnung for this district. He'd gone to at least one party. Maybe more. The unmarried girls were all tittering about him.

But causing girls to titter wasn't a sin.

Just fact.

"Besides which, this newcomer seems to have no practical skills," Amos continued. "Why else would Daniel spend so much time teaching him blacksmithing?" He grunted in disgust.

Becky studied the clouds in the sky. "Daed said that Jacob was ser gut."

Amos ignored her. "And that's not all. I just heard from some kin back in Pennsylvania, and they told me that Jacob Miller was trouble. He'd been associating with the Mennonites, and he courted a girl who wore Englisch clothing. And he got into several fights. Even got hauled into the police station once." Amos shuddered. "I even heard that he owns and operates a motorcycle. Keeps it behind his daed's barn. No wonder they sent him down here. The boy is trouble." He nodded. "Jah, definitely trouble."

Jacob? Trouble? The only trouble she found with him was the way her heart responded. And as for the allegation that he owned a motorcycle, she simply couldn't imagine that. Motorcycles were loud, noisy, and, as far as she could see, dangerous.

But she did know about the bike and the girl.

And by the way he handled Kent, she could have guessed about the fights.

"See, he's not a wise choice. You need a man who will take care of you and Emma. I'm established, Rebekah. Established." Amos nodded decisively. "I own my haus and farm. I have five hundred head of cattle. A chicken coop. I could let you sell eggs for money. I have plenty of buwe to help, and you have Emma to eventually help in the haus. I'll work up a big garden plot for you."

Becky swallowed. "But your oldest son is almost my age. You are as old as Daed."

"Age doesn't matter. And my bu says he doesn't mind about you being so young. You should see his eyes light up when I mention marrying you. I think he has a crush on you." Amos chuckled, as if that was funny.

Her stomach churned.

"But...." Mamm had told her they'd move away, if necessary, rather than force her to marry Amos. Not to mention, she'd rather remain single. Forever.

And she loved Jacob.

Maybe she'd tell him so when she returned to the house. Tell him she didn't want him to court Annie. That she was sure—really, truly sure—she wanted him to court her.

He'd told her the intent was there for a promise.

Daed approved of him.

He'd been helping with Emma.

According to Annie, he had eyes for her alone.

In spite of knowing the truth.

Jah, she loved Jacob, for sure.

She quit walking and stumbled a bit when Amos dragged her along, taking a couple of steps before he realized she'd stopped.

He released her arm.

"I'm sorry. So very sorry. You do have a lot to offer." She tried not to choke. "But, really, I'm already spoken for."

Was that a lie? Her heart had been claimed.

"You can do better with me, Rebekah." He bowed his head. "I'll be here if you change your mind. You take some time and think. You'll see that I'm right about Jacob Miller."

"You're very kind. I'll definitely keep that in mind."

But she wouldn't change her mind. Nein, it was made up.

There was a spring in her step as she turned back toward the house. And her smile wouldn't be restrained.

She couldn't wait to tell Jacob.

❧

Becky was smiling. *Smiling.* He'd done everything but handstands and splits to try to coax a grin out of her and had gotten nothing.

Of course, he wasn't the one she loved.

He should be glad that she'd found happiness. That she had someone to love and would not have to marry Amos Kropf. That had been Jacob's original goal, after all—to help Becky find someone better to marry.

And now, she had a beau.

But instead of feeling joy, his heart broke with the knowledge that he wasn't the one she'd chosen.

Jacob didn't even look at the man. Didn't want to know who he was. Instead, he watched Becky approach the gathering with that beautiful smile brightening her face, lighting her eyes. He wanted to cry because it wasn't directed toward him.

As Becky drew nearer, Jacob felt like a coward; he took his plate and went to hide someplace where he could eat in peace, even though he didn't feel like choking down a single bite.

Matthew, being the good friend he was, followed him and kept up a one-sided conversation about the goings-on at the Stoltzfuses'. With all those kinner, it sounded like a busy place, but Jacob was thankful that Matthew didn't seem to expect him to respond.

Maybe he knew that Jacob's heart had been broken in two.

He had to pull himself together. After all, he would still be working for Daniel at the blacksmith shop. Still be staying in the dawdi-haus.

Still seeing Becky every day.

Still living in Missouri.

Right now, that was too close.

How could his heart mend if it was ripped asunder day after day?

With his mind attuned to Becky's every move, he didn't even have to look up when he heard the soft footsteps headed his way.

Why was she being so persistent in tracking him down? Did she want to rub in her rejection even more?

There was no need for that. He'd gotten the message, loud and clear.

Jacob started to scramble to his feet, his full plate in hand, ready to beat another hasty retreat, when Matthew put his hand on his arm, stalling him.

He stared down at the food he'd managed only to move around and shred, his stomach churning. He took a deep breath. *Lord, help me bear this.* The ultimate rejection.

Matthew stood and faced Becky. "I think you need to leave Jacob alone. He has no need of a two-timing girl like you."

Jacob heard Becky suck in a gasp.

"Go. Now. Leave him be."

He didn't know whether to be happy or sad that she turned on her heel and walked away without saying a word.

Chapter 31

Two-timing? The term still hurt. Jacob should have known better than to allow Matthew to call her that. She hadn't been out with anyone except for Jacob, and she'd figured he knew that, but now she wasn't so sure. He was avoiding her. So much for thinking that once everyone left, she would have an opportunity to tell him about her change of heart.

His behavior had nipped that in the bud. He'd disappeared for the afternoon and shown up again only for the evening Bible reading. And he hadn't asked her to join him for the singing that night. But then, she was the one who had told him the truth about herself, and now, her worst fears were coming true.

Monday didn't get much better. Jacob made no unexpected visits to the house, and when Becky found time to venture down to the shop, Jacob was either busy talking with a customer, or he made himself scarce.

Even worse, he completely ignored her at meals and other times when he was forced to interact with the rest of her family. She blinked back the tears. She'd known he'd reject her eventually after learning the truth.

When Becky walked down to visit Annie on Monday afternoon, she found out that he'd asked another girl, Annie's older sister, Cathy, to ride home with him.

That hurt, too, even if she was thankful that Jacob would not come between her and Annie. All of a sudden, Becky didn't like Cathy very much, though they'd had no disputes in the past.

On Tuesday, Becky was setting freshly baked cookies out to cool when Daed came into the kitchen. She handed him one that was still warm from the oven and poured him a cup of coffee. Then, she swallowed her fear and spoke up. "Daed, Jacob is avoiding me. Would you send him up here to talk to me, please?" She hated to ask but didn't know how else to get Jacob to talk to her. Meanwhile, she wondered why she even bothered when she knew that his avoiding her had to be the result of finding out the truth.

She would prefer that he tell her straight-out instead of carrying on with this business of pretending she didn't exist.

"I could talk to Jacob," Daed said with a slightly amused smile, "but I won't. You work this out on your own, Becky." He touched her shoulder and winked. "He loves you. But I'm not always going to be around to solve your relationship problems." He didn't say anything more. He seemed content to sit back and watch the drama unfold.

Becky saw nothing funny about this situation.

By Friday, she'd baked a mountain of goodies— pecan pie, apple pie, cherry pie, peach pie, and several dozen cookies. Jacob seemed to enjoy the fact that she'd spent every spare moment in the kitchen. If the way to a man's heart was through his stomach, she should be paving the way directly to his.

Having put another pie in the oven to bake, Becky stared out the kitchen window. Seeing no buggies or cars outside Daed's shop, she decided to make one more attempt to talk to Jacob.

She hurried out to the shop and slipped inside. Jacob stood in the corner, holding something in his hands, working it with his thumbs.

She'd wanted to surprise him, but she barely got her two feet into the building before his gaze locked on hers.

✦

Jacob's breath hitched, and he turned away, hoping she hadn't noticed the effect her presence had on him. He pushed a button on his cell phone, then listened to yet another message from Susie. Fifteen so far, and he'd barely made a dent in them. He should do a mass delete.

And Susie had nothing to say, except how much she missed him and wanted him to come home. Well, she also told him about the parties she'd been to with Timothy.

While he was glad that she'd moved on, he wished that she didn't feel obligated to keep him informed. He wanted to move on with his own life. And why exactly did she want him to come home? So she could share in person?

If he went home, it would be to join the church. Then, he'd look for a good Amish girl to spend the rest of his life with. And she certainly wouldn't be Susie.

Trouble was, he didn't know who else it would be. If it couldn't be Becky, then who?

"Jacob?" Becky touched his upper arm.

He tried to ignore the electrical charge that shot though him.

"I'm busy." He pushed the button once more to listen to another message. This one was from Matthew, telling him he'd be coming to Missouri a bit early. Jah, he'd figured that out. "Gotta take this one." He walked away from her, though there was really no point in returning that call.

She followed after him. "I won't take much of your time."

"You've taken too much of my time already." He winced as the words left his mouth. They went way beyond harsh. Instant guilt reproached him.

She stood there a long moment in complete silence. "Jah. I guess I have. I knew you'd reject me once you learned the truth."

He shut his eyes, fighting the urge to turn around. To tell her that wasn't the case at all. To pull her into his arms and...and...beg her to tell her beau that she loved Jacob Miller.

Well, to come right down to it, he still had a chance. Bex wasn't married yet.

He still had time to change her mind.

And treating her unkindly wouldn't be the way to win her heart.

"Bex." He swung around. "I'm—"

She was gone. Somewhere in his search for perspective, she'd disappeared. Undetected.

And in her place stood...Susie?

Jacob couldn't keep his mouth from gaping as he stared at the figure. He blinked several times, hoping to clear his vision, to restore Becky to Susie's place. But it didn't work.

Maybe because Susie had colored her short, spiked hair, which was now black. She couldn't possibly hide that from her parents, not even under a kapp. And she didn't wear the long, Amish-style dress covered with an apron. Instead, she wore low-cut jeans and a tight T-shirt about three sizes too small, which exposed a belly-button ring.

He averted his gaze, his face heating, and strained to see out the dirty window to watch where Becky went. He also needed to make sure that it was not a malfunction of his imagination that had conjured up Susie. But his imagination probably would have produced a Susie who looked the way she had the last time he'd seen her, not like this. His mind must really be on the fritz.

Maybe, in reality, Becky stood in front of him.

Nein. Definitely not Becky.

"Don't look so shocked, Jacob." Susie moved closer to him. "I expected you to be happier to see me." She ran her fingers up his arm, her brown eyes dancing. A moment later, she snuggled close to him, wrapping her arms around his waist.

His hands came up automatically, but then he caught himself. She didn't belong there in his arms. For a moment, he stood stiffly, trying to find a remnant of the excitement he might have felt had she made the trip earlier. But that attempt failed miserably. Instead, he felt about as excited as he would to hold his nephew after he'd smeared cherry pie on his only clean shirt. He put his hands on her shoulders and pushed her away gently. "What are you doing here?" He hoped his words sounded kind and did not make it obvious that he wanted to push her and her belly-button ring into the nearest river—or, better yet, the nearest car, so she could drive away fast.

Susie rolled her eyes. With a jerk of her arm, she pointed toward the open door. "Is that her? Becky?"

Nobody stood there, but he nodded anyway. "Jah."

"You can't want that."

Jacob didn't answer. To be honest, he didn't know what to say. Well, he could think of a response or two, but none that would sound remotely welcoming—or even kind. What had he ever seen in Susie? He wanted to tell her to go back to Pennsylvania, back to Timothy, and to leave him be. But after she'd made the long trek, that seemed rude.

"I just dressed like this for the trip." Susie turned away. "The driver is still out there. Point me where I'll be sleeping, and I'll have the bags brought in. Then, we'll talk."

She intended to stay? She must have mentioned it in one of the phone messages he hadn't listened to yet. Jacob frowned. At least Daniel's Amish hospitality would not put her up in the pigpen. He smothered a snicker and started to lead her to the house, maybe introduce her to Becky, but a car pulled in—probably a customer—followed by a buggy. Daniel wasn't in the shop, so Susie would have to meet Becky on her own.

He swallowed. Hard. What would the two women talk about in his absence? He cringed, wondering what Becky would even think when she met Susie. Even more important, how would he ever fix his relationship with Becky while Susie was around? And how would he explain this new twist to Daniel?

"Ask Bex to show you to a room."

She harrumphed and stomped off.

Susie's arrival was the last thing he needed.

For once, he was glad that his work in the blacksmith shop kept him away from the house.

⁓⁂⁓

Becky wasn't sure what to think of the Englisch woman talking to Jacob in the blacksmith shop. Wearing black the way she was, her face appeared washed-out, as if she'd escaped the screen of one of the horror films that Kent liked to watch. Becky repressed a shudder.

It probably had not been the best idea to sneak out of the shop and leave Jacob to deal with the Englischer. But considering the woman had likely heard Jacob's unkind words—*"You've taken too much of my time already"*—she thought he deserved some inconvenience.

The Englischer had shot Becky a triumphant look, as if Jacob's remark meant something to her. What, Becky didn't know.

But that didn't matter. With Jacob tossing her love aside like yesterday's scrap metal, leaving had been her best option. He obviously needed time away from her.

If only she had someplace to go.

Wait—she did! Becky straightened as she remembered Naomi Joy's request for her to come and help for a few months. *Help is on the way.*

Maybe Tony, the driver who'd brought the Englischer, would take her to Naomi Joy's. Becky stepped over to talk with him.

"How you doing, Miz Becky?"

"I'm gut, Tony." Becky glanced toward the workshop, then looked back at the driver. "Do you have time to take me to Naomi Joy's haus today?"

"I sure do. Just unloading these suitcases for Miz Susie, and then I'll be ready when you are."

Miz Susie? That creature was Jacob's Susie? "I'll be right out."

Becky didn't ask her family, since Mamm and Grossmammi had gone to market and Daed had vanished. Probably wandered down to a neighbor's to visit. She'd just leave a note on his pillow.

The Englisch woman, Susie, came up on the porch steps, startling Becky back to the present. "Becky, is it? I'm Susie, kum to visit Jacob. He said you'd show me a room."

Becky stared at her. Jacob had never once indicated that his sweet Susie was an Englischer. He would have been wise to mention that little detail, considering what he knew about Kent.

And nothing about this woman appeared even the tiniest bit sweet.

That didn't matter. Jacob could have his Susie, sweet or not.

But a room? They didn't even have a spare bed in this house. And Jacob occupied the extra bedroom in the dawdi-haus.

Then again, if she went to visit Naomi Joy, Susie could sleep in her place, next to Katie.

Becky forced a smile. "Jah. You'll be sharing with my sister Katie. Follow me." Another detail she'd have to add to her note to Daed.

In a Christian romance Becky had read once, the villain had tried to ward off the heroine by making snide remarks about the hero's not being interested in her. For a moment, Becky worried that Susie might do the same. But then, why would she? Becky wasn't the heroine. If anyone, it was Susie. And she didn't need to bother with unkind words.

Jacob had already taken care of that part.

Becky indicated the room. "There are some hooks there for you to hang your clothes on. I hope you enjoy your stay."

Susie nodded and smiled. "Ach, I will." She hesitated a moment. "But I think I need to change clothes first. I am Amish, really."

Becky eyed her apparel and her pierced belly button. Susie's district must really be liberal. "Of course." She hoped she hadn't sounded judgmental. Really, it wasn't her place. And she had been falsely judged enough to know the consequences. Turning away, she grabbed a couple of her dresses from their hooks, freeing more space for Susie's clothes.

Thirty minutes later, she sat in the van, in a seat Jacob might have occupied when he'd come to Missouri, as Tony bore her and Emma away to Naomi Joy's. Their move would be temporary, but it would give her some much-needed time away from Jacob. Maybe even an opportunity to heal.

While he renewed his relationship with Susie.

She was glad Daed hadn't been home for her to say good-bye. She wouldn't have been able to bear it. He'd said that Jacob loved her. He couldn't have been more wrong. And Becky didn't want to cry in Daed's arms. Nein, she needed to heal from this broken heart on her own.

Besides, Daed would have told her that running away from her problems wasn't the answer. Hadn't he said virtually the same thing when she'd confessed her pregnancy and suggested giving the boppli to Naomi Joy to raise?

The van pulled into a circular drive between a modest two-story house and a big barn. A gate off to one side announced the entryway to the garden. Ach, she'd miss her greenhouse. But this would be for only a few months, to help Naomi Joy during her pregnancy.

The drive took only forty-five minutes, so Becky could easily go home sometime for a visit—if she thought she could handle seeing Jacob. If not, then maybe Daed would hire a van for the family to come and visit her at her sister's.

"Here you go, Miz Becky."

"Danki, Tony." Becky gathered Emma and their things, then crawled out of the vehicle, while Tony lifted Emma's cradle out of the back. Becky walked up the porch steps and opened the front door. "Naomi Joy?" She set her things on the kitchen floor and balanced Emma better on her hip, then held the door for Tony, who carried the cradle inside and set it down.

"Bye, Miz Becky," Tony said, tipping his hat. "Enjoy your stay. Give me a call when you're ready to go home."

Jah, and you let me know when Jacob Miller has gone.

Becky glanced around the tidy kitchen. This was the first time she'd been to Naomi Joy's home. A large wood-burning stove took up most of the tiny room, and on the far wall was a sink with an old-fashioned pump. A small table nestled against the same wall, with a chair positioned at each end.

Naomi Joy bustled in from the other room, where Becky could see a wringer washer. "Becky! You came. I didn't think you would." She gave Becky and Emma a hug. "Danki. I didn't know who else to ask. I just can't handle raw food without it triggering my sickness. Poor Samuel needs to eat."

Becky nodded. "Jah, I understand. Glad to help."

"Samuel and I are sleeping downstairs these days. I can hold Emma if you want to go upstairs and get the bed ready. The one on the left will be yours. The other room is the nursery."

"Jah, danki." Becky handed Emma to her sister. "Where is your boppli?"

"Ach, hopefully sleeping. Taking a nap while I try to get some washing done."

Becky nodded. "I'll be right down to help." She grabbed her bags and headed upstairs to the tiny bedroom tucked into the eaves. The ceiling was slanted, and the head of the bed was positioned where the ceiling was lowest. She'd have to be careful not to sit up straight, or she would bump her head, for sure.

Jacob would never be able to sleep here. The bed was too short and narrow. The ceiling so low.

Ach, Jacob. Why did she have to think of him just now? Tears burned her eyes.

Would he miss her? Enough to come after her? Would Daed even tell him where she'd gone? After all, he'd told Jacob when she had gone to McDonald's, even sent him after her. Yet he no longer interfered when she asked him for help. She was supposed to work it out on her own.

A lot of good that had done so far.

It was said that absence makes the heart grow fonder.

But then, that whole absence thing hadn't held true for him and Susie.

On second thought, maybe it had. After all, Susie had asked for a break, and now she had come for him.

And then, there was the proverb "Out of sight, out of mind," which said just the opposite.

It didn't take much thought to know which one would prevail in her case.

Chapter 32

J acob stretched his tired back as the last customer finally left the shop. He pulled off his leather work gloves and the goggles, putting them in a neat pile on a shelf. Daniel slid a handful of money toward Jacob. His weekly earnings.

"Danki for picking up the slack, Jacob."

"Jah." They both had been immersed nonstop in work. Maybe Daniel needed him as a full-time employee, after all.

He glanced toward the house with a strong yearning to talk to Becky. He really should have listened when she'd come to talk to him. But he hadn't. And now, he needed to apologize, see what she had to say, and start trying to make things right.

Try to woo her.

"You thinking of staying around here, ain't so? I could offer you a full-time job." Daniel broke into Jacob's thoughts with the tempting offer.

"Jah, maybe so. But I need to talk to Becky real quick," Jacob said as they neared the house. He hoped she wasn't too busy with supper preparations, but if she was, then he would ask her to go for a walk later.

Though, considering the unkind words he'd spoken earlier, it wouldn't surprise him if she didn't want to.

If that was the case, then he'd apologize to her right there in the kitchen, in front of her daed and everyone.

Even in front of Susie, if his daydream—more like a nightmare—about her visit were really true.

"Jah. Ach, Jacob, I was thinking. See over by those trees?" Daniel pointed to the right. "That might be a gut place for you to build a haus."

Jacob glanced that way and nodded. "I'll look it over sometime. Though what would be the point?" He pulled in a deep breath. "Someone else is courting her."

Daniel shook his head. "Nein. Just you."

"I saw her coming down the driveway like she was running back from meeting a beau." The day he'd kissed her. He still liked to relive that too-brief moment in his memory. "Then, on Sunday, I saw her walking in the field with a man. And when I asked her if I could court her, she said nein. Well, I guess she technically didn't answer."

"She's scared, ain't so? Besides, I saw her with Amos Kropf. He had some things to say to her." Daniel chuckled. "He's hardly at the point of proposing."

Jacob gave Daniel a sharp look. "I thought I saw Amos talking with you."

"Jah, for a little while before services. He went to find Becky when church let out."

She had been talking with Amos Kropf? Relief washed through Jacob for a brief moment before the flash flood of guilt hit. Ach, this made his behavior earlier so much worse.

"I need to apologize." Jacob looked down and kicked at a rock. "I messed up big time."

Daniel nodded slowly. "Jah, perhaps so."

Jacob took a deep breath and followed Daniel into the house. Katie and Leah worked at the stove while Ruthie set out the jams and other canned items. The table hadn't been set yet. Becky was nowhere in sight.

Maybe she was feeding Emma. He glanced at the cradle to see if the boppli was in there. And did a double take.

Emma's cradle was missing.

Spiders of fear made their way up his spine. "Where's Becky?"

Daniel pressed his palms into the table. "Leah?" His voice was tight.

Leah shook her head. "I don't know. I got home late from market and couldn't find her or my parents. Not sure where any of them are. She might be visiting Annie. Or maybe they all went to town together."

With the cradle? Jacob thought not. Judging from his frown, Daniel agreed.

Leah turned. "But I did find that we have a guest for a while." She pointed a wooden spoon at Jacob. "You could have let us know that your Susie planned to visit."

Ach, it hadn't been a bad dream, after all. Jacob gave a slight shrug. "I'm sorry, but I didn't know. If I had, I would have told her nein."

Evidently, his apology to Becky would have to wait. Jacob went next door to the dawdi-haus to take a shower, hoping that Becky would have changed her mind and returned home by the time he finished.

When he went back into the main house for dinner, Susie was already there, now dressed in a modest dark green dress with heavy black stockings, an apron, and a white kapp. Jacob studied her. With the kapp covering her spiked hair, she looked almost like a normal Amish girl, but he still preferred her natural strawberry blond color to the black she now sported. And he didn't like the hardness in her eyes. Had that always been there?

Susie crowded in next to him at the dinner table—on the men's side of the table—ignoring Leah's attempt to direct her to Becky's seat. Jacob tried to inconspicuously scoot his chair away from her, but grossdaedi wasn't budging, and Jacob stopped short of sitting on his lap.

"So, Susie, how was your trip?" Daniel asked as he passed her the sugar snap peas.

"Ach, it was okay. The buses, they smelled like fried chicken. I'd packed sandwiches along for my meals, but I felt like I was starving the whole time. Gut to see you're having fried chicken for dinner." She took a leg and passed the platter to Jacob. "And have you ever tried to sleep at a bus station? Some people were curled up on the floor in corners. At least I got a chair. But it still wasn't real comfortable."

Right now, it seemed a blessing that Susie had the gift of gab. She talked all the way through the meal, preventing the uncomfortable silences that probably would have occurred if Jacob had been left to carry the conversation. She flowed endlessly from one subject to the next without giving anyone much of an opportunity to say anything.

When dinner was over, Jacob pushed away from the table, but Susie snagged his sleeve. "Let's go for a ride." It was an order, not a request, and he could see the censure in Leah and Katie's eyes at her failure to offer to help with the cleanup.

Daniel's expression was unreadable. "Might want to take Shakespeare."

Becky's horse.

Jacob nodded, wondering if that was Daniel's way of making sure that he remembered Becky when he was out. Like he'd be able to forget her, even without her horse right in his line of vision.

Jacob went out to the barn and got the buggy ready, then came back inside the house for Susie. He was relieved that they would be riding together under the cover of darkness. Hopefully, tongues wouldn't wag too much. Word spread fast in Amish communities.

But he did not look forward to having to keep up his half of the conversation. He couldn't ask Susie why she hadn't told him she was coming, because she might have; he had no way of knowing, since he'd deleted the rest of her phone messages, figuring they were more of the same.

It would seem he'd made a mistake there. Not that he would have been able to stop her from coming, since she'd shown up the day he'd finally started listening to his voice-mail messages.

Before they were out of sight of the house, Susie reached over and slugged his upper arm. Hard.

Jacob glared. "What was that for?"

"'I've never felt this way before'! Are you serious? We love each other. You and me. Not you and *her*."

"You asked for a break so you could be with Timothy!"

"Did you really expect me sit quietly at home while you were in Missouri working? A girl's gotta have fun. And sitting at home doesn't quite count."

"You could have spent the time preparing for marriage. Getting your hope chest filled. Learning to bake and keep a haus."

"I *know* how to do that stuff; I just don't enjoy it. And why should I worry about a hope chest? That's what wedding gifts are for."

"Susie, if you really loved me, you wouldn't have wanted to be out with Timothy. You would have been missing me and preparing for when I returned home. You didn't. You didn't even wait until my old pillow was cold before you started going with Timothy." He flicked the reins. "I let everyone here know about you."

"Including *her*?"

"Jah. Including Bex. I wasn't planning on falling in love with her. I'd just figured I'd help her find a beau." He stopped himself from saying more. He didn't want Susie spreading rumors about Becky back in Pennsylvania. After all, he'd written Mamm and Daed to tell them about her, mainly to put them at ease regarding Susie.

"You aren't in love with her," Susie said, crossing her arms over her chest. "You're in love with me." Her voice had a petulant tone he was all too familiar with. "You just forgot because we were separated by so many miles, so many months."

Jacob blinked. Something about her statement didn't ring quite true. Was mere separation enough to make him forget someone he loved? If Becky stayed away, would he forget about her and love Susie again?

That seemed fickle. Never mind "seemed"; it was. Did fickle describe him? Ach, he hoped not.

Jacob sucked in a breath. "Let's not fight. Thank you for making the trip to see me. Let's just enjoy your visit."

Susie smirked, scooted closer to him, and started to talk again, this time telling him in detail about all the parties she'd attended since he'd been gone. Apparently, she believed she'd won this disagreement.

Troubled, Jacob stared at Shakespeare's mane and tried to imagine his life with Susie as his bride. He just couldn't. Picturing Becky by his side came so much more easily.

The next morning, when Jacob went out to the barn to help Daniel with the chores, he found an unusual frown in place of his normally pleasant expression. He looked up and seemed to sober even more, if that were possible.

Becky must not have come home. A rock settled in the pit of his stomach.

"Morning, Jacob. Appears our Becky has gone to stay with her sister Naomi Joy for a while."

At least they knew where she had gone. That was a good thing. "She didn't say good-bye."

"Nein." Daniel looked down at his hands. "But she did leave a note."

"What'd she say?" Had she mentioned him and the horrible way he'd treated her? He felt bad—worse than bad—about that.

Daniel shook his head. "Just that she was going to stay with Naomi Joy for a while. That is it."

"Where does Naomi Joy live?" He'd go for her and bring her back.

"About thirty miles away. Too far."

Jah. His parents would hire a car if it was longer than twenty miles round-trip. A horse was good for only about twenty-five miles before it needed to be changed out.

"Naomi Joy is expecting another wee one. She asked for Becky to kum. But I thought she'd refused. Guess she changed her mind."

Or Jacob had changed it for her. But if she had gone to help her sister, she'd be coming back. Eventually. Jacob sighed. Maybe that was why she'd come to the shop yesterday to talk with him. To tell him she going away for a while.

And he'd refused to talk to her.

She must be so hurt.

Especially since she'd made it clear that she believed it was because he'd learned the truth. And he hadn't denied it.

Jacob hung his head in shame. "Does this Naomi Joy have a cell phone?"

Daniel hesitated. "Nein. I don't believe so. Believe there's a phone shanty out in someone's shed that they all use. Naomi Joy mentioned it once." He shrugged. "The bishop gave me special permission to carry a cell phone on account of my business."

Jacob turned away and headed for the line of cows ready to be milked. He needed to get to work and put Becky out of his mind for a while. Later, he would ask Daniel for her sister's address and write to her.

And, while she was gone, he'd spend time in prayer about their future. At least at Naomi Joy's, she'd be away from Amos Kropf. And she'd be away from Susie.

Jah, this could be a good thing.

On the other hand, she might meet someone new.

Jacob closed his eyes. He needed to get to her as soon as he could.

❦

Becky rose early, spent some time in prayer, and then hurried downstairs, leaving Emma asleep in the cradle in the corner of her new bedroom. Naomi Joy had laid a blanket and some toys on the kitchen floor yesterday, saying that she had taught Regina to stay put and play where she could keep an eye on her while she worked. But at five months old, Emma wasn't crawling yet.

Regina was seven months old, and when she wasn't supposed to be on the blanket, she was mobile, doing some sort of crazy crawl all over the house. She moved on all fours, with her legs extended, maybe to protect her knees from the hard floor. It was really cute to watch.

When she entered the kitchen, Becky found Naomi Joy sitting at the small table, hunched over an untouched glass of orange juice and nibbling on a cracker. She looked a bit green.

Becky remembered those days well. Mamm had baked a steady supply of ginger cookies to help settle her stomach. She'd also lectured Becky about eating more meat, telling her that a lack of protein was the cause of her morning sickness.

Old wives' tales that sometimes, strangely, seemed to hold true. Becky shared Mamm's advice, at which Naomi Joy shuddered. Becky had reacted the same way. How can one be expected to eat more of anything when all food, no matter what kind, made one sick?

"Samuel's gone out to start the chores. He'll be back in when he's done." Naomi Joy reached for another cracker and glanced at Becky.

Becky nodded. "Do I need to collect the eggs?"

Naomi Joy shuddered again. "Nein. He'll do it."

Her sister had always hated chickens. Always been afraid of them, rather. Ever since a rooster had chased her out of the coop when she was seven.

If Becky remembered right, that rooster had ended up as dinner later the same week.

She hid her grin as she entered the walk-in pantry and started gathering ingredients for breakfast. She thought she'd make pancakes and bacon.

Naomi Joy poked her head inside the pantry. "I'm going to go make the bed and change Regina's diaper."

"Jah." Becky sensed that her sister wouldn't be coming back to the kitchen until breakfast was ready.

Becky grabbed a mixing bowl and started measuring the ingredients, all the while thinking of home. Daed and Mamm had discovered her note by now. Had Daed told Jacob where she'd gone? Maybe he would hire a driver and chase after her. Unlikely, considering the way he had rejected her. Plus, now that Susie was here, he'd be spending all his time with her.

More likely, she'd get a letter from Daed saying that Jacob had gone back to Pennsylvania.

Not that she'd be able to go home right away if he came for her. Naomi Joy really did need help. She'd gotten sick twice after Becky's arrival yesterday, and her morning sickness seemed to last all day, triggered by almost every smell.

But it sure would be nice to be missed.

By one person in particular.

She almost wished she could have overheard the conversations at home when they'd discovered she was gone.

Well, maybe. If Jacob didn't miss her at all, maybe it'd be better not to know.

He'd rejected her, just like she'd known he would.

She was the one with the broken heart.

That made her wonder about God. Had He rejected her, too? He knew her secrets. He'd known them in advance. Did He really give second, third, even hundredth, chances, with grace and complete forgiveness? Or would she face eternity as an outcast?

The thought that God might shun her hurt worse than Jacob's rejection. She bowed her head in silent prayer, begging God to grant her His forgiveness as freely as Daed had given his, despite his great disappointment.

She prayed until she felt peace and acceptance wash over her. Then, she turned to praise.

⤳⤳

That night, Jacob started three different letters to Becky but crumpled each one and set it aside to burn later. He couldn't figure out how to word what he needed to say: that he thought he'd fallen in love with her the moment they'd met, or at least at some point in the kitchen that first day. Daed had always told him that love was a decision, not an emotion, but Jacob figured he was a bit wrong there. Jah, he'd made a decision to love Becky. But emotion was definitely involved.

And he also needed to tell her that he was sorry for treating her unkindly. He'd been jealous, but that was no excuse. She needed to know that he'd acted on wrong information, not out of disgust over knowing the truth about her past.

He put his pen to yet another piece of paper, then hesitated. He really needed to go find her, to talk to her in person.

But he didn't know when he would be able to, or how. If his motorcycle were here…. But it wasn't. And that would clearly be frowned upon by the Ordnung. He could just hear the gossip that would create, could almost imagine the look of shock on Becky's face if he rode up on a motorbike. Besides, he wanted to establish a reputation as a good Amish man. A man worthy of marrying Becky.

This goal meant he'd have to keep Susie under control while she visited. She could ruin his reputation quickly, and he didn't want any disturbing news to reach Becky.

He could hire a driver and go by car—that wouldn't take too long. A distance of thirty miles was nothing to the Englischers. In less than an hour, he could see her.

He'd have to see how busy the shop would be today. No way would he leave Daniel in the lurch. They were usually closed on Saturdays, but orders were piled up and waiting. If he could get away after lunch, he'd ask Daniel for the driver's phone number and go.

And, if not, Becky would receive a letter by Tuesday. It probably wouldn't take more than a day for a piece of mail to reach her.

Might be better that he keep their time apart as just that. Apart. And communicate only by mail. He'd keep his prayer time unhampered. Maybe, if he asked her, she'd pray about them, too.

Jah, he'd apologize by letter and wait.

He'd write her every day. Okay, that might be too much. Twice a week, at least.

He turned his pen to the paper.

Dear Bex,....

Chapter 33

Becky lifted open the freshly washed window and peeked out at the long driveway curving toward the road for what must have been the hundredth time since she'd arrived at Naomi Joy's. Her shoulders slumped. Still no car. Every night for a week, she'd dreamed of seeing a vehicle pull into Naomi Joy's long drive—a driver, with some of her family (okay, mostly she dreamed that it would be Jacob) come to check on her. But there was no reason why any of them should. She'd told them where she'd gone, and they knew why. Rather, she assumed they did. Naomi Joy needed help. She was being the good, dutiful sister here.

No one would guess that she'd left in order to heal from a broken heart.

And so no one came.

Not even Jacob. But, of course, he would be busy with Susie.

Her eyes welled with tears. It'd be so nice if she were actually missed. She turned away from the window and went to the stove to check the meat, hoping Naomi Joy didn't notice her tears.

Naomi Joy balanced Emma in one arm and Regina in the other as she used her bare foot to straighten the colorful patchwork quilt on the floor. "Can't believe I tripped over that thing."

Becky set the hamburgers they'd prepared on the table, followed by a small plate of sliced onion, just as Samuel came through the door and went over to the inside pump to wash up. She wiped the moisture from her face, and Samuel gave her an odd look she couldn't translate, but she hoped he would attribute her watering eyes to the sliced onions.

He wouldn't have reason to guess about Jacob, either.

How smoothly was the household running now that she was gone? Was Mamm enlisting Katie's help in the kitchen more often? Did they even miss her?

With a sigh, she reminded herself that no matter what happened with her family, with Jacob, she belonged to God. And He wouldn't turn His back on her.

That was almost enough to make her smile.

Naomi Joy put both babies back down on the quilt, then poured lemonade from a pitcher into three glasses.

Becky picked up the plateful of ginger cookies she'd arranged for dessert. Her heart clenched to remember how much Jacob had seemed to enjoy her cookies. Too bad she hadn't been able to bake her way to his heart.

Becky still couldn't believe that Jacob had asked Cathy home from the singing. It seemed unfair that he hadn't sat at home in misery like she had. Obviously, he wanted to get on with his life. If only she could regroup as fast.

Why hadn't she guarded her heart against Jacob? She'd wanted to. She'd warned herself not to let him in, that he'd reject her when he learned her horrible secret.

And he had.

How long did a broken heart take to heal?

❧

Right after lunch, Jacob escaped Susie's watchful eye long enough to run his letter to Becky out to the mailbox. It had ended up being four pages long, front and back. And it had taken him a whole week to put what he wanted to say into words. He hoped he hadn't rambled too much, but he did want to share his heart and apologize completely for everything. And to ask Becky to pray with him regarding their future.

That request would surely make his intentions clear enough. She would know that he was thinking about marriage.

He realized that he probably should have mentioned how Susie's visit was going so that she wouldn't get the news secondhand.

Too late now. He'd mention that in his next letter.

He shut the lid of the mailbox and eased the wiggly red flag into the upright position, then turned around when he heard the sound of wagon wheels crunching over the gravel.

"Hi, Jacob."

He looked up into brown eyes, the only obvious difference he could see between Cathy and Annie, whose eyes were a greenish hazel. He inwardly groaned. "Hi, Cathy."

"Are you writing a letter home, Jacob? You must be so homesick for your friends." She fluttered her eyelashes rapidly, as if she had something stuck in them.

Ach, that reminded him. He needed to write to his parents. No doubt they'd heard that Susie had come to Missouri. He needed to set their minds at ease. He'd do that tonight.

"Nein. Writing to Bex—Becky. She went to visit her sister for a while."

"Will she be gone long?"

Jacob shrugged. "I don't know. I hope not. The haus seems to have a big, empty spot with her gone." Not to mention his heart. "Things just aren't the same. I plan to write her a couple of times a week. Let her know she's missed." He hoped that would get the message across to Cathy that his interests lay elsewhere.

"I imagine. I know she's a ser gut cook. Her baked goods and jams always place at the county fair. Care to take a ride with me, Jacob?" She shook the reins. "I'll let you drive. We can talk...."

Jacob's eyes widened. "Nein, but danki for asking. I need to get back to the shop."

"Maybe tonight, then, Jacob? You could kum by after chores, and we'll visit. I could get out the checkerboard, ain't so?"

Her boldness rivaled Susie's. Didn't she know that men preferred to do the chasing?

"Nein, can't tonight. Have a friend visiting from Pennsylvania."

Cathy's eyes sparkled with curiosity. "Bring him along."

Jacob shook his head. "Ach, not a 'him,' but thanks for the offer." He turned to jog down the drive.

He didn't get but a few feet from the mailbox when Susie dashed toward him. "Where'd you slip off to so fast? I've been hunting all over for you. I just heard there's going to be a party in Judah Swartz's back field. You'll take me, of course." She put her hand on Jacob's arm and glanced at Cathy, still sitting there in the buggy. "Hi. I'm Susie."

"You'll have to find your own way." Jacob shook off her hand. "I need to get back to work." He looked back when he reached the shop.

Odd how Susie stood there in the road, talking to Cathy. He couldn't imagine what they might have to say to each other. They were still chatting when Jacob went inside the shop.

❧

Four weeks later, Becky had settled into her new routine at Naomi Joy's. Another older man with a family had shown more than a passing interest in her, but she'd declined when he'd asked if he could call on her some evening.

Naomi Joy had told her she'd made a mistake in rejecting him outright. After all, she'd said, everyone knew that since she already had a daughter, her only hope would be to marry a widower.

Becky had shrugged off the hurtful comment, saying something about not being ready.

And she wasn't, really. She spent hours in prayer, pleading with God to rid her heart of love for Jacob. Until she healed from this broken relationship, she needed to avoid beginning another.

But in four weeks, it seemed strange that no one in her family had contacted her. No phone calls—though that would be hard to do with Naomi Joy not owning a phone. And no letters, either. Not one single letter.

Except from Annie. Becky reached under her pillow and pulled out the letter she'd received a couple of days ago.

She'd thought that Mamm would have written to her, at least. Hadn't she written Naomi Joy twice a week when she'd first married and moved away? Mamm might have begun writing letters for Becky and Naomi Joy both, but Becky supposed not, since Naomi Joy shared excerpts aloud but never gave her the letters. If Mamm had included Becky's name in the salutations, then surely Naomi Joy would have handed her the letter to read.

Annie wrote about all the local news, telling Becky how much she missed having her around and spending time with her, and that Susie was still visiting.

At least it seemed that Jacob wasn't courting Cathy.

Becky refolded the letter and slid it back beneath her pillow, trying to bat back the tears. Only Annie missed her. Not Mamm, not Daed, and certainly not Jacob. Nein, and his former girlfriend had come back into the picture so quickly, it set her mind to spinning.

Hours later, Becky watched through the window as the red pickup truck that carried the rural mail stopped down by the road. She got up and looked for Naomi Joy. She found her in the kitchen, wiping down the pantry shelves.

"Mail's here."

"I'll get it today. I need the exercise. Maybe I'll feel better."

Becky nodded. Naomi Joy said that every day. Those same exact words. Maybe she'd walk out to the box with her sister today. Maybe she'd have some mail, too. Nein. She would be heartbroken if there wasn't anything, and if she received a letter, Naomi Joy would give it to her. She'd do some more baking, instead. They were almost out of bread. And she hadn't made an apple pie yet for Naomi Joy.

Fifteen minutes later, her sister came back inside and sat down heavily in a chair. "Getting hot out there. Here, you have a package from Annie. And Mamm wants to know why you aren't answering any of their letters. Strange. I don't remember you getting any mail. Except from Annie."

"I haven't." Becky poured her sister a glass of water from the pump.

Naomi Joy peered down at the pages she held. "Mamm says that Daed's been writing to you. Wow, he never writes me. But you were always his favorite. Wonder where the letters have been going?"

Her family had been writing to her? Becky stood in stunned silence. And her heart asked the same question. Where had the letters been going?

Chapter 34

Jacob shoved the end of a piece of metal into the roaring fire. How long did Becky expect him to wait? Another week had gone by with no mail for him, except a note from Mamm expressing concern that Susie was still in Seymour. Jah, Jacob was about ready to put her back on the bus, himself.

Susie had lapsed into her old ways. Jacob thought he'd seen Kent's red car picking her up down the lane one evening. He'd tried to warn her about Kent, but it had only given rise to another fight between him and Susie.

Probably just as well. He yanked the metal out of the fire and surveyed it, then put it on the anvil, picked up the hammer, and started pounding it.

Susie needed to go home.

And he needed to end this ongoing silence between him and Becky. It had gone on long enough. She must be getting his letters, and unless his love meant nothing to her, she should have written back by now.

Daniel came over and caught Jacob's arm in mid-swing. "Getting a bit carried away there, son. Want to talk about what's bothering you?"

Ach, an open invitation. But what did he have to say to the father of the woman ripping his heart to shreds?

Nothing. He had to work this out on his own.

"Need a glass of water," he mumbled, then shoved past Daniel, avoiding his too-knowing gaze. But Jacob didn't go to the house. Becky wasn't there. The outside pump would be good enough.

He splashed water on his face and let it run down his arms, soaking his shirt. Then, he stuck his head under the cold flow, trying to drown his wayward thoughts.

It didn't work.

With water still pouring over his head, Jacob peered at a pair of blue sneakers that stopped beside him, clear of the water. One of the sneakers rose and then came down in what Jacob could only call a stomp.

He straightened and shook his head to get some of the water off, then wiped his face with the bottom of his shirt.

Susie stomped her foot again. "I've had it, Jacob. I'm tired of living with this family. Your cousin Daniel has given me a week's eviction notice. He told me to go home! Can you believe this?"

Relief washed over him. Daniel had handled it. Or, maybe he'd done it to throw down the gauntlet and force Jacob to decide between Susie and Becky. But there really was no decision to make. "I'm not leaving with you."

"Of course, you're not. You're still pining over your Becky. Get over it, Jacob. If she loved you, she'd be here."

"She's helping her sister."

"If you loved her, you'd be going over there every chance you had. Get over her, Jacob. You don't love her. Last chance. Kum home with me. Saturday. We'll get published and marry as planned."

Jacob heaved a sigh. "You're right. This has gone on long enough. I'll settle it."

He should have done that in the first place instead of relying on letters alone to communicate with Becky.

He wouldn't write to tell her he was coming. The element of surprise had to work in his favor.

He turned away from the pump and headed back toward the blacksmith shop with Susie on his tail, talking away, though her words sounded like gibberish. Didn't matter. Jacob was done listening. He'd arrange for some time off tomorrow. That would be a good time to visit Becky. And, one way or another, he would speak with her, even if he had to shout at her back as she retreated. It made no difference whether her sister and brother-in-law were present. He needed to tell her how he felt. She would hear him out, one way or another.

Then, he would know whether he should stay in Missouri or give up and go home to Pennsylvania.

But not to marry Susie.

He turned to face her. "Susie, we've got to talk."

༚

"I have an idea." Naomi Joy pushed her coffee mug away. "Let's go home tomorrow and visit Mamm and Daed. They'll see how you are doing, and you can explain that you've not been getting any mail. Besides, I'm feeling a little better, so I can give you confidently back to Daed. School's out now, so Katie can kum for a while."

"Tired of me, Naomi Joy?" Going home wouldn't be a good idea. Not good at all.

"Nein. I think you are fattening Samuel up. He says if he has much more of your gut cooking, I'll have to let his pants out." Naomi Joy laughed. "Maybe it'd be better for him to not have such gut cooking so he'll appreciate me more. Besides, Katie needs the practice. Someday, as a frau, she'll be expected to run a haus. And Mamm says you can practically run theirs single-handedly. She didn't worry a bit about things getting done when you were there. I think Mamm's missing you."

"Too bad I'll never be a frau." Becky punched her fist into the bread dough she was kneading. "Really no point in my going home, Naomi Joy."

"Mamm says that there's a certain Jacob Miller moping around the farm," Naomi Joy said with a wink.

Becky shrugged. "His former sweetheart came to visit. As far as I know, she's still here." She tried not to sound as bitter as she felt.

Naomi Joy's mouth dropped open. She shook her head. "Rebekah Troyer. Are you saying you used me as an excuse to run away from your problems? Not that I don't appreciate your help; I never would have survived this month without you. But I think you need to get home now and resolve your unsettled issues. Besides, much more of your cooking, and Samuel will send me home to Daed and keep you here, instead. I just can't risk that." She grinned at Becky. "That's settled, then. I'll have Samuel call for a driver, and we'll go home tomorrow."

Becky frowned at the table and considered throwing herself into Naomi Joy's arms and begging to stay.

Instead, she set the dough off to the side to rise.

"Hmm, that's interesting," her sister continued, skimming a letter she'd opened. "Mamm says that Daed talked to the bishop about you and what happened with that Englischer. She said that the bishop decided to just tell a few choice people what happened and let the truth get out that way. I guess that would be gossips at their best, ain't so? They didn't want to rehash the whole unpleasant situation by bringing it up in a meeting. Can't really blame them there."

Becky shrugged, not really sure how she felt. She didn't want the whole issue dragged into the mud, that much was certain. Wouldn't it have been better to simply forget it? Telling the gossips meant she'd be a choice topic of conversation again.

Becky sighed as she scrubbed her hands at the sink. Then, she returned to the table and tore into Annie's package.

Out fell five letters bound with a rubber band. A note was clipped to the top.

> Dear Becky,
>
> Guess what I found when I put some of Cathy's clothes away?
>
> Love always,
>
> Annie

Relief and anger warred within her. Cathy had stolen letters addressed to her? She thumbed through the envelopes. Daed's name was scrawled in the top corner of each one.

Why would Cathy steal Daed's letters? It made no sense. She flipped through the envelopes again.

They had all been opened. Opened! Becky blinked, trying to control the sudden rage that boiled within her. How dare Cathy invade her privacy? She'd have a thing or two to tell her when she returned home.

Then, another thought occurred. Had Cathy stolen Jacob's letters, too? Or had he been too busy entertaining Susie to write?

Since there was nothing she could do about it now, Becky swallowed her anger and turned her attention back to the letters. With no postmarks for reference, she didn't know where to start reading. She hoped Cathy had kept them in order.

She glanced at her sister. "Jah, tomorrow sounds ser gut." Then, she picked up the letters and went upstairs to read them in the privacy of her room.

⌘

The next morning, Jacob settled into the backseat of the driver's car. They hadn't even started the trip, and already he felt skittish and sick to his stomach.

Nerves. All nerves.

Lord, let her listen to me, please.

He hoped God wouldn't find that sort of prayer disrespectful.

But it seemed the whole courtship had been fraught with failure to communicate. He wished he knew how to have a conversation when the other person wouldn't listen. And he was just as guilty of that as Becky.

Maybe more so.

Today, he would settle that. He'd talk with her, and they would work this out.

Thirty miles. How long would that take in a car? Forty-five minutes, maybe?

He couldn't wait to see her. To talk to her. To touch her, at least on her hand. He'd gone too long without contact.

Though, if he failed in his quest, then he'd be forced to go longer. Possibly even forever.

Jacob heaved a sigh and closed his eyes. He'd spend the rest of the trip in fervent prayer.

All too soon, the driver pulled the car into a circular drive. A dark-haired man with a beard led a horse pulling a plow toward the barn. He stopped and looked at the car.

Jacob opened the door and climbed out. "Jacob Miller. I've kum to see Becky."

The man's eyes widened. "Samuel Mast. Becky and Naomi Joy have gone home for the day. You just missed them; they left maybe ten minutes ago. Fact is, Naomi Joy mentioned leaving Becky home and bringing Katie back. Not sure what they'll do, though."

For a second, frustration ate at him. He'd missed her. So much for the element of surprise. But then, Becky had gone home. Home. To him.

Okay, to her family. But still.

Jacob grinned. And fought the urge to pump his arm in the air and shout "Yes!" like the Englisch sometimes did.

Samuel nodded, seeming to measure Jacob up, making sure he was worthy of Becky. Finally, he returned the grin. "Best be heading home, then, Jacob. Sorry you wasted the trip."

"Be seeing you, Samuel."

"Jah, expect so."

Jacob turned and walked back to the car. He couldn't control his grin as he climbed into the backseat again. He leaned forward. "Home, please."

Becky would be there waiting for him.

The radio blared as the driver pushed the button to turn it on for the drive back. Jacob couldn't make out most of the lyrics, except for the recurring refrain, "We can work it out! We can work it out!"

He prayed that was a sign.

Chapter 35

Becky handed Emma to Mamm, who began exclaiming how much Emma had changed in five weeks, and climbed out of the van. She immediately found herself engulfed in Daed's strong arms. "We missed you." He squeezed her tight, then released her and stepped back as Becky's littlest sisters rushed in for a hug.

It felt good to know she'd been missed.

Becky scanned the small crowd gathered around the van as Tony opened the back and pulled out Emma's cradle and Naomi Joy talked with him about what time she wanted to be picked up.

Everyone was present and accounted for, except Jacob and....

"Where are Grossdaedi and Grossmammi?" Becky looked around again. Maybe they were just taking longer to come out. After all, Daed had come running from the barn, her sisters and Mamm from the greenhouse.

Mamm hesitated a moment. "Grossmammi fell the other day and broke her hip. She's in the hospital in Springfield waiting for a hip replacement. Don't worry, she'll be alright. He's staying with her there."

And Jacob?

She swallowed that question down. Maybe he'd gone to Springfield with her grandparents. Or maybe he was out with his Susie. Though Daed had indicated in his letters that Jacob and Susie didn't get along so well. Fighting constantly, he'd said.

Becky was hurt anew at the thought of Cathy opening Daed's letters, but she swallowed her anger down again. All these years, she'd been taught that it was necessary to forgive. Now would be a good time to exercise that choice.

She followed the family inside as Daed hoisted the cradle and carried it up to the porch.

The kitchen was filled with the intermingled aromas of fresh coffee and baking bread.

"Be gut to have cookies again. Think we're fresh out." Daed gave her another tight hug.

"I tried." Katie made a face at him. "They just got a little overdone."

"The dog wouldn't even eat them." Ruthie took Regina from Naomi Joy. "It was quiet around here without you, Becky."

"Jah, and poor Jacob." Katie shook her head. "He was all kinds of bothered to find you gone. He acted almost like a child who'd lost his favorite toy."

"Jah, that's all I want to be. Jacob's toy," Becky said, then gasped. Her hand flew to her mouth. She hadn't meant to blurt that out loud. And it had sounded bad. She ducked her head as she felt the heat rising in her cheeks.

Naomi Joy gave her a pointed look. "I can't wait to meet this Jacob."

Daed pulled out the chair next to Becky and sat down. "Jacob's gone to Naomi Joy's haus today."

At least he wasn't with Susie. Wherever she was. Becky slanted Daed a sideways glance. He straightened his legs out in front of him and clasped his hands together over the waist of his pants. "He sent Susie home last night." Daed's expression spoke volumes.

Jacob had chosen today to finally go after her? He'd allowed Susie to stay so long. With five weeks gone by, it had certainly taken him long enough. Funny he'd rented a driver to go out there and never let them know he was coming. But then, Naomi Joy had made a spur-of-the-moment decision to travel, too.

She wondered how long he'd be gone. Maybe she'd have time to run over to Annie's before he got home. She didn't want to miss him.

Butterflies fluttered in her stomach.

She considered asking when he'd left so that she could calculate when he'd arrive home, but she lost her nerve. What she'd have to say to him, she didn't know.

Buggy wheels rolled over the gravel driveway. Mamm looked out the window. "Annie's here. Did you tell her you were coming home?" She sounded a bit accusing.

"Nein. I didn't tell anybody." Becky stood and went outside to meet her friend. "Hi."

Annie smiled. "I didn't know you were coming home. Why didn't you tell me?" She jumped down and hugged Becky. When she released her, Becky saw that she waved a bundle of letters bound with a rubber band. "Cathy's not home today, so I took the liberty of going through the rest of her things. I came over to show these to Jacob and ask how he wanted to handle this. But since you're here, I'll give them to you, with my apologies. I had no idea—"

"More letters? She stole all my mail?" Becky's mouth dropped open. She shut it with a snap. She seriously needed to have a talk with Cathy about this violation of privacy.

"Apparently so. Appears that she read them, as well." Annie sighed. "I really am sorry, Becky. I didn't know. But now I need to apologize to Jacob, too. I didn't know my sister was sabotaging his relationship with you." Annie handed Becky the letters. "Is he home?"

"Nein. He went to Naomi Joy's haus to visit me." The irony of it. The day she comes home, he leaves. She shook her head and looked down at the stack of mail, anxious to read it. The envelopes were all tattered along the upper edges, where they'd been opened.

"Ach. Well, then, when you see him, please tell him I'm sorry." Annie smiled at her. "I have to go. I promised to help Mrs. Zook with some things today. How long are you home for?"

"Forever, I hope. Naomi Joy is taking Katie back with her."

"We'll have to get together and talk, then." Annie nodded. "Enjoy the letters. And again, I'm sorry."

❦

Jacob leaned forward in his seat. That looked like Becky darting into the barn. He watched the open doors, hoping for her to reappear, as the car pulled to a stop.

"Danki." Jacob handed the driver some money.

"Sorry it was a wild goose chase, man. Do you want me to come back later? So you can try again?"

Jacob hesitated, glancing toward the barn again. "Nein. Wait awhile. I may need a ride to the bus station."

There would be no point in staying if Becky wouldn't be in his future.

Jacob slid out of the vehicle and jogged over to the barn. Becky stood in front of Shakespeare's stall. The horse nuzzled her hands. She reached into her pocket and handed him a bit of carrot.

For a long moment, Jacob just stood there in the open doorway, watching her.

Five weeks was entirely too long to be apart.

She talked softly to the horse, patting him on the nose.

"Bex." His voice came out hoarse, and little louder than a whisper. He tried again. "Bex."

She jumped, her shoulders pulling back in surprise. After a moment, she turned around. "Jacob."

A becoming blush spread over her cheeks. His heart hurt. "Don't ever leave me like that again." He winced at blurting out his thoughts like that. Not exactly what he'd dreamed of saying upon reuniting with her.

She stood there in silence, perhaps not knowing how to respond.

"Ach, Bex." He moved across the floor, coming to stop in front of her. In another moment, his hands slid over her soft cheeks, cupping her face, his thumbs resting on the corners of her mouth. "Why didn't you answer my letters?"

"I never received any from you. At least—"

"I wrote you two or three times a week. Nothing came?" Not even his apology? His declarations of love?

"Nein. But Annie sent me Daed's letters. She found them in Cathy's things. And she found your letters today." Becky gestured behind her as he swallowed in disbelief. He looked beyond her and noticed a thick stack of envelopes tied together and resting on a hay bale.

"I came out here to read them in private."

Jacob shut his eyes briefly. He would have to deal with Cathy later. But now, Becky needed to know what he'd written. "I'm so sorry, Bex. So very sorry. I never meant to hurt you the way I did. I didn't reject you because of what happened between you and Kent. Really. It was just that I thought you had another man courting you."

She dipped her head, but he moved a thumb to her chin, raising it back up. "Look at me, Bex. Please? I want to see your beautiful face."

She swallowed hard. "But what about Susie? Why did she kum?" Apprehension and something else—anger?—flitted across her face.

Jacob groaned. "Ach, Susie. Who can figure her out? She started dating Englisch buwe from around here. I told her to go home. There was nothing between us. Never would be. You are the only one I'm interested in."

Becky stared up at him. "Jacob, I...." She hesitated a second. Then, the tip of her pink tongue peeked out, and she licked her lips. "Jacob...." Her voice shook. She did that distracting tongue thing again. He was going to kiss her. No help for it.

He moved his thumbs again, touching her lips, tracing them. Pressing against their softness. Becky drew in a ragged breath. His own breathing wasn't much smoother.

"Bex." He drew out her name on a groan. In the next second he cupped his hand on the back of her head, tangling his fingers in the soft strands of her hair. He slid his other hand down to the small of her back, pressing her against him.

His mouth found hers, teasing lightly, then settling in more firmly. She trembled against him. And then her lips stirred under his, responding with an eagerness and abandon that surprised and delighted him. She reached up and wrapped her arms around his neck, clinging to him, allowing him to deepen the kiss.

Jacob didn't know how long they stood there, wrapped in each other's arms and kissing, but it wasn't enough. Nein, he wanted to hold this woman for the rest of his life.

That seemed unlikely if he couldn't even get her to smile.

He needed to hear her heart, and soon.

He had to let her go.

He tore himself out of her arms and took a step back.

✧

Becky struggled to stand, let alone breathe. Her knees had turned to liquid, her toes curling in her shoes. She'd never been kissed like that in her entire life.

Jacob took another ragged breath. "Bex, is there any hope for me? Give me a reason to stay. Please."

How could she talk? She was still fighting for air. She couldn't find the strength to launch herself back into his arms, and that was where she really wanted to be. She wobbled and reached for the stall door in an effort to support herself so that she wouldn't crumple in a heap at his feet.

He backed up another step, his expression changing from hopeful to discouraged. His shoulders slumped. In another second, he spun around and pulled his bicycle from the shadows of the barn.

"Good-bye, then, Bex. Always remember that I loved you."

He disappeared out the barn door, wheeling his bicycle beside him.

Becky stood there, sucking air into her lungs. How on earth had he recovered so fast?

He loved her?

And "*Good-bye, Bex*"?

What?

Suddenly, breathing wasn't the problem. She choked on a sudden lump and found the strength in her legs. "Jacob! Nein!"

He'd already left the bicycle beside the van waiting in the driveway, and the driver had opened the back and was preparing to shove it inside the luggage compartment. Jacob disappeared inside the dawdi-haus.

"Jacob." His name caught on a sob. She'd been taught that it wasn't ladylike to run. But really, in this situation, did it matter?

Daed stood on the porch, his gaze moving from the door of the dawdi-haus, which had just slammed shut, to the driver of the car, then to Becky. His brows furrowed in a frown. But without making a comment, he turned and went back inside. Wouldn't he make an effort to stop this?

"Don't load that," Becky ordered the confused driver as she passed the van and entered the dawdi-haus. Grossmammi was in the hospital, so the house was empty except for Jacob. She ran up the stairs. "Jacob!"

If she had sinned by running, she was really sinning now. She shoved the door to his room open. And skidded to a stop in the doorway.

Jacob shoved his belongings into his suitcase on the floor.

"Nein. Don't go."

He looked up from his crouched position, his blue eyes darkening. A muscle worked in his jaw. "Give me a reason to stay, then. Saying your daed needs me isn't gut enough."

"I need you. Ich liebe dich. I...." The words came quickly, born of desperation. She leaned on the door frame for support. Tried to calm down. "Ich liebe dich, Jacob."

He rose to his feet, holding her gaze. "And say that you'll marry me, kum December."

Her breath hitched. "Jah."

He walked to her and pulled her into his arms. "Gut. Ich liebe dich. I want to marry you." He leaned down and nuzzled the side of her neck, where she could feel her pulse pounding. She shivered and snuggled closer, her arms going around his neck. "I want to spend the rest of my life with you." He kissed her neck again, then worked his way up to her jaw-line. Then, he stopped and looked in her eyes. "Marry me soon."

"Anytime. The sooner the better." She couldn't keep from smiling.

"So, all this time I've been trying to get you to smile, and all you needed was love, ain't so?" Jacob touched her lips and grinned back.

A Preview of

A Harvest of Hearts

Book Two in The Amish of Seymour Series

by Laura V. Hilton
Coming in Fall 2011

Chapter 1

S hanna Stoltzfus felt something brush against her hair, just above her left ear. She swatted at it. When she touched flesh, she jumped, her attempts to pray forgotten, and raised her head from the steering wheel to see maple-stained fingers, complete with calluses and a small cut.

The hand pulled back. "Is something wrong? Are you hurt?" a deep voice asked.

She looked up into incredible gray eyes belonging to a drop-dead gorgeous Amish man. He grasped his straw hat in the long fingers of his right hand. His light brown hair shone with natural blond highlights. She'd paid big bucks for streaks like those. He also had a strong, clean-shaven jaw. Nice. Too bad he hadn't been around when she'd been Amish. She definitely would have noticed a hunk like this. Might even have considered staying.

"Lost, maybe? I can direct you back to the main road. Where did you want to go?"

"Anyplace but here. Even Mexico sounds good." She swallowed her trepidation and aimed what she hoped was a wry smile at him. When she reached for the door handle, he stepped out of the way. "You must be the houseguest Mamm mentioned in her letters. Matthew Yoder from Pennsylvania?" She swung her legs out of the car and extended a hand. "I'm Shanna."

"Shanna." He seemed to freeze. A little smile played on his lips. "Shanna," he repeated.

She didn't know quite what to think. He said her name as if it meant something special. Then, he blinked. "I'm Matthew, jah."

He held out his hand, but before his hand could touch hers, she fixed her gaze on his brown fingers. He hesitated and then rubbed his hands together, as if to check to see if the stain was still damp. Then, he pulled back. "Shanna."

His tongue seemed to trip over her name this time. Or maybe he'd heard some negative things about her. Her stomach churned. She shouldn't be here. But where else could she go?

"I guess they are expecting you?"

"No. Not really." Shanna stood and looked up at him. The top of her head barely reached his jaw.

His gaze skimmed over her. She wondered what he thought as he studied her faded jeans, T-shirt, and flip-flops. She looked down at her toenails. Good, they were painted with pink polish. Except the paint on one of her big toes had a huge chip. She wished she could reach for the bottle and repair the damage. As his gaze traveled back up, she repressed the urge to smooth her hair. It wouldn't have done much good, anyway. She'd driven the whole way with the windows down, so it would be hopelessly tangled.

His forehead wrinkled, and there was no hint of recognition in his eyes when they returned to her face.

"You have no idea who I am, do you?"

Matthew raised his eyebrows and his gaze met hers. "No. Should I?"

Unexpected pain shot through her. Daed had made good on his threat to reject her. "Figures. He probably forbade everybody to say my name. I'm surprised he allowed Mamm to write. Or maybe he doesn't know."

Confusion flashed across Matthew's face. "So, you think your Mamm lives here, and she isn't expecting you?" He shook his head, his lips curling into a sympathetic half smile. "This is the home of Levi and Deborah—"

"Stoltzfus. Yes, I know. And I'm their oldest daughter."

Matthew's smile slipped, and he blinked, cutting off her view of those gray eyes for a brief moment.

"You know, you have beautiful eyes." She stepped closer, then turned to shut the car door. "My things are in the back. But I guess maybe we should leave them there until we find out if I'm allowed to stay. Mamm said I would be welcome, but Daed has the final say, you know." She bit her lip and tried to force her fear of the imminent confrontation out of her mind. It didn't work. And since her little brothers and sisters hadn't gathered around to welcome her, she wondered if her family was even home. She looked around for the buggy, or some sign of life other than the handsome Matthew. She didn't notice any.

"Jah. Probably should wait." He blinked again when she turned to face him.

"Well, shall we?" She walked past him, around the front of the car, and toward the porch. At the top step, she hesitated and glanced back. Matthew stood where she'd left him, watching her. He didn't even try to hide it by looking away. A shiver worked through her, but she ignored it. He'd probably never met anyone like her before. Daed always said she was too outspoken. She sighed. "I guess I should ask. Where is Daed?"

He motioned behind him. "In the shop."

"Good." Postponing a meeting with Daed would at least give her time to see Mamm and her little sisters before she was kicked off the property.

If that happened, Shanna hoped this gorgeous Amish man wouldn't witness her humiliation. She felt ashamed enough of her modern clothes, now subject to his intense gaze. She was so underdressed, she might as well have shown up at a formal event wearing boxer shorts and a paint-spattered T-shirt.

Did Mamm still keep her Amish clothes hanging in her bedroom closet?

She scowled and turned toward the house. It would take more than a good-looking man to get her to change into Amish clothes. She hadn't been able to wait to leave the Amish life behind, and she wasn't about to return to it.

Well, she would stay for the summer, if permitted. But no longer than that.

And if Daed wouldn't let her? She'd deal with that when the time came.

❖

Matthew stared at the front door, through which the green-eyed beauty had disappeared after only the briefest look back, as if checking to see if he followed her. And he probably would have, if his feet hadn't felt rooted to the ground.

He mused over their brief conversation and allowed a smile to play on his lips as he grappled with the sense that he'd glimpsed into his future.

"Shanna," he whispered her name again.

He hadn't meant to touch her hair. He'd noticed the open window, and he'd simply reached in to touch her shoulder. But she'd moved, and instead of the soft tap he'd intended, his knuckles had buried themselves in her soft, golden tresses.

Inappropriate.

Even worse, he hadn't wanted to pull back.

Matthew swallowed, lifted his legs to see if they would still move, and turned toward the shop. He couldn't remember what he'd needed to go to the house for, anyway. No point in looking like a bigger fool in front of her.

When he pushed the shop door open, Levi looked up from where he stood, hunched over and sanding a wooden chair. "Did you get the key?"

Matthew shook his head. "I forgot what you sent me for." Ach, this was worse, having to admit to his mindlessness. Heat rose up his neck. "Um, there's a girl...your daughter. She was in her car. Said something about staying."

A look of hope flashed across Levi's face. His shoulders straightened, and a bright smile lit his face and eyes. He put down the sandpaper and moved toward the door, then stopped, his shoulders slumping. "Probably not for long."

Matthew couldn't quite read any of the other emotions that flashed across the older man's face.

"Is she shunned?" Matthew asked hesitantly.

Levi shook his head. "Nein, not formally. But I hoped denying her a place in the family would bring her back home." His expression hardened. "And maybe it would have. But my frau...."

He didn't need to say more. Matthew nodded in agreement. Shanna had mentioned letters in which her mamm had said she'd be welcome. Deborah must have been going behind Levi's back and staying in contact with her daughter.

It was none of his business, but he decided to ask, anyway. "Will you allow her to stay?"

He hoped Levi would say "Jah," the fascinating creature could stay. But another part of him wanted a decidedly firm "Nein." He hadn't been around her more than five minutes, and already she'd messed with his insides.

"I don't know." Levi scratched his head. "I'll have to think on it."

Matthew chuckled. "Maybe in the barn loft."

Levi's mouth curved up in a grin. "Might be best."

"I'm teasing." Matthew moved toward the door. "I'll go get the key you wanted. Sorry I forgot it earlier."

"Jah." Levi picked up the sandpaper and went back to work. "And I'll think on it. Gives her a few more minutes with her mamm, anyway, in case I decide not to let her stay."

❖

After hugging Shanna, Mamm resumed peeling apples at the counter, where a recipe for apple turnovers was propped against the flour canister. Shanna picked up a knife to help with paring, as she had countless times before. Mamm chatted nonstop, talking about Shanna's sisters, who were at friends' houses today, and about the garden. Not one mention had been made about whether she was permitted to stay. A piece of apple skin dangled from the peeler, ever lengthening as Mamm worked the apple around and around. It had always been a challenge for Shanna to try to pare the entire apple without breaking the strip, like Mamm did.

She'd never succeeded.

Yet another sign of failure. Another reason why she'd never be an Amish frau.

That, combined with the old-fashioned clothes and her intense dislike of the wringer washer. She'd hated that thing ever since getting her hair stuck in it as a young girl. Shanna had always been afraid that the contraption would pull her whole head through the rollers, try to press it flat, as it did the garments, and leave it abnormally shaped.

That was almost reality. Spiritually, she was abnormally shaped; God had never intended her to be Amish. It must have been a fluke for her to have been born into an Amish family.

Shanna pushed the thought away. Why was she even thinking about this stuff? She'd settled it long ago, for pity's sake, so that she could enroll in college to earn her nursing degree. So that she could live and work in the real world. And wear real clothes. And...well, there were many other benefits of being Englisch.

Yet those scrubs she had to wear to her clinicals could hardly be considered real clothes.

Her stomach felt as if a whole flock of Canada geese had landed in it, honking, with wings flapping, as they did when they passed through during migration. It had to be the fault of that young man—the one who'd come out to her car and caused her heart to flip-flop like the bottoms of her sandals.

Matthew Yoder.

A good Amish name, for someone who appeared to be a good Amish man.

As if she'd summoned him by thinking his name, the door opened, and Matthew strode into the room, heading straight for the key rack that hung on the wall. Not that there were many keys hanging there. Why would they have need for keys? Absolutely nothing worth stealing, except maybe Daed's tools, and he was out there now with them, so Matthew would have no need to unlock the shop.

She watched as Matthew lifted down a long key. The barn key. One of the doors there led up to a loft she'd never been allowed to enter. She didn't know what Daed kept in there, just that he'd built stairs to replace the ladder leading up to it.

Matthew palmed the key, then turned toward the door, moving with an even stride. Not once did he look in her direction.

Had Daed said something to dispel the friendliness he'd shown her earlier?

Mamm turned around. "Ach, Matthew. I didn't realize that was you. Kum meet Shanna. She's our oldest. Attends college up in Springfield."

Matthew hesitated by the door, then turned, his gaze skimming over her. "Welkum, Shanna." His tongue didn't trip over her name so much this time. And he didn't indicate they had met in the driveway.

"This is Matthew Yoder from Pennsylvania," Mamm continued. "He came down in the swap I mentioned in my letter, where we traded buwe with a community in Lancaster. Matthew is looking for farmland hereabouts."

"I hope you can find some," Shanna said. Farmland wasn't readily available in this part of Missouri, as far as she knew. But then, she didn't keep track of such things. She wasn't in the market for land.

Matthew grinned. "I have my eye on a piece not too far from here. Belongs to an Englischer, so the haus would need some work to be made suitable."

She knew that meant taking out the electrical lines, removing the screens from the windows, and installing a woodstove, among other things. All silly rules. Why no screens? Okay, she knew the answer: to keep God's view unobstructed. But, really. He could see through screens! And keeping the bugs out would hardly prevent people from going to heaven. Shanna shifted her feet to hide her shrug.

"The barn isn't adequate, so we'd need to have a barn raising to replace that, too," Matthew said, as if he hadn't noticed her reaction. "But that's if I get the property. I'm praying on it."

"Might not want to pray too long. Someone might buy it right out from under you," Shanna quipped.

"Then, that would be God's will, ain't so?" Matthew looked into her eyes and held up the key. "I'd best get this out to Levi."

Mamm put the apple she'd just peeled in the bowl beside her. "Tell him that Sha—his daughter is home."

So, Daed had forbidden them to mention her name. Nausea roiled within her, and vomit rose in her throat. Why was she subjecting herself to this? She shouldn't have come. Maybe one of those pay-by-the-week establishments in Springfield would have room. If she could afford it.

Matthew's gaze stayed locked on Shanna. "Ach, he knows. I'm sure he'll be up in a bit."

His expression told Shanna nothing. The Canada geese resumed their wild flapping in her stomach. She wasn't sure if it was more due to the compassion in those beautiful gray eyes or the news that she'd be facing Daed long before she was ready.

Mamm picked up another apple. "Don't worry yourself. He'll let you stay."

Shanna wasn't too sure.

A thump sounded on the front porch. Then another.

Shanna clutched her stomach, afraid she'd be ill. The next second, Daed stood in the doorway.

About the Author

Laura Hilton graduated with a business degree from Ozarka Technical College in Melbourne, Arkansas. A member of the American Christian Fiction Writers, she is a professional book reviewer for the Christian market, with more than a thousand reviews published on the Web. Prior to *Patchwork Dreams*, she published two novels with Treble Heart Books, *Hot Chocolate* and *Shadows of the Past*, as well as several devotionals. Laura and her husband, Steve, have five children, whom Laura homeschools. The family makes their home in Arkansas. To learn more about Laura, read her reviews, and find out about her upcoming releases, readers may visit her blog at http://lighthouse-academy.blogspot.com/.